ACTS OF LIFE

by Merita King

Published by Merita King
Eastleigh
Hampshire
United Kingdom
© Merita King 2013 all rights reserved

Cover art by J L Stratton. Copyright 2013

Acts of Life

ISBN 978-0-9570520-6-2

OTHER WORKS BY MERITA KING

The Lilean Chronicles: Book One ~ Redemption
The Lilean Chronicles: Book Two ~ The Sleeping
The Lilean Chronicles: Book Three ~ Changing Faces
The Lilean Chronicles: Book Four ~ Avalanche Effect

Floxham Island ~ Sinclair V-Log AZ267/M

ABOUT THE AUTHOR

Merita King has loved the science fiction and fantasy genre in both books and movies since she was a young child. She has been greatly inspired by years of watching movies and reading books and has wanted to make a contribution to this genre for many years. Her stories all contain a strong spiritual thread as she believes that spirituality is universal and crosses all boundaries. She believes that the creative process is largely intuitive and can be very effectively blocked by too much pre-planning. "Plot lines, characters and events all come to me intuitively," she says, "and this makes the act of writing a constant pleasure." She is a psychic medium and lives alone in Hampshire, UK.

DEDICATION

For Laurie, for her friendship and unfailing loyalty

CHAPTER ONE

Jake Elloway yawned as wakefulness embraced him. With a groan he threw back the sheet, he swung his legs to the floor, frowning as he realised something was wrapped uncomfortably around his left foot. A smile spread across his face as he snickered and saw the pink lace panties. She could not have been more than twenty-two and was just as he liked them; blonde, large breasted and so crazy about him that she would do anything he asked.

"Hank old buddy," he said aloud to the empty room, "your attention to your duties is beyond reproach. Thanks man." Hank was his Personal Assistant, and Jake decided he deserved a bonus in his next paycheck.

Being a famous vidicom movie star may have its drawbacks but it has its benefits too and Jake indulged in them all as often as he could. Hank knew all about those little extra duties that could not be found on his contract and helped ensure his employer was able to live his privileged lifestyle to the full. Henry Davenport, or Hank as his friends called him, did all the things a vidicom movie star's personal assistant would do and he was the Elloway family's most trusted employee. Jake knew he relied on Hank to a huge degree but he was generous and made sure he compensated him well for his devotion to duty.

The girl selected for him last night was perfect and he would be very grateful as usual. She gave him a good time and there was no need to fetch his ever-willing Assistant to escort her out for nearly three hours. That was almost a record; Jake's dalliances with his specially selected fans normally lasted around and hour and a half, two hours at the most before Hank would discreetly escort them to a waiting car with a signed photograph for their trouble. Hers were the perfect lips for a blowjob, Jake decided and he had not been wrong. He would remember the sight of those red lips around his penis for a long time to come.

With one practised movement, he tossed the panties into the laundry basket and headed to the bathroom to shower. Today was his last meeting before taking off for three months character research and he did not like to be late where business was concerned. He enjoyed a good reputation within the film industry as someone who always turns up on time and gets the job done and he felt no compulsion to change that now. Besides, the Entertainment Council were to have their annual meeting in a few weeks to give their final votes and Jake knew he needed to court their affections.   The success of all celebrities and entertainers depends upon their votes and he knew if he wanted to continue his climb up the rankings, he could not afford to piss anyone in the business off by being late for a meeting.

He thought back over the past year as he washed himself and could not think of anything he had done that might cast a cloud over his chances with the Entertainment Council. They vote once a year and discuss how each celebrity has performed, both as an entertainer but also in their personal lives. Any social mishaps or public misconduct would lose him a vote and he could slide down the rankings. Jake wasn't about to give up his position on the leader board just yet so although he liked to indulge himself from time to time, he always made sure he did so discreetly. Although not in a position of leadership, he was up there in the top five percent and worked hard at his job to maintain his position and he always hoped to climb further.

Hank was waiting for him in the kitchen, sipping china tea and continually checking his watch. He smiled as Jake entered and poured him some coffee.

"Morning Jake," he smiled. "Did you umm, sleep okay?"

"Hank old buddy," Jake grinned, "I owe ya one. Thanks man."

"You're welcome," he grinned. "Now what's it to be this morning, French toast or croissants?"

"Croissants please. Have you packed everything?"

"Everything is done Jake, don't worry. You can check your bags yourself if it'll help you to stop worrying."

"No it's okay, I trust you buddy. I'm still not totally keen on this y'know."

"I know but there's much more to it than just researching for your next role. Think how the Entertainment Council will view what you're doing; the attention to detail you're showing by going to all this trouble just for a role in a movie will bring dividends at next year's voting."

"Yeah I know," Jake sighed. "It's just the thought of three whole months locked up in some greasy trash can with a bunch of equally greasy labourers. I just hope there's at least one nice looking chick amongst them."

"There are a couple actually," Hank smiled. "I spoke to some guy last night who assured me that a couple of the women on board are easy on the eye."

"Well that's a bonus. Let's hope they're movie fans too huh?"

"Indeed. Now eat up, we have to be off in twenty minutes. I'll go tell Matt to bring the car around."

The smell of the cream leather upholstery in his top of the range hover limo always pleased Jake. The generously proportioned seat hugged him as he sat back and sighed.

"Good morning Mr Jake Sir," the grinning reflection of his chauffeur Matt said. "A beautiful morning for your trip into space huh?"

"Morning Matt," Jake replied as he wondered if he was ever without a smile on his face. "Let's hope the weather up there is as good." He looked at his Hispanic chauffeur and realised he envied him in many ways. With a wife who adores him, a beautiful baby daughter and an extremely well paid job that brings him into contact with one of the most powerful entertainment dynasties in the business, his life seemed blessed in ways that his own wasn't. All of that without the constant pressure to be perfect all of the time. Matt doesn't have to worry about offending the Entertainment Council, Jake thought to himself as they sped out of the Elloway Mansion and headed into the city. The demands of his position as a celebrity were sometimes a little burdensome and at such times, he found himself longing to rush out of a bar and punch someone in the face in front of everyone and not give a damn. The ever-present mob of fans could be annoying and his beaming smile was not always natural. Sometimes he found it almost unbearable to resist the longing to yell at people to just fuck off and leave him alone but he knew the Entertainment Council would think all their Christmases had come at once if he did.

Traffic was surprisingly light as they sped into the city and as the skyscrapers loomed towards them, Jake pondered on the trip he was about to embark upon. The movie role he'd been offered seven months ago didn't at first excite him as it was a bit of a departure from the roles he'd become known for. Being famous as an action hero meant he was used to being the lead character in every movie he made and had not played a secondary role to another actor in the last ten years, so when this role came along his first instinct was to turn it down. As always Hank was there with his sensible wisdom and helped him see the situation in a different light. The character he was to play was not the lead and not only that, he dies before the end and Jake was not at first willing to play a second level character who ended up dead. Hank explained that although Vinnie was not the lead character and despite the fact that he dies before the end, the emotional depth of his role would prove to viewers and more importantly, the Entertainment Council, that Jake had real acting talent beyond muscles and a pretty face.

They had argued about it for a while. Jake just was not interested in playing sidekick to the ageing has-been who was to take the lead role and Hank had to use his powers of persuasion to the full.

"But Jake, Vinnie's role has such emotional depth that everyone will be blown away by your performance and they'll realise that you've got more than just a six pack and biceps. You have been playing those pretty faced hero types for years and not once have you been able to play a character that has any genuine emotional depth. This is just what your career needs right now."

"Come on Hank, the guy dies two thirds the way through and he doesn't even get the girl."

"For goodness sake Jake don't you realise the opportunity the role of Vinnie is offering you? This is a chance to prove to those naysayers out there that you have some real talent and can act beyond the roles you normally play. You've become type cast, can't you see that?"

"Type cast?" Jake replied in shock.

"Yes Jake, type cast. You are thirty-six years old and soon you'll be too old to play the hero who saves the world, gets the girl and never sheds a tear. What will you do then huh? You need to be able to play different roles, display a wider understanding of the many subtle nuances of human nature and emotion and make that character shine using real acting talent and not just your muscles and pretty blue eyes."

Reluctantly at first, Jake accepted the role of Vinnie the cargo hand on an intergalactic freighter who gets involved in saving the last inhabitants of a dying world. Since this role was new to him, he agreed to spend three months working on an intergalactic freighter in order that he research Vinnie's job and lifestyle. Today he was to meet with Adam Maydell, the movie's Director and together, give a press conference before boarding the shuttle for the short flight to the Mayan Queen, in orbit above Earth. Jake was a little apprehensive about the trip and not just because he was worried he might not get too much sex. Hank would not be there to advise him; he would be alone with the crew and have to get along with them and actually get his hands dirty working with them for three months. He gave a deep sigh as the jet-black hover limo came to a stop outside Adam Maydell's office building.

There was quite a crowd gathered and Jake automatically smiled as Hank opened the door and stepped aside. Security guards held the crowd of women back and Jake waved to them as he stepped from the limo. Photographers jostled with each other for position in the press section to the right of the door and he grinned and waved as the flashes lit up the street that was still slick with the early morning rain. His name rang out from a hundred different directions at once and he turned this way and that, smiling and waving. He gave a few autographs and humbly accepted a few kisses before allowing Hank to usher him through the door to where Adam Maydell was waiting.

Adam Maydell hugged Jake affectionately and shook hands with Hank before stepping aside and ushering them into the elevator that took them up to his spacious office. One wall was made entirely of glass and as the room was on the twentieth floor, Jake's heart always did a flip if he got too close to that window. Without waiting for Adam to offer, he helped himself to coffee and smiled as he noticed Adam was sporting a bright red cravat today, which meant he was in a good mood. Adam always wore a cravat and the colour was a direct indicator of his mood. The brighter the colour, the brighter his mood and today he was vibrant red. On his desk, alongside photographs of his two kids, Jake noticed a photograph of a young blonde in an extremely tight pair of shorts. She did not have quite big enough breasts for his taste but he knew right away he would happily take her to bed and he secretly envied Adam for making such a catch since his very public divorce. Adam knew it too and loved

6

to flaunt his conquest for he knew Jake would sooner piss glass than bed any woman of his once he finished with her. Jake had no interest in taking anyone's leftovers and Adam knew he had scored a point up on him for it. It's a guy thing and despite it, they were great pals.

They spent a good couple of hours talking about the role of Vinnie and how it would stretch Jake and allow him to display real acting talent and Adam was able to illustrate just how to play up the emotional depth of the character. They went over a couple of scenes and Adam's legendary skill in helping actors stretch themselves helped Jake to learn how to allow the emotion of the character to shine through and say what needs to be said without him having to climb mountains or wrestle grizzly bears or save maidens from volcanoes. It was a total departure for him; he's not an emotional man in himself so this was a real learning curve but he soaked it up and by the time they called it a day and left for the press conference, Adam was confident Jake would blow the entertainment world out of their seats when he played Vinnie.

The limo cruised silently to a halt outside the spaceport building, its curvaceous, almost sexual lines catching the eye of the passengers as they stepped from the vehicle. Cameras flashed and news reporters yelled Jake's name as they strolled through the automatic doors that opened with a satisfying swish as they approached. No fans screamed outside this time; the spaceport security team were obsessionally vigilant and kept them all outside the main gate to the complex. It was wonderfully cool inside and Jake sighed with relief as the man standing before him extended a hand and smiled.

"Mr Elloway. My name is Miles Clutterbuck and I'd like to welcome you to Al Grazia Spaceport."

"Thank you Miles," Jake smiled back as he shook the proffered hand. "A beautiful place you have here."

"It is indeed Sir, thank you. Now if you'd like to follow me I'll show you to a private room where you can relax and freshen up before your press conference."

"Lead the way."

Miles led them through the building and over to a door at the far end of a short corridor. "Here we are Mr Elloway. There's a bathroom through there and you have fresh coffee in the jug. That door there takes you through into the boardroom for your press conference so you may hear a little noise as everyone gets themselves seated. Someone will come and let you know when they're ready for you. If there's anything at all you need, just press this button by the door and I'll be here right away."

"Thank you Miles, we'll be most comfortable here," Jake replied as he headed for the coffee and plate of cute looking little cakes. After pouring himself a drink he indulged in four of the delicate little pastel coloured confections. Hank poured a coffee for himself and took a tentative sniff of one of the cakes before taking a tiny bite. He chewed and then raised an eyebrow appreciatively before helping himself to two more.

Jake looked out the window just as a shiny black shuttlecraft took off and headed up into the clouds. This was a big change for him and he sighed as he realised what he was about to do and thought back to when he was a sixteen year old naive boy who wanted to be an actor. If anyone told him back then that in another twenty years he would be going into space to research his latest role, he would have laughed. He remembered how disappointed his father had been when he finally told him he did not want to go into the family business because he wanted to be an actor. Although Leonard Elloway had not yelled or punished Jake for refusing his offer of a place in Elloway Soundalight Enterprises, he knew he was disappointed because he did not speak to him for a week.

Jake hated the way his father ignored him when he was a kid. His biggest driving force back then was to make Leonard proud of him and every time he did something wrong or disappointed him, his father chose to ignore him rather than punish him and it had the desired effect for Jake seldom made the same mistake twice. He remembered so many times running to his secret den at the bottom of the garden and crying his eyes out after days of silence from his father and then the joy when he finally spoke to him again. Leonard Elloway was a hard worker and was the reason the family was so wealthy; his invention of the Soundalight Vidicom Transducer transformed the way vidicom movies were made and brought him the respect from the entertainment industry that he'd craved for years. Looking back now, Jake decided he would rather his father had beat him than ignore him and he never quite forgave him for those days of silence.

Once he had been able to show his father that he was truly serious about becoming an actor, Leonard had put the full weight of his position and wealth behind him and had personally financed his first three movies and he even co-starred in one of them with him. One day he had shown Jake some footage of movies made over five hundred years ago, before the time of vidicom or holographic cameras and Jake was awe struck. His favourite had been a rather silly tale of some good looking thug who liked to illegally race cars with his friends and the ever present but hapless cop who never quite managed to catch him. There had been ten of those movies made, all with the same characters but it was the tenth and final episode that Jake had loved so much. The good looking but brainless thug finally got his comeuppance when the now ridiculously over muscled cop managed to corner him in a barn out in the middle of nowhere and shot him right between the eyes. Leonard told Jake that according to old logs, there had been talk of an eleventh episode with one of the thug's many illegitimate kids taking his place. Just as filming was due to begin, one of the main actors had been jailed for indecently assaulting his ten year old son while the actor who played the cop was so hyped up on the illegal steroids he used to make himself so hugely muscular, that he could hardly function and even had to be helped to dress himself. That had unfortunately made those movies taboo and none of the movie making companies around in those days wanted anything more to do with the series. They were a suspicious bunch and so the eleventh episode never made it to the screen.

Jake begged his father to make a version of that movie with him in the role of the thug and Leonard was so taken with the idea that he agreed so long as he could co-star as the cop and so long as he caught him in the end. Jake agreed and took his first role as an up and coming hover buggy racer who steals parts to illegally enhance his buggy's performance and secretly sabotage's his closest rival's buggy, which crashes and kills him half way through the race which Jake's character wins. When knowledge of his illegal activity surfaces, Jake's character goes on the run in his enhanced hover buggy and Leonard, as the cop, has to chase him all over the American United Western Hemisphere until he finally catches up with him and arrests him. It was the one and only time Jake got to hit his father, even though the fight scene was staged and none of the blows actually hit home and Jake realised now, all these years later that making that movie brought him and his father much closer than they had ever been before. It was the first time, Jake realised as he gazed out of the window, that his father showed he respected him.

A discreet knock at the door brought him back from his reminiscing and he turned to see a tall and rather broad man enter and smile.

"Good morning Mr Elloway, I'm Paul Anders, Managing Director of Al Grazia Spaceport." He extended a hand, which Jake shook.

"Morning Mr Anders, I'm delighted to be here and thank you for your hospitality today."

"You're very welcome. Now everything is ready next door for your press conference so whenever you're ready?"

Jake looked at Hank, who nodded and put down his coffee. They entered and the room exploded with camera flashes and shrieks of 'Jake, Jake' from every direction. He went into automatic celebrity mode as they all took their seats and he made sure to smile warmly to everyone as he scanned the crowd for a nice piece of ass. Hank kicked him under the table and frowned. Jake grinned and hissed his apology as he waited for Adam Maydell to begin the proceedings with his speech.

When Adam sat down, Jake stood and cleared his throat. "Thank you all for coming ladies and gentlemen. It is always gratifying that so many show such an interest in my work and I feel honoured to be able to do what I do. As you're all aware, today I'm leaving Earth for three months but none of you yet knows why. Well, I'm proud to announce that Galactic Vidicom Pictures have signed their commitment to a new movie production that I'm delighted to be a part of. The role I'll be playing is something of a departure for me and in order that I'm fully prepared to bring the character to you all in as truthful and honest a way as possible, I shall be spending the next three months aboard an intergalactic freighter as research for my character's job and lifestyle. I'm very much looking forward to becoming part of the crew of the vessel and I fully intend to be an active member of staff and not just a passenger. Now I'm happy to take any questions."

Everyone in the room leapt up and arms waved frantically. Jake pointed to a pretty redhead in the front row and smiled at her. She blushed.

"Can you tell us more about the character you'll be playing in this new movie?"

"The character is named Vinnie and he works aboard an intergalactic freightliner as part of the crew. During a routine delivery, something happens that plunges them into a desperate fight to save the inhabitants of a dying world." He smiled at the redhead and she nodded and smiled back. "Okay who's next?" A sea of frantically waving hands filled the room once again and Jake picked a rather serious looking brunette with fabulous breasts. He smiled at the breasts, "yes ma'am?"

"In what way is this new role a departure for you?" she asked without a smile.

"Well you see Vinnie isn't the hero, world saving type of guy I normally play. He's just an ordinary guy who works for a living and hopes to do well enough to buy a decent home, meet a nice woman and have a happy family. Playing Vinnie will necessitate me using much more than just muscle to get his personality across. He will allow me to show everyone a far more serious side to my acting. This role has great emotional depth and I hope to show you all that I really am more than just a pretty face and a six pack." The brunette nodded and as she sat down, Jake thought he saw a faint smile on those pink glossy lips and he just couldn't help himself from wondering what they'd look like around his penis. "Who wants to be next?" This time he picked on a thin young guy with a moustache. "Yes Sir?"

The questions went on for almost an hour and Jake graciously smiled and answered them all, even when that guy had decided to ask him about some nasty rumours concerning vote rigging with the Entertainment Council. Every celebrity and entertainer has to run the gauntlet of vote rigging rumours; it is a side effect of the entertainment ranking system and although everyone is sure such things do go on, no one has ever been able to successfully prove it and get a celebrity thrown out of the rankings. Such a move would certainly end an actor's career for to be able to get any movie roles, an actor needs to have a place in the rankings. Even bottom place will do, so long as he is visible on the ranking table, he is able to accept roles and make movies. Of course, all the movie making companies want the actors higher up the rankings but everyone starts at the bottom and there are incentives for companies to encourage them to hire the lower ranked actors. Jake remembered the first time he became visible on the ranking table and smiled. The Elloway family had thrown a huge party to celebrate and he had been so proud. It had taken him three independently financed movies to get enough votes from the Entertainment Council to get his place on the very bottom rung of the ladder and he was proud of himself. Oh, he knew his father had persuaded one or two people to give him a chance to prove himself but he had done the acting and won the votes by his own talent and hard work.

He took the time to pose for photographs and sign autographs and was delighted to see the serious brunette amongst the throng. He shot a look at Hank who glowered at him as he mouthed 'NO' silently and grinned, then took her into his arms and allowed a hand to stray just a little too far down her back as they both grinned at the camera. She smiled up at him and he kissed her lightly on the lips. He shot another look at Hank, who by this time had a look of thunder on his face. Reluctantly he let the brunette go. After fifteen minutes of photographs, autographs, handshakes with wide-eyed lads hoping to be just like him one day and much kissing of pretty young things, he allowed Hank to steer him from the room.

Paul Anders, the Managing Director, was waiting for him with a smile. "Everything is ready for you Mr Elloway. Here is your galactic passport and your baggage is already aboard the shuttle. If everyone would like to follow me, I'll escort you to the departure gate." He led the way along the corridor and through the main concourse of Al Grazia Spaceport where several hundred regular passengers called out, waved, and took photographs as he passed by, smiling and waving graciously. Jake had the smile and gracious wave down to a fine art after his years in the limelight and everyone agreed that no other celebrity they knew of could do it as well. The speed at which that smile could appear in the presence of a fan, and the equal speed it would drop away once the fan was gone, was legendary. Jake was looking forward to three months of not having to be nice to everyone all the time but he was also scared for that very same reason. Having been in the limelight every day for the past twenty years and although it was a pain in the ass at times, he knew it would be weird not having it for three whole months.

"Here we are Mr Elloway," Paul Anders exclaimed as he showed them into a room with expensive looking leather seating and huge glass doors that led out onto the array of twenty landing pads, seven of which had craft of various sizes on them. "I'll wait outside while you say your goodbyes. When you're ready, knock on the door and I'll come and escort you to the shuttle." He smiled and left the room.

Adam Maydell approached, his hand extended. "Take care buddy, I'll miss ya."

"You too," Jake replied as they hugged.

"You'd better give me your cell phone now," Hank said.

"I'd better call Mom and Dad first. I promised I would." He dialled the Elloway Mansion and waited. His father answered. "Hi Dad. I'm just about to board the shuttle."

"Hey son, how did the press conference go?"

"Fine. There was just this one dude that went on about vote rigging but otherwise it was fine."

"That's par for the course I'm afraid. You're always going to have that issue thrown at you, all actors and entertainers get it. Just smile sweetly and refuse to be drawn into a fight about it."

"Yeah that's what I did," he replied. "Is Mom there?"

"Yeah she's hovering, trying to rip the phone from my ear. Take care son. Work hard and be humble okay? I love you."

"I will. Thanks Dad, I love you too."

"Jake? Baby is that you?"

"Hi Mom. I'm just going to board the shuttle now but I couldn't leave without kissing my Mom first could I?" he teased as he heard her sniff. "Hey come on Mom don't cry. It's only three months."

"I know, I'm just being silly. I'm proud of you baby. You show them Jake. You work hard and show them there's no actor with more integrity and real ability than Jake Elloway okay?"

"I will. I have to go now. Take care of Dad okay? I love you Mom." He switched off his cell phone and handed it over to Hank.

"Take care Jake. I envy you buddy."

"You do?"

"Hell yeah. I would give anything to go into space. I wish I was coming with you man."

"Well I'll see if I can get them to take you for a ride one day huh? Maybe for your next Christmas present."

"That would be awesome."

"Thanks Hank, for everything okay? I just wanted to make sure I thanked you in case, well you know. In case anything goes wrong up there."

"You're welcome. Break a leg huh?"

They hugged and Hank let Paul Anders back in.

"Right Mr Elloway follow me." He pressed a plate at the side of the huge glass doors and they opened with another satisfying swish. "Your shuttle is this one right here on pad four."

"That shiny little black number?"

"That's her."

"Nice."

"She's my personal shuttle craft Mr Elloway and she is very nice indeed. You will be very comfortable."

"Wow thank you."

"It's my pleasure. Here we are, after you." He stepped aside and Jake hopped up the three steps and into the shuttle. The interior was fitted out in the palest cream leather upholstery. The seats were big and even though Jake is a big, muscular man, he settled into one nearest the window and had more than enough room to stretch his legs out and relax his body without feeling squashed.

Paul Anders checked his seat belt and smiled. "I bid you goodbye Mr Elloway. Enjoy your trip and I look forward to welcoming you home in three months." He extended his hand and Jake smiled as he shook it.

"Thank you Mr Anders. See you in three months."

CHAPTER TWO

The shuttle lifted effortlessly off from Al Grazia Spaceport and headed up into the light cloud cover that dotted the summer sky. Jake looked out of the window and watched as the scene below him shrank and was lost below the misty clouds. He had never been into space before, despite the fact that travel to other worlds was commonplace and he felt a mixture of emotions. The strongest of these was fear, followed closely by apprehension, with excitement struggling to keep up from the rear. He was scared because he suddenly realised how alone he felt without his ever-faithful entourage behind him and he worried about how the crew would receive him. For the past twenty years he had been used to being adored by everyone and he hoped that his new companions were movie fans, even if they did not particularly like his movies. If they at least liked movies there would be some common ground to work with.

Hank told him that some of the crew were not from Earth and he was curious to meet them as he'd never met someone from a different planet before, although he knew that many lived and worked on Earth and there were even a couple of pretty well-known actors from other worlds. Five years ago he had almost landed a role in a movie that would have entailed him working alongside a woman from Albazilon 7, but the finance fell through and it never happened. He suddenly wondered what he should call them; he wasn't sure if the word alien was acceptable or insulting. He cursed aloud for not thinking to ask Hank about that.

"Is everything all right Mr Elloway?" a voice from up ahead called out.

"Huh?" Jake replied, leaning forward to try to see who was speaking to him.

"Is everything okay? You seemed a little um, upset?"

"Oh yeah, I'm okay thanks. I just realised I forgot to ask my Assistant something. Sorry for my language."

"No need to apologise. You'll be hearing all sorts of language from the crew and not all of it pretty at times. Is there a problem I could help with?"

"Well I umm, I've never met anyone who's not from Earth before and I just realised I forgot to ask how I should refer to them. Is the word alien okay or is that insulting? I don't want to upset anyone."

"The word alien, although not overtly insulting, is not used in general conversation unless one is talking in abstract terms. Remember that everyone is an alien to someone so if you refer to the people you will be working with as aliens, you are assuming that you regard them as somehow less than yourself. They are simply, people from other worlds, as you are to them."

"That makes sense, thank you umm, sorry I don't know your name."

"Oh forgive me, I forgot to introduce myself. My name is Shib. It stands for Synthetic Humanoid Intelligent Being."

"Synthetic Humanoid?"

"Yes Sir, I'm what you might call, an android."

"Really? Wow. Oh, I'm sorry; I didn't mean to be rude. This is all so new to me."

"You've never met an android before?"

"Well no."

"But we're everywhere. Have you not ridden on a hover bus, caught a cab or taken in a delivery from a postal worker?"

"Well, no. I guess I live something of a privileged lifestyle so I don't have to do any of those things."

"It's interesting that you should describe it in those terms Mr Elloway. I find humans very interesting and take every opportunity to meet and talk with them. It helps me to learn about them so that I can interact with them in a more real way so they can be comfortable with me."

"How do you mean, in those terms?"

"Well, you say you've never realised androids are so commonplace on your world because you've never had to do any of the things that would bring you into contact with us, and yet you say your life is privileged."

"Oh shit. No, I didn't mean my life is privileged because I've not met guys like you before. I meant it's privileged because I don't have to wait for a bus or hail a cab. Because I have plenty of money I have my own transportation and staff who work for me and my family and they do all the stuff like taking in postal deliveries etc."

"Ahh I understand now. Thank you for explaining. You know humans are very complex beings and I do struggle to understand all of the subtleties of their interactions with each other."

"Well you're always welcome to come and find me if you need help with anything. Actually it's a comfort to know there's someone I can talk to who won't be offended when I show my lack of experience."

"Thank you Sir, I will take you up on that offer. I work on board the Mayan Queen piloting the shuttles and driving the loaders and although the crew are hard workers and are always polite to me, it will be helpful to have someone to talk to on a less formal footing."

"Anytime buddy."

Jake looked out of the window and gasped at the sight of the Earth beneath him. This was something he had only seen in photographs or in vidicom movies but nothing could have prepared him for the sight of it. The beautiful blue green planet curved away in both directions and he felt a lump rise in his throat as he tried to comprehend what he was seeing. Down there he was a big noise but up here he realised he was a mere speck in a huge universe and he felt the weight of that realisation.

"Wow," was all he could manage to say as he fought the emotion rising within.

"Do you think it's beautiful Mr Elloway?"

"Do I think it's beautiful? Are you crazy Shib? It's the most awesome sight of my life."

"I must admit I find the concept of beauty most difficult to understand. How a man can look at a woman, call her beautiful, and then look at a lump of rock, covered in clouds and say that is also beautiful, is beyond me. I fail to see the connection."

"It's how it makes you feel Shib," Jake snickered. "Beauty is felt, not seen."

"Ahh so it's an emotional thing? No wonder I find it such a difficult concept. I don't have emotions."

"That's more of a blessing than a curse buddy," Jake replied. "Believe me. By the way, why aren't we floating around? I thought there wasn't any gravity up here."

"The shuttle is fitted with a Contra Wave Gravity Processor which simulates gravity. All space craft are fitted with such devices so you will be able to move around normally."

"Ahh okay, that's a comfort. Oh look, is that the Mayan Queen? Wow she's huge."

"Yes Sir that's her. We'll be on board in a few minutes."

Shib brought the shuttle into the huge belly of the Mayan Queen and set down on the pad with the gentlest of jolts. The shuttle bay doors slid shut and Jake heard a loud hiss.

"That noise is the shuttle bay being refilled with air so that you can breathe. When you hear the siren, it's safe for you to exit the shuttle."

Jake unbuckled himself and stood up, just as Shib appeared from the cockpit. He looked into the face of the android and smiled as he extended his hand. Shib shook it and was about to speak when a loud wailing siren boomed through the shuttle bay.

"Ahh there's the siren. It is now safe for you to exit the shuttle Mr Elloway. I'll fetch your baggage." He dialled a key code into the pad alongside the hatch and waited while it lowered. Jake looked out, expecting to see people waiting to meet him and was more than a little surprised to find no one there. With more than a little trepidation, he stepped down the ramp and looked around the grey and uninspiring interior. Two other shuttles stood on pads, one with its side open to reveal pipes, wires and connectors so he guessed it was being serviced or repaired. The shuttle bay was huge and as he looked around, he tried to get a feel for the place but it just did not feel like home to him, not yet anyway. He sighed and hoped he would get through this experience positively.

Shib appeared with his baggage and smiled. "I'll show you to your quarters and then give you a tour of the ship and introduce you to your co-workers."

"Okay. Thanks buddy," Jake replied quietly.

"Would I be right in guessing that you're feeling apprehensive?"

"You're very observant," Jake laughed. "I thought I was a better actor than that."

"You're current emotion is understandable but unnecessary. Follow me." He led Jake out of the shuttle bay and ushered him into a lift. Up one deck, he led the way along a series of corridors before stopping at a door halfway down on which was written 'Jake Elloway' and pressed a code into a pad to the side. The door slid open with a slight squeak and Jake got his first look at his accommodations. All of his conversations with Hank had not given him any idea of what to expect but having been used to the height of luxury for so many years, the room he now found himself in was something of a shock. It was no more than ten feet square at the most, with a single bunk along one wall, a single closet, a small table and chair. Behind a partition was a basin, toilet and two shelves. Everything was grey and the whole placed smelled of abandonment. The lack of a welcoming party and now this dreary room made him realise he was not going to be a celebrity whilst on board the Mayan Queen but he smiled politely to Shib, who put his bags down on the bunk.

"Your key code for the door is 279854," Shib said as he handed him a slip of paper on which the number was written. Jake pocketed it and thanked him. "Now let me show you around. On the wall at every intersection of corridors and every lift, there are maps of the whole ship, showing you where you are. It's quite easy to follow. There are three decks, the lower one being the engineering section, stores, and the shuttle bay at the rear. The middle deck has living quarters, kitchen, dining, recreation room and the connection tunnel to the barge. The upper deck contains the bridge, security headquarters and medical bay. The barge is a separate section to the main body of the ship that houses all of the cargo and freight."

"Okay that sounds easy enough to follow," Jake smiled.

"The only sections of the ship that you are not allowed to enter are the bridge and security headquarters, unless of course Captain Nagle invites you. Now let's go get some lunch shall we?" Shib led the way to the kitchen and introduced Jake to Zeke Mackie, Head Chef of the Mayan Queen. They shook hands and Jake was relieved to find Zeke quite a movie fan. He smiled a lot and smelled of sweat and onions but he was a friendly guy and Jake knew right away he would get along okay with him.

"Welcome aboard Jake," Zeke grinned. "I'm looking forward to talking movies with ya. Now how about something to eat, what would you like?"

"Oh umm, how about a sandwich?"

"Sure thing. How about a nice thick Hagglin steak sandwich?"

"Hagglin? I've never had that. What is it?"

"It tastes a little like a cross between pork and beef."

"That sounds wonderful," he smiled. "That'll do nicely."

"Okay, coming right up," Zeke grinned and disappeared through the door, behind which Jake could just glimpse a rack of saucepans and several five gallon drums of something. Ten minutes later a slim girl appeared carrying a plate on which was Jake's sandwich. She smiled shyly as she laid it in front of him.

"Your sandwich Mr Elloway," she whispered and blushed. Jake looked at her and realised within five seconds that she would happily leap into bed with him. Within a further five he realised he did not want to go there; she was not his type at all and she seemed just a little too young. Maybe if he got desperate towards the end of the trip. Maybe.

"Thank you very much," he smiled. The sandwich was wonderful; the rich meat was indeed like a cross between pork and beef but it had a rich smoothness unlike anything he had ever tasted.

"Wow this is wonderful."

"Thank you Jake," Zeke bellowed from the other end of the room. "Aamy? Could you be a good girl and get those vegetables prepared for tonight's dinner?"

"Oh sure Zeke, no problem," she replied and with a last look at Jake, she turned and ran back into the kitchen.

Zeke came and sat down as Jake ate his sandwich. "Jake? It's only fair that I warn you that Aamy is absolutely crazy about you and she might sometimes be a little umm, well how can I put it?"

"Forward?" Shib offered and Zeke smiled.

"Yeah that's it exactly. She's a very emotional girl and it's her first job since leaving her home world and she's kind of like a daughter to me and I umm, well I."

"Don't worry Zeke," Jake replied. "She's not my type and she's far too young anyway. What is she? Fifteen?"

"She's twenty three actually but yes I understand why you might see her as so young. She is a little naive but then that's how her people are. I hope you're not offended by my directness but I feel responsible for her y'know?"

"No offence taken Zeke. I can understand where you're coming from and I promise you'll have nothing to worry about."

Shib took Jake down to the engineering section and introduced him to the Chief Engineer. "Jake, this is Asmion Nefulan, our Chief Engineer. Everyone calls him Nef. He's from Damiklon Prime and there's nothing he can't fix, repair or rig up. He's a mechanical genius.

"Hello Jake," Nef smiled and extended his hand and Jake noticed his six, slightly webbed fingers. His voice was weird too and his surprise must have showed. "I can see we have a virgin amongst us Shib. How wonderful. Fresh meat." He laughed and clasped Jake's hand and shook it vigorously. "Sorry to have a joke at your expense Jake but up here you have to take your fun where you can. You've obviously never met anyone from another world before huh?"

"Am I really that bad an actor?" Jake laughed. "First Shib see's right through me and now you too? Maybe I'm in the wrong trade after all. I hope you aren't offended but you're right, this is my first time meeting anyone from another world."

"Not offended at all. I'm from Damiklon Prime as Shib correctly told you. We live both in water and on land on our home world, and as you've already noticed, my hands are rather different to yours and I have these too," he said as he pulled the collar of his overalls aside to reveal what looked to Jake like gills.

"Wow, so you can breathe in water too?"

"Yes, we have the ability to breathe in water and in air too."

"That's awesome," Jake grinned. "I'd love to be able to do that."

"Many from Earth envy us those very capabilities Jake. You will also have noticed my voice sounds strange to your ears?"

Jake nodded. "On Damiklon we don't talk in the same way Earth people talk. To your ears, our communications with each other would sound a bit like singing. We have to learn to speak in a different way if we want to work away from Damiklon, much like Earth people learning to speak another language if they wish to travel to another continent." Jake continued nodding, he was fascinated. "Inter galactic law also states that I am required to show you this." Nef pulled up his sleeve to reveal a four-inch long tube strapped to his upper arm. "I have a pair of retractable fangs and a venomous bite and this is the only antidote. All Damiklonians are required to carry it by inter galactic law and to show it to all personnel with whom we will be in extended contact. The security guys from upstairs check it every week so you don't have to worry about it."

"Wow," was all Jake could think of to say. Nef laughed.

"You and I are going to be great friends Jake. I'm in the room next door to yours by the way so I can help you settle in and get to know everyone. Now, let me show you the heart of the Mayan Queen. Just through here." Jake followed him deep into the engineering section to see the ship's engines. They were huge and although not mechanically minded, being a man meant he was interested and listened intently to what Nef told him. Nef introduced him to his staff and he even found himself signing a couple of autographs. After being on board less than two hours, he was beginning to feel right at home.

Shib took him up to the middle deck and along the connection tunnel to show him the cargo hold where he would be working and introduced him to his work buddies.

"This is Dredge and he is your supervisor while on board. You will take your orders directly from him whilst on duty and it is to him you will answer for everything you do while working."

"Hello Jake, welcome to the Mayan Queen."

Jake shook his hand and smiled. "Thank you Dredge. I'm very grateful to you all for letting me come aboard."

"The work is hard but not difficult. So long as you're happy to take orders and do as you're told, you'll fit right in."

"Oh I will, I will."

"This is Manlee 18 and this is Ace Chaplin. They are your co-workers and they will show you what is expected of you."

"Hello Jake, welcome," Manlee 18 said as he shook his hand. Jake looked into his eyes and saw a depth of experience he could not begin to fathom. There was no way to describe how but he just knew this guy had seen things and done things that would give other folks nightmares.

"Good to meet you Manlee."

"Hi Jake," Ace Chaplin grinned and shook his hand vigorously. "Man this is awesome having you here. I love your movies."

"Well thank you Ace, it's a real pleasure to meet you."

"We will expect you here at 0800 in the morning." Dredge said. "The guys here will be holding your hand for the first couple of days until you get to know your way around, so I won't hit you with work stuff this afternoon. See you in the morning."

"In the morning guys," Jake smiled as he followed Shib back along the connection tunnel. "Wow that guy back there seems a little umm, stiff?"

"You mean Dredge?" Jake nodded. "He is a very serious man and he expects his staff to do their job to the best of their ability. He doesn't have much understanding of the way people sometimes blur the lines between right and wrong and he expects those working under his supervision to obey him without question. He's from Regnor Prime and it's their way. Leadership is never questioned on Regnor. They are warriors and expect others to be as precise as they are about what is right and what is wrong. He can get a little stressed at times but so long as you work hard and don't question his leadership, he will treat you fairly."

"Okay, thanks Shib. I knew I couldn't expect life aboard to be a party. It's been a long time since I've had to take orders. I'll get used to it. By the way, that guy Manlee seems umm, well there's something about him you know? I saw something in his eyes. A kind of darkness. Am I imagining things?"

"No you're not imagining things Jake. Manlee is from a planet called Zylom 2. His people don't have different genders like most other races do."

"Really? So he isn't actually a he?"

"Technically no but Zylomians make a choice when they leave their home world to be known as either he or she, for the benefit of the other races they encounter who aren't used to a genderless humanoid. Manlee 18 made the choice to be known as he. You can safely forget his genderless state and consider him just another ordinary man."

"Okay thanks."

"He has suffered quite a lot in the past from bullying. That is why you see the darkness in his eyes. We have another Zylomian on board too. Hefton 24. He is Captain Nagle's first officer and again, he has chosen to be known as a man."

"This is certainly an education for me Shib," Jake sighed and ran a hand through his hair.

"Don't worry Jake; you'll get to know everyone in time. You won't be the new kid for long. Now let's go up to the top deck and show you the medical bay. I have to tell you about the head nurse you'll be meeting. Her name is Faline d'Extallio and she is from Azullon 4. Azullonians have a very different attitude to sex than Earth people do."

"Really? How different?" Jake was immediately interested.

"On Azullon, sex is considered to be nothing more than a momentary physical enjoyment and they will happily engage in sexual encounters with anyone they find physically appealing. Most males find this prospect unavoidably exciting, until they realise that Azullonians do not equate sex with love or affection. Earth men particularly find the prospect of a woman engaging in sex with any male she finds appealing, to show a lack of moral standards and it can lead to some aggression between males who all may be seeking the woman's undivided attention."

"I understand."

"You must be aware at all times that whilst she may choose to agree to a sexual encounter with you, she does so with several other males on board as well. There must be no accusations as to her moral standards and no in fighting with other men she engages with. This is something Captain Nagle made quite clear would not be tolerated."

"Don't worry Shib," Jake smiled. "I'll be a good boy."

Jake almost fell on the floor when Shib escorted him into the medical bay and introduced him to Faline d'Extallio, the Head Nurse. She was gorgeous; almost the perfect female form as far as he was concerned. She was slim, with massive breasts and blonde hair that reached down to her rather small but very pert ass. Her rounded but muscular thighs and slightly tanned skin gave her a truly exotic appearance. Her almond shaped black eyes held his gaze and then to his total surprise, she slowly looked him up and down. He felt like she was undressing him with those eyes and it turned him on.

"Welcome Jake," she smiled, her voice soft and delicate. "It is a pleasure to meet you."

"Thank you, I'm very happy to be here."

"Anytime you have a medical problem, you come here and see us. Our doors are always open, night and day."

"I'll remember. Thank you."

"I have your medical record here and I see you have an allergy to animal hair."

"Yeah that's correct."

"Come and see me when you have some free time and I will cure you of this affliction if you wish."

"Really? You can cure it? That would be awesome. My mother has always wanted to get a dog but because of my allergy she's had to go without."

"It is simple to cure and will not cause you any pain."

"Wow, thank you. I'll take you up on that offer."

"Until then Jake," she smiled and held him with those eyes again and Jake knew with every fibre of his being that he was going to be having sex with her soon.

Shib led the way back down to the middle deck.

"I'll show you the recreation room now Jake."

"Okay thanks. Wow she is one hell of a woman Shib."

"Her appearance pleases you?"

"Hell yeah," he snickered.

"Would you mind explaining to me what it is about her appearance that is so appealing? I've asked several of the other males on board and the only answer they give is to do this." He held out both hands, palms up and Jake roared with laughter.

"Well Shib, it's her breasts that do it for me. I find large breasted women attractive and the blonde hair makes it all the more perfect."

"Why are large breasts preferable? The women I've spoken with all say that when they're too large they are uncomfortable and can cause them back pain."

"Well I umm, I don't know really. Men regard them in a very different way to women. We see them as sexually attractive whereas they don't. It's just one of those weird things I guess."

"Could we discuss this further when you have some free time? It would be a tremendous help to me in understanding the people I work with."

"Sure buddy, anytime."

"Thank you very much. Ahh here's the recreation room." Jake found himself inside a large room filled with seating and gaming stations. A bar ran along the far end and venders stood along one wall dispensing anything from snacks to vidicom movies and everything in between. "The bar serves beverages from 7pm each evening. You do have an allocation of twenty five beverage credits each month, and anything over that you will have to pay for."

"Oh I don't touch alcohol Shib."

"Never?"

"Not a drop. I have to keep myself fit and healthy to do what I do, which means no drinking, smoking or recreational drugs. I don't even like to take pain medication if I can avoid it. It poisons the body and drains your strength little by little and in the movie business, your looks are everything so I have to abstain."

"That's very disciplined of you. The bar here does serve non-alcoholic and fruit based beverages too, so you should find something you can safely enjoy. Let me introduce you to everyone." He led Jake over to the small stage that sat at the end of the room and called out. The room fell silent and Jake went into automatic smile mode.

"Ladies and gentlemen, I'd like to introduce you to Mr Jake Elloway. As you all know he is going to be working among us for the next three months as research for a movie role he will be playing in the near future."

Jake smiled and waved a hand to the twenty or so faces that looked at him. Roughly half had smiles on them he noticed with a little disappointment, whilst the other half looked at him impassively. A couple called out hello and he made a great show of saying hello back. A guy at the back of the room called out and Jake turned to look.

"Can you play tapshots Jake?"

"Tapshots? Umm no I haven't heard of that. What is it?"

"It's a game played with two sets of dice," Shib explained. "I'm pretty confident that you'll be introduced to it before too long. Just a word of warning though, don't challenge Ace Chaplin to a game and if he should offer, refuse."

"Why?"

"Because he's an expert and he'll have the shirt off your back," a short muscular guy at the front replied and everyone laughed.

"Ahh okay, thanks for the warning," Jake replied.

"You want a drink buddy?" another guy asked.

"Sure, something non-alcoholic though please," he replied.

"No problem, come sit down."

"I'll leave you here while I go up to the bridge and inform Captain Nagle that you are safely aboard and have met everyone."

"Okay and thanks Shib." Jake sat and chatted with the guys and found several of them were movie fans, although only a couple admitted to being fans of his. He felt at home talking about movies and soon began to relax amongst his new companions.

Shib entered the bridge and approached Captain Nagle's chair. "Sir, Mr Elloway is aboard and has been allocated quarters. I've given him a tour of the ship and introduced him to key members of staff."

"So, the Elloway kid is finally here huh?" Captain Nagle looked up at Shib.

"Yes Sir. Would you like me to bring him here to the bridge to meet you all?"

"Hell no Shib, whatever next? If I can get through the next three months without having to spend any time in that bastard's company, I'll be a happy man. It's bad enough knowing he's on my ship at all and amongst my staff without me actually having to acknowledge him. No. Keep him away from me Shib. I want nothing to do with him. If it weren't for the money Galactic Vidicom paid us and the promise of a place in the credits of his next movie, I wouldn't allow him to set foot aboard any vessel of mine."

"Very well Sir."

"Where is he now?"

"He's in the recreation room."

"Keep an eye on him Shib. The moment he steps out of line I want to know about it okay?"

"Of course Sir."

CHAPTER THREE

Jake was delighted to discover that some of the guys had set up a gymnasium at the far end of the cargo hold, and by the time everyone began to move into the dining room for dinner, he had promised to help several of them with their workout routines. He'd found a couple of pretty girls amongst the general workforce and felt confident he would not have to go without some ass for too long. One of them, a curvaceous brunette with pointed ears from some planet or other he could not remember the name of was obviously keen and he grinned to himself at the thought that he would be having sex with an alien within the next three months. He wondered what Hank would make of that. The other girl was not so obviously keen but she was beautiful and he wanted her, so he paid her plenty of attention. As they were going into dinner, one of the guys named Crib called him aside.

"Hey Jake. Be careful buddy."

"What's up Crib?"

"That gal. Y'know the redhead? She's already spoken for. I just don't want you getting into any difficulty here. You gotta work with these guys for three months okay? She's dating a big Zamoran from engineering and those guys are pretty territorial."

"Aww hell, that's a damn shame. She's hot."

"Yeah tell me about it. Most of the guys on board would like to have her but she is a no go area with that big guy of hers around."

"Okay, thanks for the heads up. You never know though, she may dump him and then she's fair game huh?"

"If that happens then you can join the back of the line buddy; there's plenty here who saw her first."

Jake laughed aloud and sat down. Over dinner he got to know a couple of the guys a bit better and found a couple he reckoned would turn out to be decent buddies. Several of the crew he had met so far seemed quite disinterested in him and that phased him a little. Being used to public adoration for so long meant he had little experience of being disliked and he did not quite know how to handle it. In the end, he decided they were just morons and forgot them. Aamy made sure she waited his table and kept looking at him in a way that made him extremely uncomfortable. She was attractive and he would take her to bed if there was no one else here willing but there was something in the way she looked at him that made him keep his distance. He was just wondering what it was when Crib nudged his arm.

"I think you've made your first conquest there Jake."

"What?"

"Aamy, the little Terramoran waitress over there. You can't tell me you haven't noticed the way she looks at you."

"Yeah I've noticed," he grinned, "but there's something about the way she looks at me that makes me hold back. I don't know what it is though. She's a little intense don't you think?"

"Aww c'mon buddy, don't play the innocent with me. You really can't see it?"

"See what?"

"She's in love with you man."

"What? No way, you've read her wrong." Jake thought about it and the more he thought, the more he realised that Crib was right. It showed in her eyes when she gazed at him and he now knew what it was that put him off. It was the love in her eyes that did it. Jake was not into being in love and it put him right off. He did not need or want the baggage of a woman being in love with him.

"Hey there's no way I'm up for that kind of commitment and besides, Zeke has already warned me off."

"Really?" Crib grinned. Jake nodded.

"Yeah. He said she's like a daughter to him and he wouldn't want her to get hurt. He didn't say it in so many words

34

but I got the point. He was warning me off. That's okay cos I'm definitely not into the love thing. No way."

"Wow that old buzzard. I'd never have thought that of him. She's pretty though don't you think? I would love to, you know. If I had the chance."

"Hell yeah so would I but not with her feeling the way she does. That's a complication I don't need."

After dinner, Crib and Jake went back to the recreation room and began his indoctrination into the world of tapshots. By the time he went to bed he had grasped the basic principles. He went along the corridor to the shower room he shared with three other guys and was happy to find the water hot and plentiful. His bunk was not nearly as comfortable as his bed in the Elloway Mansion but he managed to drift off to sleep within thirty minutes. His dreams were filled with images of the nurse on her hands and knees while he pumped at her from behind her pert little ass. The hot redhead lay on her back underneath them both and cried aloud as the nurse's tongue brought her swiftly to a bone crunching orgasm. Jake awoke, swiftly threw back the bedcover and with just three firm strokes his penis exploded onto the floor of the dank grey room.

At eight o clock sharp Jake was in the cargo hold ready for his first day at work. Dredge was surprised to see him turn up on time and his surprise showed.

Jake grinned as he greeted him. "Morning Boss, hope I'm not late."

"Mr Elloway. You made it on time. That's good. Come with me and I'll get you issued with all your gear." He led Jake to a small room and issued him with overalls, boots and gloves. "Here is a key to your locker. It's number 751 in the room next door. Take off any jewellery and put this around your neck." He handed him a flexible metallic tube with tiny green lights all the way along. "This is linked to the ship's computer so we know where you are at all times when you're working. This can be a dangerous job at times and if we have to evacuate the hold quickly or get a team together to deal with an emergency, we need to know where you are instantly."

"Okay, that makes sense I suppose," he replied as he put it around his neck with a little caution. "Does it give me an electric shock if I misbehave?" he grinned. Dredge stared at him without expression and the grin fell from Jake's face.

"Just a joke Boss."

"You have ten minutes to get changed and then I'll hand you over to Ace and Manlee. They will show you what you will be doing today," he said and turned and walked away.

Jake went into the room next door to find his locker. "Jeez don't they have humour where you come from buddy?" he thought as he stripped off his clothes.

Ace proved to be much better company than Dredge and Jake soon relaxed. The guy was crazy about movies and Jake's movies in particular and he felt right at home with a fan fawning all over him.

"I always wanted to be an actor Jake. I love movies and I'm gonna be an actor one day. Hey maybe I can be in one of your movies huh? I could be your helpful sidekick. Every hero has a sidekick." He kept on and on about it and then began making up a whole storyline for their first movie together. It was funny but Jake had to admit the guy had a natural creative flair and he made a note of one or two of his ideas that he felt he could use in future movies. This guy could prove useful so he encouraged his fantasies and listened closely.

An alarm sounded and he looked up. "What's up?"

"A delivery has arrived," Ace grinned. "C'mon. Follow me." He jogged to the far end of the cargo hold and Jake followed. "Beyond this wall is the loading bay. All deliveries are unloaded there and then we move them into here for storage.

We need to suit up to go in there as the bay doors are open. In here." He led the way into a small room and helped him into a space suit. "Just breathe normally Jake. Air is pumped into your helmet automatically so as you breathe, more air is pulled in. Don't try to force it; just pretend it isn't there okay?" Jake nodded and grinned. This was so cool but he was scared. "Okay now step into these Mag Soles. Push down so they click. That's it. Great job. Okay let's go." Ace led them out into an adjoining room where a little truck was waiting. "Step into the back Jake, right there and put your feet onto those two plates, see em?" Jake stepped onto the plates and felt his feet, clad in the heavy Mag Soles, firmly anchor into the bed of the truck. "Great job. We don't want you floating off in there today. Okay ready to go?" He pushed a button on the wall and a loud hiss could be heard as air was pumped from the room and the wall slid back. A huge room lay before him and at the far end, the loading bay stretched from one side to the other. The rear bay doors were open and another huge space ship was floating nearby, a train of barges floating out from a hole in its belly and heading right towards them. Jake was transfixed at the sight but what held his gaze most was the sight of the Earth below them. With nothing but his helmet between himself and the void of space, he gazed down at his home world and felt everything around him melt away until there was nothing but him and the Earth below. As he looked, he felt tiny, insubstantial as the immensity of the universe hit home but at the same time he felt god like, gazing down on the world he dominated so easily, and realising how many of them down there were looking up and thinking of him up here.

"Jake. Buddy wake up." Vigorous shaking brought him back to reality and he turned to see Ace grinning at him.

"Sorry," he replied. "It's just so awesome. Seeing it like this is just," his voice trailed off and he shrugged.

"I know it is," Ace smiled, "and it never stops being awesome no matter how many times you see it. You get used to it, but it's always awesome. Now hold this, we have work to do and you've already seen how much of a sense of humour Dredge has. Let's get to it huh?"

Two hours later the loading bay doors closed and Jake heard the loud hiss that told him the room was refilling with air. The siren blipped three times and Ace took off his helmet.

"Good job Jake. Let's get these suits off and then I'll show you how to get this stuff into storage next door." Diligently, Ace showed Jake how to check each crate with the manifest and allocate it a storage position according to its contents. Anything volatile or dangerous was stored in a particular place but as this latest delivery was non-toxic and not dangerous, it could be stored in the next clear space alongside all of the other crates and drums next door. Each crate and drum then had to be tagged and entered into the digital storage manifest along with its position in the cargo hold, before being stacked and stored.

The Mayan Queen holds all sorts of weird and wonderful things stored in its cargo hold. From rare delicacies from the farthest systems of the galaxy, to life saving drugs distilled from plants only found in one smelly swamp on Telzier 5. Fabrics, jewellery, huge rolls of metal sheeting as thin as a hair but immensely strong, tiny digital devices and electronic circuitry parts all sat side by side in the cargo hold. Drums of chemicals, toxic to Earth humanoids but essential to the well-being of several other races were stored in a separate section alongside volatile liquids in their special cooling drum jackets. A trapdoor in the floor of this separate section could be opened to enable the ship's crew to jettison the dangerous cargo in the event of an emergency. Each drum was fitted with an automatic charge designed to detonate after 20 seconds of zero gravity, ensuring that in the event of such a jettison, nothing dangerous could land upon a planet and cause a tragedy. All the cargo hands check the contents of this section hourly to ensure all the monitoring devices show acceptable readouts.

"You must keep out of that section Jake," Ace told him when he asked what was housed in the secure area. "You have to have special training to work that section and as you're only gonna be here for three months, it ain't worth going to the expense and trouble of putting you through the training."

"No problem buddy," Jake replied. "I'm more than happy to keep away from the dangerous stuff."

"Okay let's do one more round of checks and then we can sign off for the day."

The cargo hold crew work a six-hour rotating shift pattern. Eight in the morning until two in the afternoon, two until eight in the evening, eight until two in the morning and two in the morning until eight. The crew do five days on each shift, after which they get five days off. Although he had only worked for six hours, Jake was tired. It had been a long time since he had done any physical work and he was glad he had the rest of the day to himself. He decided to make use of the on board gymnasium and spent a couple of hours working out with Ace, Crib and a couple of the others he'd met the evening before.

He was just about to leave to take a shower when the hot redhead walked in wearing tight shorts and a skimpy top. She did some stretches and then picked up a dumbbell and started doing squats.

Her perfect ass took his breath away and although he knew he shouldn't, he couldn't help himself.

"Hey honey. You're not getting the best out of your muscles that way. You want me to show you how to change it slightly to get more improvement from your workout?"

She hesitated before nodding. "Umm okay, thanks."

"No problem. Here, hold it like this and when you squat, hold your pelvis like this." He slid a hand down her back and the other down her belly and eased her pelvis forward. "Slowly now.

It's more effective if you do it real slow okay? Now up again, that's it, and down. You should be able to feel it working this muscle here," he smiled as he put a hand on her inner thigh. At that moment, the door opened and a couple of guys Jake had not met walked in. He said hello and they nodded in response as they looked from him to the redhead and back again. He knew what they were thinking but he didn't care so he turned back to her.

"That's it, slowly now, keep your pelvis forward. Good girl. You'll get a lot more out of your routine by doing it that way." He gave her his best celebrity smile and she blushed.

"Thanks very much."

"Anytime honey," he replied with a grin and left the room, the eyes of both guys burning into his back. Back in his room, he stripped off his clothes and laughed to himself as he showered. It was obvious those two were jealous at how easily he had got himself into close proximity to such a hot girl. He reckoned she had better taste than to look at two greasy bums like them anyway and with his looks and charm and his celebrity status, he felt confident he would be into her panties before too long. The hot water relaxed his muscles and he remembered the feel of her skin as his hand had slid along her thigh and he let himself wonder if she would have objected had he slid his hand a little higher and touched her crotch. She had a nicely prominent round ass and those little shorts she wore showed it to perfection. If he achieved nothing else while he was stuck here, he was determined he was going to get her out of those soon and he laughed at the thought of doing it right there in the gym, with her sitting on him as he sat at the bench press. Thoughts of those breasts filled his mind unbidden, the dark nipples in his face as she bobbed up and down on him, his hands clasped around that ass as she climaxed. He let out a groan as his body shuddered and he felt the slick wetness on his hand. The redhead faded away and he breathed hard as the hot water rained down on his muscular body. Jeez, if he didn't get some ass soon he would go blind.

He dressed and went to get something to eat. He looked around and saw Crib wave a hand, so he wandered over and sat down.

"How was your first day at work buddy?"

"It was fine. I'll never forget seeing the Earth through the loading bay doors though. Man that is just awesome."

"It sure is."

"Hi Jake. What would you like?" The quiet voice belonged to Aamy and Jake turned to see her smiling and looking at him that way again.

"Oh hi. Could I just have one of those delicious sandwiches you gave me yesterday? What is it called again?"

"Hagglin steak?"

"That's the one. I'll have that please." He smiled and made an effort to look away until he knew she had gone. Crib laughed.

"She wants you Jake."

"Oh stop," he replied and Crib laughed again.

"But she's so in love buddy."

"Crib, I swear if you don't stop," he laughed with him. "Hey that hot redhead came into the gym earlier. My god those teeny little shorts she was almost wearing. They could kill a guy."

"I know," Crib nodded. "That sort of cruelty shouldn't be allowed by galactic law."

"I tell you what though buddy. She has the softest skin on her inner thigh," he laughed.

"Jake you didn't," Crib's eyes widened in shock. "Tell me you didn't."

"Of course I didn't," he grinned. "I just helped her with her workout that's all. She was doing some squats and was wasting energy so I showed her how to do them efficiently. Two other guys were in there. Hey what do you take me for huh?"

"Believe me Jake when I tell you she is a no go area. You may get away with this one mistake seeing as how you're a stranger here but the next time, you're dead meat."

"It was innocent. I was just helping her with her workout, that's all."

"It doesn't matter. You touched her didn't you?"

"Yeah. Just a little."

"No go means no go. Don't ever touch her again, even innocently. Not if you value your balls that is. That boyfriend of hers is extremely territorial and will definitely react violently if he thinks anyone has strayed into his territory and touched his woman. I hope for your sake the two guys who saw you don't blab to him just for the kicks of seeing you get a beating."

"You're over reacting Crib. It was nothing. Ask her yourself."

"Damn Jake, you've got one hell of an education coming. It's gonna be fun being around here for the next three months."

After dinner that evening, Jake joined everyone in the recreation room. He was fully expecting to get roped into another game of tapshots but he learned that this was movie night. Everyone turned their seats around as a huge vidicom screen lowered from the ceiling. The lights dimmed and the screen burst into life.

"Hey look guys," a voice from the back yelled, "it's our Jake." The room filled with laughter and Jake groaned inwardly but laughed along with them.

"Oh no guys, you don't wanna watch me," he feigned modestly while secretly pleased that they were to watch him in action.

"Hey buddy, how can you climb a volcano, fly a space cruiser and kill seventeen Cronorsian Magnols with pants as tight as that huh?" More guffaws filled the room and he laughed with them.

"Last time I saved a girl from a burning building she turned out to be seventy five years old and as wrinkled as my ball sac," another voice from the back yelled. "How come you always rescue the hot babes dressed only in their lacy underwear?"

Crib was crying with laughter and Jake had to admit, it was funny.

"Maybe if you took a look at your face you'd have your answer," he yelled back and more laughter filled the room.

The movie played and the guys yelled their commentary all the way through and Jake took it all with good humour, glad that they were treating him like a friend and accepting him so readily. After the movie finished he got himself a drink; a colourful concoction of seven different fruit juices mixed with Antalian glacier water. He took a tentative sip and raised his eyebrows appreciatively.

"Hey Jake," a guy from the next table called, "have you ever worked with that guy Doug Divayne?"

"Yeah I made three movies with him," he replied.

"Really? What's he like?"

"He's okay but he can't function without his daily drug supply."

"No? You're shitting me. Really?"

"No shit," Jake replied. He then regaled them with stories of his encounters with Doug and his drug problem and whilst he never actually lied, he did perhaps exaggerate a little. They listened, entranced by the stories of the now ageing but still very famous and well-loved actor.

"I didn't know he was a druggie," Crib said. "He always seems pretty together whenever I've seen him on the news broadcasts."

"Of course he does," Jake nodded. "He's together because of the drugs. Without them he'd be a wreck. Do you remember that movie a few years back when some guy died halfway through filming and there was something of a scandal about it?"

"Yeah. It was touch and go whether the movie would get finished. I went and bought that movie just because of all that scandal."

"Well, between you and me," Jake replied, "rumour in the business is that one day he didn't get his fix before filming had to start and he had to get on set without it. They were filming on top of a high building and he had to pretend to fight a guy near the edge. He was so bad that he pushed the guy and he fell twenty storeys and died. Apparently everyone always makes sure he gets his fix before he's called onto set now."

"My god," several voices chorused.

"Apparently there were several near misses too," Jake grinned. He was in his element having everyone hanging onto his every word and he worked the crowd like the professional he knew he was. They listened intently and he kept them entertained for over an hour with stories of the other famous actors he had worked with and how they all have some flaw which makes them less worthy than himself. Just as he was about to launch into a tale of the very first movie he ever made, the door opened and a huge man walked in. The room fell silent and Crib went white.

"Oh shit, I warned you Jake."

"What?"

"He's the redhead's boyfriend and from the look on his face I'd say those two blabbed on you."

"But nothing happened," he said, shrugging his shoulders and raising his hands to emphasise his point. He looked at the man as he locked eyes with him.

The big Zamoran was a mountain of a man and reminded Jake of the Neanderthals from the museums he had been to. This was potentially awkward and embarrassing so he swallowed hard whilst trying to look calm and realised with some trepidation that it was likely he was going to get a beating. His eyes were huge; much too big for his face Jake thought as he held

44

his gaze and tried to think how to get out of this with his pride intact.

"You," he said quietly as he pointed at Jake.

Jake pointed at himself and feigned surprise. "Me?"

"You," the mountain repeated and took a step forwards.

Jake resisted the temptation to step back and held his ground. "What's up buddy?" he asked and smiled.

The mountain took another step forwards and the crowd gently melted into the walls, leaving Jake standing in the middle of the room with the mountain walking towards him. Feeling very alone, he suddenly wished he had some of the skills he displayed in his movies and knew he really should do something to impress the people here. After all, he is as an action hero so he cannot really flake out of this one with everyone watching. His public image would never recover.

"You wanna drink?" The mountain was now nose to nose with him and Jake could smell the anger coming off him, and he supposed the guy could smell the fear from him.

"You touched my girl and now you're gonna get hurt."

"What?" Jake feigned surprise again. "What girl?"

"In the gym," the mountain replied. "You touched my girl."

"Oh you mean the gal with the red hair? She's your girl? I was just helping her out with her workout routine that's all, so she can get more benefit from it. Believe me buddy, I didn't mean any harm." The mountain sniffed and Jake knew he was gaining the upper hand. "Hey buddy, she's beautiful and you're a lucky guy but I would never step on your toes okay? I have my career to think of y'know. I can't afford to be stupid like that."

This seemed to pacify the mountain a little. He let out a sigh and stepped back.

"You leave her alone you hear? You're new around here so you made a mistake. Next time is no mistake. Next time is a choice and you'll get hurt."

"I hear ya buddy," Jake smiled and raised both open palms in a placating gesture. "I've never met people from other worlds before so I guess it'll take time for me to learn all the rules. Hey, sit and have a drink with the guys huh?" The mountain sighed again and then to everyone's total surprise, he sat down asked for a Glamorian Cider. Jake fetched it and sat down opposite and grinned. "Great, now tell me about yourself. I'm Jake by the way," he smiled and extended a hand.

"The guys call me Titch," the mountain responded and Jake laughed as they shook hands.

By the time Jake went to bed, he'd learned all about Titch and his customs and he decided to be wise and leave the redhead alone for he knew he'd not be able to withstand a beating from her mountainous boyfriend. He reckoned he handled the situation wonderfully and felt proud of himself as he settled into his bunk. It was warm and comfortable as he lay on his back and thought back to when he was a wide-eyed teenager desperate to be an actor. In those days he was unknown and had worked hard despite his father financing him and he felt proud of his career. There was no doubt he was one of the best loved actors around and certainly one of the best looking and he'd been voted Best Male Ass of the Year twice in a row and had three awards from women's digital magazines for his toned body and physique. With his jet-black hair and bright blue eyes, he could do the smouldering gaze to perfection and he knew women found him attractive. His life was blessed in many ways and he had always been extroverted and confident about himself and very driven in his desire to succeed as an actor. Because of that confidence, he knew what his good points were and he was good at selling himself. A smile crossed his face as he realised he had successfully talked his way out of a certain beating from the most mountainous man he'd ever laid eyes on and had the guy drinking with him and chatting like buddies. This made him feel invincible and he drifted off to sleep with a smile on his face.

"You did well guys," Captain Nagle smiled. "It's just a shame he talked his way out of a beating. He's a better actor than I thought."

"We were sure he was gonna get it from Titch," the man on the left grinned and his companion nodded. "He went purple with rage when we told him."

"Never mind, I'll have a think and get back to you."

"Sure thing Captain, anytime," they smiled and left the room. Captain Nagle slammed his fist down on the table when he was alone.

"Damn you Elloway. Damn you. I'll find a way you bastard, just you wait."

CHAPTER FOUR

Kreeve engaged the covert stealth optimiser and set off in pursuit of the Mayan Queen. The huge hulk came into view and he settled the Barclay into position one hundred kilometres behind.

"We're in pursuit Captain. Holding at one hundred kilometres."

"Good. Now we just wait."

"Why wait?" Kreeve argued. "Why not jump them now and get on with it?"

"Patience Kreeve. There's no hurry. Maria, where are they headed?"

"The Sigma System. At their present speed they'll arrive in eight days and fifteen hours."

"Okay. We'll hit them at four days out. That way they've nowhere to run."

"They'll be in sector 16230/1890 sub section alpha 83903 during day four Sir," Maria reported. "There's no inhabited planets in that area so they won't be able to summon help and we'll have plenty of time to do the job and get out."

"That's perfect. I'm going to have another run through with the guys downstairs. Call me if there's a problem."

Ilyas Da Costa left the bridge and climbed down the steps to the large open loading bay below where his band of rough but loyal workers spent most of their time. The Barclay was a small ship and it was a bit of a squeeze with fifteen of them on board but they got along pretty well and most importantly, they obeyed him without question. They came from many different planets but they worked together as a tight team and in this business you need workers you can trust to obey quickly. He had not started out his working life as a pirate; he had been in the military and done ten years in the Deep Space Tactical Unit, or DSTU's as they are known. He'd made a lot of useful contacts during his time and when he was finally discharged after a fracas involving the daughter of an Allucian diplomat, he drifted for a year or so before bumping into a couple of hit and run guys in a bar on Sindlom 3.

Over the next ten years he built up his unit into one of most successful and feared pirate ships in the business. He never dared to guess what the price on his head was these days but whatever it was, he knew it was a lot. He still has a couple of bullets buried in him from sharp shooting Mercs and he has an impressive collection of scars, the best of which split his face in half from top to bottom. He got that from a legendary Merc called Tank who, much to Ilyas's relief, had been murdered two years ago. He liked the way it scared people when he shoved his face into theirs and sneered.

"Okay boys let's go over the job again huh? Who's got the map?"

"It's here Boss," a small wiry man called Ink replied as he spread it out on the table. They spent a couple of hours going over the details of the job and discussed as many possible scenarios as they could think of that could suddenly occur and botch things up.

"That's great. We still have four days to tighten things up as much as we can. Is everyone adequately armed?"

"Yes Sir," a large hairy man who smelled of sweat named Bow replied.

"And are those docking dollies fixed?"

"All but two Sir," Ink nodded, "and they'll be done within another day or so."

"Supplies?"

"We're okay for now but we can loot the Mayan Queen for anything we're short of."

"The shuttle?"

"Patch is still servicing her but she'll be ready on time."

"Great job guys. Okay I'm off to bed. Don't stay up too late huh?"

"G'night Captain."

The crew of Mayan Queen settled into their daily routine, unaware of the danger that lurked a few kilometres behind them and oblivious to the danger that awaited them three days ahead. Jake Elloway finished his second day on duty and only dropped three crates of cargo in all that time. He spent a couple of hours in the gym with a couple of the men and then headed up to the medical bay to see about getting the hot nurse to deal with his annoying allergy. Thirty-one years ago he'd found out he was allergic to dog and cat hair when his mother decided to buy him a puppy for his birthday. Within two days he was in hospital fighting for air and covered in a rash from head to toe. The puppy went to live with their neighbour and Jake cried for a week. Since that day, his entourage expertly shielded him from any sources of animal hair and although he was used to it, he often thought of that puppy and felt as though he had missed something huge. When the nurse told him she could cure him of this burdensome affliction he was delighted and although she had said it would not hurt, he didn't care if it did and he promised himself that when he got back home he was going to buy his mom a dog and get one for himself too.

The medical bay was quiet when he entered and looked around.

"Hello?" he called but got no immediate response. Before he could call out again he heard soft footsteps coming up behind and turned, only to find himself gazing into the face of the gorgeous nurse, Faline d'Extallio. He couldn't help but smile.

"Hi there," he grinned at the breasts. "I thought I'd take up your offer of a cure for my allergy."

"Hello Jake," she smiled, her almond eyes crinkling at the corners. "Of course. Come with me." She led him through into a small cubicle which contained just a single examination bed. "Strip down to your underwear and lie down. Would you like me to leave the room while you get undressed?"

"Oh no that's okay," he grinned. "I'm not shy." He was down to his underwear within ten seconds flat and settled himself. Faline dimmed the lights and pressed a switch in the wall and Jake heard soft sounds come to his ears as blobs of colour gently floated around the room. She looked down at him and again let her eyes travel up and down his body and he felt confident that what he saw in her eyes was appreciation.

"Now Jake just relax and close your eyes. I am going to heal you but you must relax. Listen to the music and let it carry you away." She climbed astride him and he opened his eyes to see those massive breasts sway slightly above him. Without warning he felt a twitch in his crotch as her ass settled into his groin.

"Close your eyes Jake and relax. Forget your body for now; there is time for other things later. Listen to the music." He felt her hands settle gently onto his chest and tried to relax.

"Listen to the music. How soft and soothing it is. Let it carry you away to the stars." He concentrated on the sounds and became aware of a warmth in the middle of his chest. Gentle at first, the heat increased and flowed throughout his body. After a couple of minutes, he felt as if his whole being was melting and it became a little uncomfortable.

"Concentrate on the music Jake, just let go of everything and listen to the sounds. Nothing else matters but those sounds. Trust me, you are safe here. Open your heart and listen."

Jake listened to the sounds and tried hard to focus on them to the exclusion of everything else. Within a few more minutes, he felt as if he had no body at all; it was as if he was just life force suddenly freed from the confines of the body and he felt more vibrantly alive than at any other moment in his life. What felt like a tingling electrical charge coursed through his being and with each passing second he felt his life force growing in strength and expanding until he felt as if he was everywhere in the universe at the same moment. The flow of energetic life force soared around his being until he felt himself vibrating. At first it seemed to be marking time with his heartbeat but it gradually increased until the vibration was so fast he wasn't aware of it any more. He felt life force flowing out through the top of his head, round and down his body and back in through the soles of his feet and up through his body in a continuous flow. It felt as if at any minute he could turn around and see the face of God himself.

"Jake? Jake, wake up." The soft voice reached through to his consciousness and he held on with his mind as it pulled him upward towards wakefulness. He opened his eyes to find himself still lying on the examination bed in the side room of the medical bay, a blanket over him and Faline standing by his side.

"Did I dream all of that?" he asked as he rubbed his eyes and ran his hands through his hair.

"No, you didn't dream it Jake. It is a unique experience yes?"

"Wow it was amazing," he sighed. "I can't even begin to describe it. What did you do?"

"I am from Azullon 4. We are adept at healing the body by connecting directly with the life force of our patient and correcting its flow pattern. When your body is suffering it affects the flow of your life force energy and by correcting that flow, we enable your body to cast off the affliction. You are a very healthy Earth male Jake. You keep your body well. You are now cured of your allergy and the infection that was just beginning in your bladder is also gone. Your problems lie not in the body now Jake. It is your heart that needs to be healed now."

"My heart?" he frowned.

"Yes. The pain from your childhood is still with you and until you can cleanse yourself of it, it will always have a measure of control over you. I can help you with that if you wish but it will require you to face those demons from the past head on and allow your life force to express its feelings openly before you can be free of it."

"Oh," he sighed as he looked away. Jake was just a boy when he had learned to control his emotions. Both of his parents had indulged him due to their continued inability to have any more children, but they had been strict disciplinarians too. His father punished him by ignoring him whilst his mother would lock him in his room, sometimes for a whole day and had spent many hours crying his eyes out and learned to lock those feelings away once he became a man. The decision had been made years ago and he would never feel those feelings again. He was however, always aware of their presence within him and often longed for them to go away. Sometimes he found himself yearning to be loved and to forget those boyhood tears but he'd never found the courage to face that part of himself and as he had grown older, that part became locked further and further away.

"Take time to think about it and come back to me if you decide you want to deal with this okay?"

"Okay," he nodded and smiled. "Thank you. You're amazing and I'm very grateful."

"It is my pleasure Jake," she smiled back. "You are very beautiful," she said as she looked him over with her eyes again. "Your body is beautiful."

He pushed the blanket off and sat up. "So is yours," he smiled as he followed her example and let his eyes travel up and down her body.

Aamy smiled as she exited the lift and headed towards the medical bay. This morning she had decided to ask Faline if she could help her with her confidence so that she might approach Jake without feeling like a shy little kid. The nurse was nice and she was happy to take her a sandwich up for lunch each day as it gave her an opportunity to have a chat with her. She was so happy Jake was on board and was desperate for him to notice her and want to spend time with her. Although now twenty-three, she had been in love with him since she was thirteen years old and saw her first vidicom movie. He played a cop who had to chase down a murderer, whilst avoiding getting killed himself. The character had fallen for the daughter of the latest victim and she had taken it upon herself to aid him in his quest to bring the killer to justice. At first, Jake's character had not wanted her interference but as the movie went on, he fell for her and when she was almost killed by the murderer and was only saved by him taking a bullet in her place, she fell into his arms and they kissed passionately. Aamy spent many hours imagining being that woman in the movie, even tried to dress like her, and never thought she would ever get to meet Jake in person. She was so surprised and delighted when Captain Nagle announced that he was to spend three months with them researching for a role that she nearly fainted on the spot and Zeke had got worried and asked her if she was okay.

The medical bay door was open when she approached so she walked in and looked around for Faline. There was no one around and she thought perhaps there had been an emergency and Faline had forgotten to shut the door as she rushed out, so she placed the sandwich down on the counter top and turned to leave. Just as she turned, she heard a noise from one of the examination rooms. It sounded like groaning and she was intrigued to know whom it was that sounded so ill so she tiptoed over and bent to look through the keyhole. Her eyes widened in shock as she saw the naked figure of Faline on her back on the examination bed, writhing as Jake, also naked and sweating, thrust hard between her legs. Faline groaned again and then Jake cried out as his body shuddered. Aamy watched in horror as Jake fell onto Faline's breasts and sucked at her nipples as she clasped her hands around his ass and pulled him hard inside her. She leapt away from the door and ran from the room, knocking a tray of instruments to the floor in her haste to leave. She ran down the corridor, took the lift to the middle deck and raced to her room to vomit into the toilet. Once she finished bringing up her insides, she fell onto her bed and cried her eyes out.

Jake stepped into the shower and grinned at the memory of the awesome sex he had enjoyed with Faline. She was insatiable and he had managed to climax three times in succession before she was satisfied. He was normally a one shot man but Faline brought out something in him that drove his desire to heights he never knew existed. Laughter filled the shower room as he remembered and realised that he would enjoy being in a relationship with her if the sex was always that good. Jeez, he decided he would even consider being faithful to her if the reward was that good. He had been married once, a long time ago but it didn't last and they divorced after just a year. It was when he was eighteen and stupid and had got a local girl pregnant. At the time, he was beginning to be noticed as an actor so he could not afford any public scandal so he hastily married her. Trouble was she lost the baby after three months and their relationship worsened after that. The divorce was amicable and he took good care of her financially so he held on to his rapidly growing reputation and had not lost any votes from the Entertainment Council over it. Since then he decided marriage was not for him and he had enjoyed life as a famous and good-looking single man. There had been three relationships in the intervening years but none lasted more than a year. One claimed he beat her, which was not true but as he could not prove it, he ended up losing three votes that year and it took him two further years to make up the loss. The other two both tried to sue him for paternity and sold their stories to the media but tests quickly showed he wasn't the father of their babies, so he came out unscathed and actually won public sympathy over it. He could not trust women after that so he was very choosy now and only ever used them once and then forgot them. No promises, no feelings and no disappointments.

His mother Jacqueline Elloway often snipped at him for not making her a grandmother and he guessed she was pushing him to settle down. He knew he would have to at some point but he could not see the rush; he is only thirty-six, there is time enough for that yet. It would happen when it was right and he felt sure that when he got home and could surprise her with a dog, she would stop nagging him to get married. He finished his shower and dressed, intending to go to the recreation room to meet the guys. There was a knock on his door and he found Shib standing there.

"Hey buddy, come on in."

"Am I disturbing you Sir? I can come back another time if you are busy."

"No, no. Not at all. Oh and call me Jake huh? What can I do for ya? Sit down, please."

"Thank you. I was hoping you could explain more to me about sexual and romantic attachment between humans. I hear my co-workers talking and would like very much to be able to contribute positively to such discussions."

"Sure, what do you want to know?"

Jake spent the better part of an hour explaining in graphic detail to Shib about his experience of sexual attraction and romance and paid particular attention to making sure he understood the very subtle but important difference between the two. He even helped him to understand some of the crude language he heard his co-workers using and he finally explained the mystery of the open hands gesture when referring to why the nurse was so attractive.

"Y'see Shib. When a guy is talking about a woman and makes this gesture," he said as he cupped his hands, palms up in front of him, "he's saying that she has big breasts and a lot of Earth men find bigger breasts sexually appealing."

"I see," Shib replied as he copied the gesture a couple of times. Jake laughed loudly at the sight. "Thank you very much Jake, this has been most instructive and educational. May I return again at some time and continue this conversation?"

"Sure buddy, anytime. Now let's head off to the recreation room and see what's going on shall we?" They left and headed down the corridor. As they approached the room next to Jake's, the door opened and Nef appeared.

"Hey Jake, how are you getting on?"

"I'm settling in nicely, thank you."

"Would you like to come in for a drink?"

"Well thanks; I'd love to if you have anything without alcohol."

"I never touch the stuff either but I do have some wonderful Limagian Nasra juice I keep for special occasions."

"Sounds wonderful. I'll see you later Shib."

"Enjoy your drinks gentlemen."

Jake followed Nef into his room and noticed with some envy that his quarters were at least double the size of his own. He understood that Nef is a permanent member of the crew, and someone in a position of authority but he is a celebrity and he reckoned he deserved a better room than the one he had but he was not going to complain so he complimented Nef on the decor.

"Wow nice room Nef. I like your style buddy," he said as he admired what looked like a collection of wicked looking daggers on the wall. "These are awesome. Are they from your world?"

"Thank you, yes they are Damiklonian war daggers. Many generations ago we were warriors and our ethic was one of fight and die fighting or be regarded as a coward. Since those days, we've evolved past such aggression but we still remember those times as a part of our history. We believe that while we no longer hold that ethic as valid for us now, to remember it will help us to maintain our evolution away from it.   The daggers are now merely ceremonial but important nonetheless. We use them in a ceremonial form of martial art. It helps to keep our speed and agility sharp."

"Really? I'd love to see that."

"You would? I can give you a brief demonstration if you'd really like me to. Choose a dagger for me would you? Be careful, they are lethally sharp."

"Awesome," Jake grinned and approached the display on the wall. There must have been twenty or more in the collection, of all different sizes and designs. He chose one of medium size that sported an S shaped blade and two pointed prongs. "This one Nef. Show me how you use this one."

"You have flair Jake," Nef smiled. "An excellent choice. This is what we call the Bringer of Tears. It was used in close quarter combat, normally in pre-arranged duals. As you see, there is a pointed spike coming from the hilt on each side of the blade and running parallel to it.   These spikes are a certain distance apart for a very specific purpose. Watch."

Jake sat and watched, entranced as Nef stood ramrod straight, eyes closed and breathing deeply. Then with lightning speed, he gave the most amazing display of agility Jake had ever seen. He twisted, leapt and ducked, thrust and sliced and finally lunged the dagger forward at eye level with a loud cry. The whole display took no more than two minutes but Nef was breathing hard.

"You see Jake, these spikes are so designed so that when the move is executed perfectly, not only does the blade slice right into the brain but the spikes pierce the eyeballs. On Damiklon, it was thought that to render your opponent blind was the greatest of victories and anyone not killed but blinded by an aggressor carried a weight of shame for the rest of his life. Back in those days, to be killed in battle meant your loved ones could remember you with honour, but to be rendered blind, and therefore unable to battle again, meant you were a burden to your loved ones. Hence the name Bringer of Tears."

"That was amazing," Jake replied with genuine awe. "Incredible. Thank you for showing me. Wow I'd love to learn to do that."

"I'd be happy to teach you if you like. You can learn the movements even without a blade. It will help your agility and speed.

"Awesome, thank you."

"Okay stand up and hold your arms like this," Nef smiled.

Jake was exhausted when he and Nef went in to dinner but it was the most fun he could remember in ages. He had offered Nef the temporary position of Personal Martial Arts Trainer, with an official mention in the credits of any movies he used the skills in, in return for teaching him and Nef accepted happily. They agreed to spend two hours every day training and Jake was delighted. He even offered him a permanent job amongst his staff with an excellent pay package and Nef said he would consider it. Jake tried to persuade him; telling him he could start his own training school and as he would be the first Damiklonian to work on Earth, there would be no competitors taking his customers. Nef seemed hesitant to say no right away so Jake decided to keep at him about it until he either agreed or declined and in the meantime, he would be getting the benefit of his knowledge.

"Anyone know what's happened to Aamy?" Crib asked when Jake sat down at his table. Everyone shook their heads.

"The little waitress?" Jake asked. "Something happen to her?"

"I don't know," Crib shrugged, "but she was late on duty this afternoon and she's not waitressing tonight. Zeke's keeping her in the back of the kitchen."

"Maybe she's love sick," Jake grinned and Crib snickered.

"At least you don't have to try to ignore her tonight buddy," he replied and Jake laughed. "So how was your day?"

"Great thanks. I got my allergy sorted out by that wonderful nurse," he replied and winked at Crib who snickered again and shook his head. "And I also started a new martial arts training regime."

"Martial arts?" Crib asked. "You managed to persuade Nef to teach you his shit?"

"Yeah. I'm definitely gonna be using those moves in future roles. It's awesome, you should try it."

"Several guys have asked him to teach them but he's always refused. How come you managed to persuade him? You must have one heck of a cute ass buddy." The whole table roared with laughter and Jake grinned.

"I guess I have the gift of persuasion huh? I offered him a job too actually."

"A job?"

"Yeah, as my personal trainer. He'd make a fortune on Earth. There's no one from his world living or working there so he could have his own business with no competitors."

"And what did he say?"

"He said he'd think about it."

"Really? He didn't turn you down flat?"

"Nope. I guess he will end up turning me down but he is at least gonna think about it and you never know, he might accept."

Zeke came up to the table and took their orders. Jake noticed he looked a little flustered.

"Is everything okay Zeke?" he asked. "Someone said Aamy is not well today."

Zeke looked at him without a smile and then suddenly bent down so he was nose to nose with Jake.

"You tell me Jake. What did you say to her?"

61

"What?" Jake replied and felt the weight of everyone's gaze on him. "I haven't said anything out of line. In fact, I haven't spoken to her at all today. I haven't even seen her today. I didn't come down here for lunch."

"She wouldn't tell me what the problem was; just that she hates you and never wants to set eyes on you again. I know I asked you not to touch her but I didn't mean for you to break her heart."

"I don't know what's up Zeke," Jake shrugged. "I really don't know anything about it. I haven't even seen her today and I've never said anything bad to her. Honestly buddy I've no clue what this is about. If you find out then tell me would ya? Bring her out here so I can ask her what I'm supposed to have done."

"She doesn't want to see you Jake and I don't want her any more upset than she already is. Just keep away from her for a while and we'll see how she is." He returned to the kitchen and Jake looked around the table to see all eyes and ears on him.

"What?" he challenged angrily and they looked away.

Shib entered just as a couple of pretty girls were leaving and Jake noticed him look at them. He grinned as he remembered their conversation earlier.

Shib saw him and wandered over. "Hello gentlemen. Did you see the rack on those two?" he asked as he cupped both hands in front of himself. The man at the end of the table spat out his drink and soaked the man opposite him and everyone roared with laughter. Jake thought Crib was going to pee his pants laughing.

"Don't tell me," Crib said when he could finally talk, "he's been talking to you Jake."

Captain Nagle listened intently and smiled. He was pleased at how things were beginning to pan out and he was sure things would develop further without much prompting from him.

"Thank you both. I'm grateful to you. Keep me posted okay? I want to know everything he does that affects any of my crew negatively. He's only been here three days and already he's nearly caused a riot from the Zamoran, he's made several storage errors at work and he's dropped three crates of Dolmerian Ale which I have to pay for. Now he's upset our waitress and chef, has tried to poach my chief engineer and he's even corrupted my android." The two men grinned and Captain Nagle scowled.

"Sorry Captain," the man on the right said. "It was just so funny."

"I'll bet it was," he replied as he paced up and down, "but the laugh will be on him soon. So help me I'm going to have him, you see if I don't. Keep your eyes and ears open huh?"

"Yes Sir," they nodded and left him alone.

He wandered over to the shelf above his desk, picked up the small photograph, and smiled. She smiled back at him, her long dark hair tumbling down her shoulders and he felt a lump rise in his throat.

"You will have justice," he whispered as he stroked a finger down the photograph. "I promise you, he will pay."

CHAPTER FIVE

Ilyas Da Costa stood with his men around the table in the loading bay of the Barclay and studied the map. They were having a last run through of the details of the job and he was finally satisfied that they all knew what they were to be doing.

"Okay guys, today's the day. You all know what you're doing. I don't want any fuck ups today please. Lew, you're piloting the shuttle. Ink, you'll be making sure those docking dollies do their job. Once we're docked, Patch and Ink will blast a door open for us. Once we're in, we go straight to the bridge and take control. Once we have control we can take things at our leisure and make sure we get what we want and get out without any problems. Any questions?"

"Where will we be entering the ship Captain?"

"Ahh yes, thanks Johnson. Ink and I have been discussing this and we've decided to dock at the rear, directly on top of the medical bay. We'll be closest to the bridge there. I know it would be easier to blast our way through either their shuttle bay or loading bay doors but we'll be furthest away from the bridge there and we don't want anything to go wrong as we're making our way to the other end of the ship. Once we have the situation under control we can get what we need from the cargo hold without worrying about running into any brave cargo hands trying to be tough. Okay guys, let's arm ourselves up and get ready to go. I'll be on the bridge. Two hours and we're off. Be ready." He ran up the steps and entered the bridge.

"Okay Kreeve, let's do it. Catch them up buddy."

"Yes Sir," Kreeve grinned as he gunned the Barclay's engines to close the gap between them and the Mayan Queen.

"Maria, keep an ear on their transmissions. If they see us before I want them to, I want to know about it."

"Yes Sir," she replied. "They haven't seen us yet. All is silence from their end."

The Barclay, invisible behind its covert stealth optimiser barrier crept silently up behind the Mayan Queen like a predator waiting to ambush its prey. Kreeve expertly manoeuvred into position a hundred metres to the left of the hulking cargo freighter and flipped the Barclay into autopilot.

"We're in position Captain. One hundred metres and holding. Ready for stage two Sir."

"Good job. If everything goes to plan, we should be in and out within a couple of hours. If we run into difficulty, I'll call. Otherwise maintain transmission silence."

"Yes Sir."

Ilyas leapt down the steps to the loading bay and looked at his men. Ink handed him his guns and he nodded. "Okay guys, let's go shopping." They leapt into the shuttle and closed the hatch. Ilyas pressed his communicator. "Kreeve, open the bay door now please." The door slid back, squeaking and grinding and Ink made a mental note to service it as soon as he had some free time. "Okay Lew, let's be off."

Lewis Marcuse, co-pilot for Ilyas Da Costa for the past two years lifted the shuttle off the pad and headed out the rear end of the Barclay. A gentle arc to the right and they saw the huge hulk before them. The shuttle didn't have the luxury of a covert stealth unit so they all knew that time was of the essence here. The shuttle shot towards the Mayan Queen and Lew brought it expertly into line atop the medical bay. Ilyas was confident of gaining entry quickly.

"We're in position Sir," Lew yelled and Ink got to work furiously with the docking dolly controller. The docking dolly is a portable docking device designed to allow one ship to ride piggyback style on top of another. This is useful in an emergency, or when the usual docking procedures or loading bays and shuttle bays are out of action. It is basically a flexible tunnel which attaches to the host ship via four legs. Suction maintains the dolly in position and the legs have an explosive anchor system. As soon as the device locks into position and the suction is activated, the dolly legs fire explosive anchors into the hull of the host ship, which further hold it in position. Within three minutes, they all heard the distinct sound of the explosive anchors and Ink grinned and nodded.

"We're on. Patch, come on let's open a door huh?" The two men raced along the tunnel and set the hull breach mechanism in place. This device contains a network of a dozen small charges that explode in a very controlled way. Rather than causing everything to blast away in all directions, these devices keep the blast contained in one direction only. With all twelve charges set to explode inwards towards the centre of a circular pattern, they blast a roughly circular hole in most hulls up to four feet thick. The charges were set and the two men backed off. Ink held the triggering mechanism in his hand. Ilyas nodded and the ceiling of the medical bay blew in.

Faline was preparing to treat a patient who had a broken wrist when the explosion rocked the ship. Luckily, she and her patient were in a side room when the portion of ceiling blew in so they avoided being crushed. She ran into the main medical bay to see men sliding down on wires from the hole in the ceiling. One look at the guns they carried told her they were not friendly so she stood still and locked eyes with one of them.

"Well hello there baby," he hissed as he looked her up and down. "I might just keep you alive, for a while anyway. Hey Captain, I found me some spoils of war."

"Keep your mind on the job Johnson," Ilyas replied, "or you'll have me to answer to and believe me, she ain't worth that."

"Yes Sir," he replied somewhat reluctantly.

Ilyas grabbed Faline and stuck his gun in her side. "Move," he commanded and shoved her forwards. He steered her out of the medical bay and marched her down the corridor towards the bridge. Seeing the keypad by the side of the door, Ilyas realised he would need a code to enter.

"Open it," he ordered as he dug his gun into Faline's ribs. She reached out and entered the code and the door slid open. Ilyas entered with Faline and grinned as the bridge crew looked up in surprise that quickly turned to horror as they realised what was happening.

Captain Nagel stood and looked at the man holding a gun to his head nurse and frowned.

"Who the hell are you and what do you want?" At the same moment, Hefton 24 and Arsh Baglin leapt from their seats and lunged for the men. Twelve guns pointed at them and they sat back down.

"I wouldn't do that if I were you gentlemen," Ilyas hissed. "If I were you I'd behave myself and do what the nice man wants." Before he could continue, gunfire rang out behind him. He turned and saw two dead security officers and grinned. "Good job boys. Go check if there are any more lurking in there." Johnson, Wells and Moody nodded and left the bridge to check the security station next door. Ilyas looked around at the bridge crew. One captain, one first officer, another man who was probably the helmsman and a cute chick, most likely comms or navigation.

"Well now, looks like we got ourselves a real party going on huh? Ink, check em for weapons."

The patient, still in agony with his broken wrist slipped out of the medical bay and headed down to the dining room, which was half-full as it was getting near lunchtime. He looked for the most senior officer there and found Shib and Nef.

"Hey guys," he called out. "Hey guys please," he yelled a bit louder and everyone looked at him. "Didn't you hear that awful bang from upstairs?"

"We heard something yeah but we had music playing and we weren't sure what it was," a bald headed man nearest to him replied.

"There's some men come aboard with guns. They blew a hole through the medical bay ceiling and dropped down on wires. They've taken Faline hostage."

"What the fuck?" Zeke replied in shock as murmurs went around the room.

"I think they went to the bridge, in fact I'm sure they did. They couldn't have gone anywhere else other than down here and you obviously haven't seen them."

"Well who the fuck are they and what do they want?" a voice from the back of the room called and several pairs of shoulders shrugged and more murmurs went around the room.

"Pirates," Zeke replied. "I'll bet a month's pay they're pirates."

"Pirates? Nef asked. "But what would they want with us. Pirates don't normally target freighters unless they're known to carry weapons or currency. Mayan Freightlines is well known not to carry such things. We're of no interest to pirates."

"In any normal circumstances I'd agree with ya but things are different now ain't they?" Zeke replied.

"How do you mean?"

"Well now we have a famous celebrity on board. Him and his family are worth a lot of money back on Earth and he's a real big noise in the movie business. Their family owns property on several different planets and I'm willing to bet that his Mom and Pop would pay handsomely to get their little boy back."

"Oh shit," Nef sighed. "Of course, that has to be it. We have to hide him."

"Why?" a voice from the back asked.

"Why?" Nef repeated with a frown. "Because we're not gonna just hand him over, that's why? Are you nuts?"

"If they want him, let em have him," another voice from the back yelled. Nef was dismayed to hear several grunts of agreement and several heads nodding. "I never did like his movies anyway."

"But that's crazy," Nef yelled. "You really mean to tell me you'd happily hand him over to them without a second thought? Thank fuck my safety isn't in your hands, assholes."

"He's been nothing but trouble since he got here," the same voice retaliated. "He's upset Aamy, who was crazy about him and now cries her eyes out whenever his name is mentioned. He manhandled Titch's girlfriend and almost made him blow his stack, and that was after he was warned to leave her well alone. He's damaged several crates of cargo which we will have to pay for out of our pay and he even tried to make you go and work for him and leave your buddies here. Why the hell should we protect him huh?"

"Because it's the right thing to do you moron," Nef yelled and ran from the room.

He knew Jake would be in the gym by now so he raced down the connection tunnel to the cargo hold. As he ran, he tried to think of what they should do. Common sense told him they should hide, but where? As he entered the cargo hold, the answer came to him. He sighed with relief and raced to the gym. Jake was doing squats with Titch and talking movies and they both looked up as he entered.

"Hey buddy, wanna join us?"

"No man. Come on, you have to hide."

"What? Hide?"

"Please Jake, we don't have much time. They'll be here soon. We have to hide you."

"Who will be here and why do I have to hide? Hide from what?"

"We've been boarded by pirates."

Titch dropped his dumbbell and looked shocked. "Shit, are you sure?"

"It has to be, who else would blast their way in through the medical bay roof?"

"But we haul cargo, not weapons or money," Titch replied.

"Yeah I know but now we're hauling rich celebrities too," Nef replied.

"Oh fuck." Titch looked at Jake. "You gotta hide buddy."

"Come on Jake," Nef urged. "You can hide out amongst the crates. We're carrying a Yolician Funeral Canoe. You can hide in there until we figure out what to do. Me or Titch here will bring you food and water and you can take some P-Gels with you."

The three raced from the gym and down through the long expanse of the cargo hold. Halfway down Nef stopped and started climbing the storage racks and urged Jake to follow suit. Titch brought up the rear in case Jake missed his footing and they were at the top in under thirty seconds. Slowly Nef began to make his way between the crates to the very middle of the stack where the huge Yolician Funeral Canoe lay in its own huge crate. He indicated to Titch, who ripped the lid off with his bare hands and pushed it aside.

"Inside here Jake, there's plenty of room. Titch, find some P-Gels would ya?" Titch nodded and disappeared, only to return within three minutes with a handful of clear bags filled with what looked like tiny particles of clear sand. Each bag had a tube leading from the top which ended in a small cup.

"Here ya go Jake. If you need to pee, use these." He turned as he heard another crate being torn open and saw Titch helping himself to armfuls of small packets of field ration packs.

"Ahh well done Titch. Here Jake, this isn't gourmet but it's food. Keep quiet and wait for me or Titch to come get you when we've thought of some kind of plan okay?"

Jake looked at him wide eyed. Everything happened so fast there wasn't time to really digest what was going on and he realised now that he was scared shitless and didn't know what to do. Pirates? He could not begin to comprehend what they would want with him until he remembered Nef saying the ship was now hauling rich celebrities. So he was to be kidnapped huh? He wished very much that Hank was here and he wished even more that Nef and Titch were not going to leave him here hiding in the dark on his own for god knows how long.

"Shit guys," he said, the shaking in his voice evidence of his fear. "Oh shit. What do I do? I can't run away can I? I'm in space for fuck's sake. I can't hide forever."

"Don't panic Jake," Nef said. "Titch and I will think of something. Just hold on to yourself okay?"

"Don't leave me alone too long guys huh?" Jake begged.

Nef smiled. "Hey buddy, we'll be back to check on you when we can. I promise okay?" He noticed Jake's chin begin to wobble and he felt sorry for him. He put a hand on his shoulder. "We'll fight for you buddy. I'll fight for you."

"Me too," Titch nodded in agreement.

Titch pulled back the lid and Jake found himself in semi darkness and alone. Thin slivers of light pierced the cracks in the wooden planking of the crate and Jake was grateful it was not totally dark. He heard Nef and Titch climb down and run off, their boot steps fading into silence. His body shook, the adrenaline coursing through his veins making him light headed, and his heartbeat thundered in his chest and throbbed in his ears. As the silence overwhelmed him, he put a hand over his mouth and closed his eyes in a vain attempt to stop the hot tears he could feel on his cheeks. At once, and unbidden, the memories of all those hours he spent locked in his room after his mother's regular angry outbursts came flooding back to his mind and he burst into tears, unable to fight back as the fear washed over him. There was no way he wanted to die yet and he certainly didn't want to die out here in space without his family and without his fans. Thinking back through all the movies he had made, he realised that all of the heroes he portrayed would be out of this situation within hours and still get the girl at the end. Forcing his emotions under some degree of control, he wondered what some of those characters he'd become known for would do in this situation, and he realised that whatever it was, they were only able to do it with the help of camera trickery, safety wires and body doubles. His movie heroes were all smoke and mirrors and he had none of those things at his disposal now to help him get out of this alive and with his pride intact. The hot tears flowed as he cried at his own inability to live up to his public image. He knew his fans thought he was every bit the hero he portrayed on screen and he realised that everyone on board would be expecting him to be able to look after himself, although some of them were probably sensible enough to realise the movies aren't real. Surely they must realise he can't really take bullets and survive with just a sexy scar and surely they must realise that when he jumped across that wide chasm in the movie about the space ship crash, that it was a body double doing it and he'd been on a wire anyway?

Nef and Titch climbed down the stack of crates and ran out of the cargo hold and deep into the engineering section. Once Nef was happy they were in the best hiding place, they sat and tried to think what to do.

"What the hell are we to do Titch?"

"Maybe we could say he never came after all," Titch offered hopefully. "Maybe we could say he got sick and put it off until we get back from this run."

"Maybe that would work if everyone on board could be trusted to lie with us," Nef replied.

"They might. He's a movie star ain't he? People like movie stars."

"Would they? Would those two who told you about Jake helping your girlfriend in the gym lie with us to save him? Would they?"

"Dammit," Titch hissed as he realised the wisdom of Nef's words.

"Would Aamy lie with us to save him?" Nef continued. "I don't know what he did to upset her but I believe him when he says he didn't knowingly do anything or say anything to hurt her. She's so crazy about him that she'd probably be upset if he just didn't say hello one morning, or if he looked at another woman and smiled too much. Would she lie to save him?"

"And knowing how protective Zeke is about her, I doubt we can rely on him either," Titch added and Nef nodded.

"Maybe we could get Crib on our side. He seems to be friendly with Jake. They always sit together at dinner and they always seem to be getting along well. Now we need to think of what we're going to do. Come on Titch, think."

"The obvious thing is to get him off the ship, but how? And where to?"

"We could steal a shuttle I suppose."

"But where would we go? How far can those things travel?"

"Shit," Nef hissed. "We're too far out for our shuttles to be any use. They're not built for the long haul."

"I'll bet theirs is though?" Titch replied and Nef looked at him wide eyed.

"Hey yeah, I'll bet it is too. Pirates need to be able to run, and run quickly, and far. We could steal theirs while they're busy searching for Jake."

"You can pilot?" Titch asked. "You never told me that."

"No I can't but Shib can pilot anything and he's become good friends with Jake."

"He's good friends with everyone," Titch remarked. "Would he come over to our side do you think? He's an android remember and they can't take sides."

"That's true but one of their programmed rules is that they mustn't do anything to cause harm to come to humanoids."

"So we can't expect him to help us kill those pirates then," Titch said.

"No but if we tell him they are out to harm Jake, he will feel obliged to help us keep him safe," Nef smiled. "Jake is part of Shib's circle now so he'll feel obligated to ensure his safety."

"Okay so let's go find him," Titch said. "And Crib too. That way, Jake has friends around him."

"We could ask Ace Chaplin too, he's crazy about Jake's movies. I'll bet he'll be only too happy to tag along."

"Okay," Titch nodded. "You go find Shib and I'll find Ace and Crib and we'll meet umm, where shall we meet?"

"In my quarters. My door code is 33848. One hour okay?"

Ilyas Da Costa grinned at Captain Nagle. "Well Captain Nagle, what a situation we have here huh?"

"Who the fuck are you and what do you want?" Captain Nagle hissed.

"Captain Ilyas Da Costa is my name and I'm very happy to meet you Captain Nagle. You've got something I want. Something I intend to take from you and if you try to prevent me, then I shall kill you and your staff, one by one until I do get it. Am I making myself clear?"

"This must be a mistake," Hefton 24 said. "We are a freight liner. We don't carry arms or currency."

"Ahh but you are carrying something extremely valuable today," Ilyas replied.

"What?" Arsh Baglin snapped. "What the fuck is it?"

"I heard that the Mayan Queen has gone into the movie business," Ilyas grinned.

"Jake Elloway? Nagle replied in shock. "You want Jake?"

"I do indeed Captain and I mean to have him."

"Fine, take him. You're welcome to him," Nagle replied.

Hefton 24 looked at him in shock. "You're just going to pass him over? Just like that?"

"Of course I am. I never wanted that bastard on my ship in the first place."

"But Captain," Arsh exclaimed. "Why did you agree then?"

"Because Galactic Vidicom paid Mayan Freightlines a whole wedge of cash as an incentive and the boss of the firm told me I had to. They also promised the company a mention in the credits of the movie. Believe me if was down to me, I'd have refused point blank."

"Well I'm very happy to hear that you're so keen to hand him over," Ilyas smiled. "So where is he?"

"I've no idea," Nagle replied. "But he can't have disappeared can he? He's aboard somewhere. Bodecki, make a general announcement to all decks asking Jake to report to the bridge immediately." Stella Bodecki hesitated, looking first at Arsh and then back to Captain Nagle.

"Bodecki, do you have a hearing problem?"

"No Sir," she replied and turned to the comms panel and flipped switches. "All decks, this is a general announcement. Would Jake Elloway report to the bridge immediately please? Repeat, Jake Elloway to the bridge immediately." She flipped off the comms and looked at Captain Nagle.

"It's done Sir."

Nagle glared at Ilyas, who glared back. "Good," Ilyas smiled. "So now we just wait. Sit down everyone; we might as well be comfortable while we await our celebrity guest. If he's not here in twenty minutes, we're gonna tear this hulk apart and its crew along with it."

Nef ran along to the shuttle bay searching for Shib and was relieved to find him discussing the servicing schedule of the shuttles with an engineer. He called him aside so they could talk in relative privacy.

"Shib. Would I be right in thinking that you like Jake Elloway?"

"Well as you know Nef, I don't have emotions, but I can admit that I freely choose to spend time with him whenever possible and that I regard him as a valuable member of my circle."

"That's great buddy. Would I also be right in assuming that if you knew his life was in danger you'd do what you could to help keep him safe?"

"Of course. Why are we having this conversation Nef? Is there something I should know about?"

"And would you still be keen to help him, if it meant you having to lie?" Nef stared at Shib, who stared back as his artificial brain considered the question, which Nef realised, must be causing him some problems.

"As you know, lying goes against my programming. If, on the other hand, refusing to lie meant that Jake would be in danger, then his position within my close circle would force me to agree to lie. Saving life takes precedence over lying where my programming is concerned. Does that answer your question?"

"Thank heavens. Yes buddy, it does," Nef sighed audibly with relief. "We've been boarded by pirates who mean to kidnap Jake."

Shib looked shocked at this news. "Pirates? But what would they want with us? We don't haul weapons or currency?"

"Exactly," Nef nodded. "So it has to be Jake they're after. Now Titch and I have hidden him. He's safe for a while but he can't stay hidden for long. We want to steal the pirates' shuttle and make a run for it. Titch is finding Ace and Crib, who are also friends with Jake to see if they'll help us. We need you to fly the shuttle. None of us can fly and without you, we can't stop them taking Jake. Please help us. It means that you'll have to keep this a secret and lie if anyone asks you where Jake is." Another agonising few seconds passed in silence as both men locked eyes, waiting while Shib's artificial brain digested the information.

"I will help you Nef. If I were able to experience human emotions I would say that I regard Jake as my friend and I will help you."

"Thank you buddy, thank you very much. I've arranged to meet Titch in my quarters. Let's go there and wait for him and plan what we're going to do."

Titch headed off to the recreation room and found Crib and Ace locked into a game of tapshots.

"Crib, Ace, I need to talk to you guys."

"Give us a few minutes Titch, I'm losing my shirt here," Ace hissed. Titch wasn't in a waiting mood so he went up to the table and picked Ace up bodily and tucked him under his right arm. He then picked Crib up and walked out with them tucked under his arms. The whole room whooped and whistled.

"I wanna play mommas and papas and you're gonna play with me," Titch said as he ignored their protestations and marched down the corridor towards Nef's quarters. He punched in the code and entered, before dropping them onto the floor.

"What the fuck is happening," Crib said as he stood and brushed himself down.

"Have you lost your marbles Titch," Ace asked.

"Sorry guys but I need to speak with you and I ain't got time to waste waiting for you to finish playing that stupid game."

"Okay big guy, what's the problem. You have our attention," Ace asked as he sat down on Nef's bunk.

"We've been boarded by pirates."

Both men went white and exchanged glances. "What the fuck?" Ace exclaimed. "Pirates? Are you sure?"

"Holy fucking shit," Crib said as he ran a hand through his hair. "Pirates? Jeez I heard someone talking about it earlier but I assumed he was joking. I never thought we'd run into them. What the fuck do they want with us? We don't carry guns or cash?"

"No but we're carrying Jake," Titch replied, "and he's worth a fortune. Nef and me reckon they're here to kidnap him and we don't feel like letting em have their way so we're gonna steal their shuttle and make a run for it. You want in?"

"Oh fuck," Ace replied with a sigh. "Of course, it has to be him they're after. We've nothing on board they could possibly want."

"Nef and I hid Jake but he can't stay there forever without being found if they decide to search the ship, which they will when they realise he isn't around. We don't have a lot of time and we need to know if you want to help us at least try to get him away. Some of the guys on board make it quite clear they don't like him and we don't feel confident that they won't just turn him over to them. I think that's the wrong thing to do and so does Nef. He's talking to Shib now to see if he'll help us fly the shuttle. Of course if he refuses we're sunk cos none of us can pilot but at least we're trying."

"I'm in," Ace said.

"Me too," Crib agreed.

"Awesome, thanks guys," Titch smiled.

A knock at the door startled them. Titch went to answer it and found Manlee 18 standing there. Without waiting for an invitation, he marched right in and faced the three.

"I want to help you too."

"Help us with what?" Ace replied.

"Help you get Jake away to safety," Manlee replied. "I'm sorry; I listened from outside the door. I don't know if he regards me as a friend or not but I can speak from much experience of bullying and I won't stand by while another person is bullied for personal gain. I couldn't live with myself if I stood by and did nothing while he is kidnapped for ransom. After what I went through I couldn't let someone else go through that without trying to help. He may not be the nicest guy in the galaxy but no one deserves to be mistreated and bullied."

"Thanks Manlee," Ace replied. "You of all people know what it would mean for him if we handed him over. I'm real glad you're with us buddy."

They sat and talked about their proposed plan until Nef entered with Shib. When he saw Manlee 18 sitting with his friends, Nef looked shocked.

"It's okay Nef," Titch said, "Manlee is with us."

"Really? Are you sure buddy?"

"Yes," he nodded. "I can't stand by and let them take him to be held against his will and possibly even tortured and killed. I know what that's like and I couldn't sleep at night if I didn't try to help."

"Shib is with us too, so we're good to go now we have a pilot." Everyone smiled with relief at the news. Nef was just about to continue when the comms siren sounded.

"All decks, this is a general announcement. Would Jake Elloway report to the bridge immediately please? Repeat, Jake Elloway to the bridge immediately."

"We don't have much time guys," Nef said. "We need to come up with a plan."

"They will have attached their shuttle to us by way of a docking dolly set up. As you said, they've piggy backed onto the medical bay and gained entry that way. We will need to get up to the medical bay, climb up through the docking tube, lock it off to prevent decompression when we leave and then fly off in the shuttle," Shib told them.

"It sounds simple when you say it like that," Nef replied, "but we can't just walk up there with Jake, especially as we've no weapons."

"Stealth will be the order of the day, Manlee said and everyone nodded. "So we need to find a way to get there without being seen. Any ideas?"

"Actually yes," Shib cut in. "We could use the crawlspace between the inner hull and the insulation layer. It's just wide enough for a man to walk. We can climb the decks by way of the hull braces that join the inner and outer hulls; they're just like ladders and will take us all the way to the medical bay."

"So how do we get in there?" Ace asked.

"There are entry panels all over the inner hull for access in the event of a hull breach. We need to be able to access the crawlspace to check and effect repairs to the outer hull and the insulation layer."

"Awesome, let's do it," Nef said. "Is everyone agreed?" Everyone but Titch nodded. "Titch?" Neff asked quietly. "You don't wanna leave your girl do ya buddy?"

"I'm sorry guys," he said sadly. "I can't leave with you but I will help you all the way until you're safely away. I'll do anything I can to help but I can't leave without her and we can't ask a woman to come with us on a trip like this."

"That's okay buddy," Crib said. "We understand. Thank you for helping us."

"Okay, so where's the nearest entry point to the crawlspace from the cargo hold?"

"In order to access the upper decks of the main ship, we will have to enter the main ship's crawlspace and not the one on the barge section. That means we will have to make it through the cargo hold and up the connection tunnel to access the nearest panel. Where is Jake hiding?"

"In the Yolician Funeral Canoe."

"Okay so that's about a third the way down the hold. We will have to find a way to make it up the cargo bay and through the connection tunnel without anyone seeing us. Any ideas?

CHAPTER SIX

Ilyas ordered the bridge crew to sit down so Ink could tie them up securely. Captain Nagle refused at first, stating that as he was happily handing Jake over to them, there was no need to restrain him or his crew.

"Listen Captain," Ilyas sighed. "I'm the guy with the gun here, so I reckon that puts me in charge and I'm ordering you to sit the fuck down." An intense glare pushed his point home and the Captain reluctantly returned to his chair. He was happy to hand Jake over but he wasn't happy to push this pirate captain over the edge and be shot for his trouble.

"Good boy," Ilyas grinned. "Ink?" he nodded his head in the direction of the Captain's chair and Ink nodded back. Once Nagle was secured to his chair, he let Faline go and ordered her over to the far side of the bridge.

"Ink, secure her in restraints as well. If we don't get what we want then she'll be an acceptable substitute. Like you said Johnson, spoils of war. Man I love my job," he said as he looked her up and down. "Where are you from baby?"

"Azullon 4," she replied quietly. The pirates looked at each other with eyebrows raised as grins spread across their faces.

"Really?" Ilyas grinned. "Well, well, well, it looks like we're gonna be having ourselves a party guys when this is over."

"I sincerely doubt that," Faline replied as she glowered at him. He walked over and knelt down in front of her.

"Oh you do, do you?" he asked and slapped her hard across the face.

"Hey," Arsh Baglin yelled. "There's no need for that. We're letting you have Jake. Leave her out of this."

"We have ourselves a hero here guys," Ilyas said as he strolled over to Arsh and looked down at him. "Are you willing to die to save her? Well?" Arsh glared at Ilyas for a few seconds and then looked down at the floor with a sigh.

"I thought not." Once the crew were restrained into their chairs Ilyas approached Stella Bodecki and looked her up and down. Her tanned complexion and slim body pleased him and he smiled.

"Hey baby what's your name?"

"Stella Bodecki," she replied without emotion.

"Well Stella. I must say you're a beautiful woman. Are you Hispanic?"

"Half," she replied.

"Nice," he nodded as he continued looking her up and down. "I've always had a penchant for Hispanic women. Ever since I lost my virginity to Maria Vargas back when I was a rookie in the military. Wow, she was one hell of a woman, as I'm sure you are. You're gonna enjoy yourself as the Captain's woman." Stella looked down at her feet and tried not to cry. She didn't want to be the Captain's woman, at least not that one. There was only one Captain she wanted to give herself to and he was not a pirate.

Ilyas was getting irritated at the wait. A glance at his watch told him the twenty minutes was up. He turned to Stella and glared.

"Time's up pretty lady and I don't see no Jake Elloway rushing in to rescue you all. Open a comms channel to all decks." She hesitated and looked at Captain Nagle, who nodded before indicating her hands restrained to the arms of her seat.

"Ink, loosen one of her arms." Ink rushed over and freed her right arm. "Okay honey; flip them switches like a good girl," Ilyas ordered. She opened the channel and Ilyas smiled. "Attention all personnel. This is Captain Ilyas Da Costa of the pirate vessel Barclay. I have your Captain and bridge crew under guard. I require everyone to assemble in the shuttle bay immediately. Anyone found in any other area of the ship will be shot on sight. Jake Elloway is to surrender himself into my care immediately and any personnel knowing his whereabouts is to inform myself or one of my men." He signalled to Stella to close the comms channel. "Secure her back into restraints Ink. Okay guys, we wait for ten minutes and then we tear this place apart. Anyone found wandering around is to be shot. I want Elloway and I mean to have him."

Jake's eyes adjusted to the gloom and he began to relax. The sounds of people walking around as they worked their shift in the cargo hold echoed round the huge room. Try as he might, he could not help but think about this new situation that arose so quickly before there was time to prepare himself to react better. He decided to try to keep his mind occupied on something else, so he thought back over the movies he had made over the years and tried to remember one that had something of a similar event in it. The only one he could think of was the one where he played a soldier fighting in a war on some god-forsaken planet that had been invaded. His character was captured along with his whole company of men and they had to escape and get to freedom and continue the fight. Of course, it was a great help when they found the lock to the cell was old and easily broken. They were then delighted to find their captors were knocked out cold with one fake punch to the head and they were further blessed that their captors conveniently left their shuttle standing idle right outside the camp. He gave a deep sigh of frustration at the way life is never quite as convenient as it is in the movies. As he was mentally making his way through the movie where he played a cop looking for his partner who had disappeared, he heard the call asking him to come to the bridge. For a split second he almost obeyed but fear rooted him to the floor of the canoe. Images of men with guns running through the cargo hold and climbing the stacks of crates filled his mind and he began to shake.

"Oh shit," he whispered to himself. "What the fuck do I do? Someone help me please. I don't wanna be in this shit, I wanna be at home making movies and doing what I do."

He thought of his parents back home on Earth, oblivious to the danger he was now in and wondered how they would react if he never came home to them. If the pirates demanded a ransom, he knew his parents would pay up. Being one of the most well known movie stars in the whole of the business, he knew Galactic Vidicom would put the money up to help bring him home. Even his fans would get a fund going if it became public knowledge, which he was sure it would; stuff like this never stays secret for long. This made him feel a little better but the knowledge that not all of the crew aboard the Mayan Queen would necessarily fight to help him, dismayed him.

"Morons," he hissed. "The whole damn lot of em."

He thought back to his last conversation with his parents. The quick phone call before he boarded the shuttle now seemed like a lifetime ago but he was glad their last words had been good ones. Thinking back over his life, he decided that overall, he had done a lot of good. Over the years, he had done a lot for charity and even had an American Humanitarian Achievement Award for his work with Dream Makers, the charity the Elloway family set up to help terminally ill children realise their dreams. He had met and had his photo taken with so many kids over the years the charity had been going and he felt good that meeting him was the dying wish of so many kids. A small laugh escaped him at the memory of his Mom, dutifully polishing all eleven of his EnWatch Awards given by the Entertainment Council each year for those entertainers who show the most progress in their points throughout the year. Every week she did the rounds of his awards, the Living Legend Award taking pride of place in the specially designed glass cabinet that stood proudly in the entrance hall of the Elloway mansion. The President of the American United Western Hemisphere presented him with the it at the grand ball in the presidential palace. His handshake with the President was all over the media for weeks after that and he thought his Mom was going to burst with pride.

Just as he was about to rummage around for one of the ration packs he heard another comms announcement, this time telling everyone to go to the shuttle bay and that if anyone knew where he was, they were to tell the pirate captain or be shot. He heard running footsteps as the crew working below downed tools and ran off towards the connection tunnel that led to the main ship and the shuttle bay. Total silence surrounded him and he went cold as he imagined himself standing on the floor of the cargo hold, alone in the eerie silence. Memories of similar feelings in those far off days when his mother used to lock him in his room whenever he had been naughty as a kid again came back to him. All at once he was seven again, locked in his room for stealing a freshly baked cookie off the rack and crying his eyes out, his pleas and apologies steadfastly ignored until she let him out again hours later. He angrily swiped away a tear that trickled down his face and took a deep breath.

"For fuck's sake I can't just lie here and wait to be found. I have to do something," he whispered aloud. The only problem was, he couldn't think of what he should do that didn't involve giving himself over to the pirates. Maybe he should give himself up, he wondered. Maybe they would treat him okay and let him go when the ransom was paid. He then remembered a movie he had made where the daughter of a rich businessman was kidnapped for a huge ransom. The detective he had played was hired to help find her and when the family paid up, they tried to kill her anyway. If it were not for his character's timely entrance, she would have been dead. With this memory, he decided he didn't trust these pirates to let him go even after getting the ransom money. Overall, he reckoned they would have to kill him so he could not identify them, after all, the man had said his name on that last comms announcement. Captain Costa or something, Jake couldn't remember. He wrestled with the awful choices; either lie here and starve to death or be found later by the pirates when they search the ship or give himself up now and hope they don't kill him. Neither of these options thrilled him but he knew he had to make a choice.

He was just about to struggle out of the canoe and give himself up when he heard someone climbing the crates towards him. Oh shit, they'd found him already. His body began to shake as he gasped and fought with his fear, the noise getting nearer and nearer. Suddenly the lid of the crate moved and he found himself looking up into the face of Titch. He sighed as the realisation that a man he thought was a buddy had given him away.

"Come on Jake, hurry up and get outta there. We don't have much time," Titch hissed.

"What's happening?" he asked as he struggled into a sitting position. "Do they know where I am?"

"Don't be a moron," Titch hissed. "You're going on a little trip with your buddies okay? Now hurry the fuck up or do I have to carry you?" Jake heaved a sigh of relief as he realised that they had not given him away after all. With some difficulty, he dragged himself out of the canoe and climbed down to the ground with Titch. Nef, Shib, Ace, Crib and Manlee 18 were waiting for him.

"You okay Jake?" Nef said as he looked at him.

"Well umm," he faltered, "I've had better days y'know."

"We're gonna try to get you away. It might not work but we have to try. You'll have to do as we say and be quiet okay?"

"Sure, no problem at all. I couldn't stay up there much longer without going crazy. I was about to give myself up when Titch arrived. A minute longer and I'd have been gone."

"We're gonna try and steal the pirates' shuttle and make a run for it. I have to say though, we might not make it and even if we do, they could chase us and get us anyway, or even fire at us. If you'd rather not, say so now cos we have to get moving."

Jake thought for a whole two seconds before replying. "Let's go."

"Then follow me gentlemen," Shib replied. "We have to enter the crawlspace at the other end of the connection tunnel. As this cargo hold is in the barge section, which is separate to the main ship, the crawlspaces don't connect with each other. We have no choice I'm afraid. Let's be quick and quiet." They ran as quietly as they could, up the cargo hold and into the connection tunnel and listened for any sounds that might indicate someone was around. Silence met their ears and Shib moved forward towards the panel he could see in the wall ten feet ahead. He reached into his pocket and retrieved his panel connector. With a last look around, he made a dash for the panel and within ten seconds he was ushering the group into the crawlspace between the outer and inner hulls. He entered behind them and reconnected the panel. Everyone sighed with relief.

"That's the most dangerous part over. Now we just have to climb up to the top deck using the hull braces. Okay gentlemen, start climbing and be quiet."

The group began the climb up to the top deck of the ship via the hull braces that connect the inner and outer hulls and prevents the two hulls twisting and buckling. Between the two hulls, an insulation layer sandwiched between two airspaces ensures the super freezing temperatures of space do not penetrate to the inside of the ship. The outer of the two airspaces is filled with Marganoid Gas that reacts with cold temperatures to produce heat, which is then pumped to a heat exchanger and used to supplement the ship's power system. The hull braces are spaced at four-foot intervals, meaning that the friends had to help each other to make the climb. As Titch was the biggest, he went up first and then hauled each of the others up after him. It was slow going but they got into a rhythm and despite Ace losing his footing once, they made it up to the middle deck without incident.

"We must be extra quiet up this last section gentlemen," Shib whispered. "The pirates are holding Captain Nagle and the crew in the bridge and they are due to begin searching for Jake anytime now. If they hear us, we have nowhere to run and our plan will be scuppered. Best to be slow and quiet than try to rush and make a noise." The group nodded and grunted their agreement and the climb continued.

"I did something like this in a movie once," Jake whispered and Ace snickered.

"I was just thinking of that too. Funny how art imitates life isn't it?"

"Or life imitates art in this case perhaps," Jake whispered back.

"Shut the fuck up ladies," Titch hissed. Jake and Ace grinned at each other.

Above them they saw the top of the ship begin to curve away to their left, indicating they had reached the top deck. Shib indicated for them to step onto the narrow walkway of the crawlspace and look for the access panel.

"Here," hissed Manlee. Shib crouched and retrieved his panel connector from his pocket. He was just about to start opening the panel when they all heard voices and everyone froze.

"Check everywhere," a voice they recognised from the comms announcement ordered. "Don't miss anything." Sounds of boot steps came to their ears followed by doors opening and closing and cupboards being ransacked.

"Empty Captain," another voice reported. The boot steps retreated down the corridor to the lift. They heard the swish of the lift door opening, followed by another swish as it closed and then the gentle hum as it descended. Shib was just about to open the panel when they heard more voices.

"There's too many for the lift," he mouthed. "We'll have to wait until we're sure they've all gone down."

They waited in silence for the lift to return, trying to hear what the pirates were saying but they were too far away to hear clearly. They heard Jake's name twice and some raucous laughter before the hum of the lift came back to their ears. Another swish, boot steps, swish and then the hum of the lift descending. They listened but heard nothing. They waited but the lift didn't return. Shib looked at Nef standing beside him and raised his eyebrows. Nef nodded and Shib opened the panel as quietly as he could. He slowly eased it aside and peered out into the medical bay. It seemed deserted so he climbed out and beckoned the others to follow. As they were extricating themselves from the crawlspace, he looked up and saw the open mouth of the docking dolly. Once everyone was out, he refitted the panel and looked up into the hole. A thin cable hung down from the shuttle and he guessed the pirates had used it to lower themselves down. He grabbed hold and effortlessly climbed up using just his hands and disappeared from view.

Seconds later, he reappeared and nodded. "Come on."

Titch came over and crouched on the floor. "Come on Jake, climb onto my shoulders."

"Hey buddy," Jake said, "thank you, for everything."

Titch stood and shook hands with him. "You get away safely Jake and remember me huh?"

"Always buddy." Titch dropped to the floor and Jake climbed onto his shoulders, holding onto the cable for balance. Titch stood and Jake jumped up the wire and hauled himself the last few feet until Shib was able to grab his arms and pull him onto the horizontal walkway. Using this crude but effective method the group made their emotional but hurried goodbyes to Titch and got into the shuttle.

Shib ushered everyone into the main body of the pirate's shuttle and checked the docking dolly controller. He pressed a switch and a door slid across the hole; the audible thunk telling him it was safely locked in place, preventing decompression of the Mayan Queen. Another switch brought the shuttle's own hatch sliding into place, and with a final switch, the whole docking dolly assembly fell away from the shuttle.

"Okay we're free gentlemen," Shib reported as he rushed to the pilot's seat. I recommend you all find somewhere secure to sit. This might not be a completely smooth ride."

"Why not?" Jake asked.

"Because this is just a shuttle. There must be a main ship somewhere close by; I believe he called it the Barclay. As soon as we depart, it will undoubtedly see us and might very well fire on us."

"Oh shit," Jake hissed.

"Don't worry Jake," Shib replied as he flipped switches and readied the shuttle for a swift getaway. This is a powerful craft, a fighter in its day and capable of quite a speed. It's also very manoeuvrable so if they do fire on us, we can get out of the way quicker than a bigger ship can. Ahh, I can see what I assume is the Barclay on the sensor screen so at least I know which direction to go in. We don't want to run smack bang into the side of it do we? Okay, hold on please, let's go." He gunned the engine and Jake was flattened against the back of his seat as it shot off into the void like a missile.

Kreeve stretched and yawned as he sat and waited in the cockpit of the Barclay for Ilyas and the others to get back with Jake, and whatever spoils they could lay their hands on. A beep made him sit bolt upright in his seat and lean over to the sensor display. The shuttle had disengaged the docking dolly.

"Jeez that was quick man," he hissed. "Well done Captain, you asshole." He went to rise from his seat, intending to go down to the loading bay to lock the shuttle down as soon as it landed and glanced out of the window. What he saw rooted him to the spot. The shuttle suddenly took off at top speed in the opposite direction.

"What the fuck?" he said aloud as he watched the shuttle disappear into the vacuum of space. "What the fuck are you up to Ilyas Da fucking Costa?" He grabbed the comms headset and flipped the switch, despite Ilyas telling him to maintain transmission silence.

"Captain? What the fuck are you doing out there? Captain, this is Kreeve. What the fuck is going on?"

A few moments of static then Ilyas's voice came back at him. "Kreeve? What are you on about? I thought I told you to keep quiet."

"You did, but you failed to tell me you lot were going to fuck off in the opposite direction. What am I supposed to do now? Sit here and jack myself off till you decide to come visit?"

"What?" Ilyas exclaimed. "Kreeve for fuck's sake buddy, what the hell are you on about?"

"Captain," Kreeve hissed slowly to emphasise his frustration. "I've just watched you disengage the docking dolly and fuck off in the opposite direction at top speed. I want to know what you're up to and I want to know now."

"But we're still on the Mayan Queen looking for Jake. The asshole is hiding somewhere and we're about to start shooting his pals until he gives himself up."

Kreeve swore aloud as the realisation of what had happened hit home.

"And I know just where he's hiding."

"Kreeve, don't make me angry buddy please. Pilots are ten a penny y'know. Make sense for once in your life huh?"

"He's stolen the fucking shuttle and made a run for it, is that sense enough for ya?"

"What?" Ilyas yelled. "Shit, shit, shit. I'm gonna wring that fucker's neck. Okay umm, get ready to give chase. We'll steal one of the Mayan Queen's shuttles to get back to ya."

Kreeve disengaged the covert stealth optimiser and readied the helm for a quick getaway before leaping down the steps to the loading bay and clearing a space for the Mayan Queen's slightly larger but slower shuttle.

Ilyas and his men were working their way down through the middle deck of crew quarters when the call from Kreeve came through. When he realised what had just taken place he stood rooted to the spot as the rage built up within. Ink would go to his grave swearing on oath that he saw the Captain's face go dead white with fury.

"That fucking asshole," he spat. "Fuck the ransom, I'm gonna slit his fucking throat."

"What's happened?" Ink asked.

"He's only gone and nicked the shuttle and made a run for it."

The men looked at each other in disbelief. "Jake?" Moody asked.

"Yeah," Ilyas replied wide-eyed. "He's stolen my shuttle and run away. Can you believe that?"

"Shit," Ink sighed. "I knew this was gonna go wrong."

"So what do we do now?" Johnson asked.

"We keep searching, that's what?" Ilyas replied as he marched into the next room along the corridor.

"But why? If he's already gone why stick around here?" Ink asked.

"Because it might not be Jake that's taken the shuttle. It might be a decoy to lure us away. Are you really so devoid of brain cells that you can't figure that out?"

"Sorry Captain," Ink replied. "Moody, Johnson, you two take that room over there, Patch and Lew, the next one along and be thorough but don't dawdle." He paired up the rest of the men so the search could be done as swiftly as possible and within thirty minutes they'd found all the crew quarters, the recreation room and kitchen empty of personnel.

"Captain?" Lew asked as Ilyas went to step into the lift to the lower deck. "Shouldn't we search the cargo hold before going downstairs? If Jake is hiding in there and we go downstairs, he could use the opportunity to hide somewhere else and we'd be going round in circles forever chasing him.

"Okay, good call Lew," Ilyas nodded. "Patch, Moody, you stand guard here by the lift so nobody can come up from below. If anyone gives you any trouble, shoot them."

"Yes Sir," they chorused and took up position by the lift.

The rest ran down the connection tunnel and into the vast cargo hold. They searched the various rooms around the perimeter before doing a quick scan amongst the stacks of crates and barrels.

"It would take weeks to search this lot thoroughly Captain," Ink said and Ilyas nodded.

"Yeah, we'll just have to do a quick scan and hope I guess."

"Psst," a voice hissed and Ilyas looked round to find Lew indicating with his head to look up. Everyone looked up to see the stack of crates in one section slightly askew from their proper positions.

"Looks like someone's been climbing up there Captain," Lew remarked and Ilyas nodded.

"Well done buddy. Okay Ink you're the best climber, up ya go." Ink nodded and began to climb as silently as he could. The others talked loudly down below in an effort to mask any noise of his ascent. Once at the top he readied his gun and peered over the top stack to see a huge crate in the middle with its lid pushed aside. He hauled himself up and took a deep breath before lunging towards the opening, gun held out in front. Ration packs and P-Gels lay strewn about the bottom of what looked like a huge canoe.

"This is where he was hiding Boss," he called down to Ilyas. "There's a huge boat in the middle here and there's ration packs and P-Gels in there and the lid's pushed to one side. He was here, I'll bet my old mother on it but he ain't here now."

"Okay good job buddy," Ilyas replied. "Let's go downstairs and do the engineering section and then go meet our friends in the shuttle bay huh?" They ran back along the connection tunnel and took the lift down to the lower deck. The engineering section was small and revealed nothing of interest so they made their way to the shuttle bay, which by now echoed with the murmurs of the Mayan Queen's entire crew.

The murmurs stopped when they entered and Ilyas grinned.

"Lew, take five guys with you and go fetch the bridge crew down here. Keep them restrained at all times okay?" Lew nodded and headed back with five volunteers. Ilyas smiled at the crowd.

"Good afternoon ladies and gentlemen. I'm Captain Ilyas Da Costa of the pirate vessel Barclay and I've come to relieve you of Jake Elloway. Unfortunately, it seems that he has managed to elude us by stealing our shuttle and I'm mighty annoyed about that. So, who is gonna be the first to volunteer to make sure that shuttle of yours over there is fully fuelled and ready to go?" No one moved so he made a show of shouldering his gun and a man ran forward.

"I'll just do it now," he muttered and ran towards the nearest shuttle.

"Good boy," Ilyas grinned. "Everyone else move over to the side and out of the way." He leaned back against the wall and tried to relax as he waited for the bridge crew to arrive. A few minutes later the door opened and Lew marched the bridge crew in.

"Well hello again Captain," Ilyas grinned. "It seems we have a slight change of plan. I'm sure you won't mind coming along on a little trip with us will you?"

"What?" Captain Nagle replied. "I'm not going anywhere with you. I told you you're welcome to take Elloway so take him and fuck off."

"Now now, that's no way for a respected captain to speak in front of his faithful crew. It seems that our dear Jake has managed to steal our shuttle and make a run for it, so we intend to steal one of yours and chase him down and slit his throat. And you lot are coming with us as insurance."

"Insurance for what?" Arsh Baglin demanded.

"Well firstly, to ensure your crew don't sabotage the shuttle and secondly as payback for all my trouble. If we don't find him so I can pay him back personally for all this trouble he's put me and my men through today, you'll pay for him since you are his hosts. That makes you responsible for his actions whilst on board the Mayan Queen." Ilyas grinned at Captain Nagle.

"Look, I'll go along with you if you insist but there's no need to take the whole bridge crew. Let them stay behind."

"A noble gesture Captain and one I'm sure your crew admire you for making but no. You're all coming along. The more the merrier. Looks like we're gonna be having a party gentlemen. Now move it," he gestured towards the nearest shuttle. Once the bridge crew were restrained inside the shuttle, Ilyas went looking for the man who had volunteered to check the fuel levels. He found him disengaging the fuel supply generator.

"It's fully fuelled now," the man said. "Fully fuelled and ready to go."

"Good. Who can operate these shuttle bay doors?"

"I can."

Ilyas approached the crowd huddled against the wall. "Everyone now move quietly out of the shuttle bay please. We don't want you floating off when the doors open do we. The

Captain and crew of the Barclay thank you for your hospitality." Once everyone had gone, he turned back and nodded to the frightened man.

"Okay buddy, open these doors would ya?" The man nodded and ran to the operation module and secured the door. Ilyas climbed into the shuttle, secured the hatch, and smiled when he heard the hiss of decompression. Lew lifted the shuttle, turned it around on the pad, and waited for the bay doors to open enough for him to squeeze through.

CHAPTER SEVEN

Shib expertly adapted to the controls of the unfamiliar shuttle and aimed towards a nearby system he could see on the long-range scanner. In the back, everyone waited until the pressure equalised, then let themselves out of their seat restraints. Jake heaved a sigh of relief at having got away but this was short lived as he realised that they were still out in the void of space and could not just run into the nearest police station for safety.

"Where are we gonna go?" he asked. He looked around at his companions who all looked vacant.

Nef shrugged. "I haven't the faintest idea. Shib, is there anywhere nearby we can head for?"

"There is a system within range," Shib replied. "There are two habitable planets there and we have enough power to reach the first of those if we maintain this speed. If we slowed a little, we might make the other one but I wouldn't recommend slowing down. Once the pirates realise what's happened, they'll come after us and their ship might very well be as fast, if not faster than this shuttle."

"Okay let's head for the first and hope we can get to safety there. What's the system called?"

"Tellizon," Shib replied. "Tellizon 3 and 4 are habitable. The orbit of Tellizon 3 puts it out of our range, so although Tellizon 4 is further away as the crow flies, its orbit puts it right in our path and saves us having to take a left around its sun."

"Do you know anything about Tellizon?" Crib asked.

"Nothing I'm afraid," Shib replied.

"I do," Manlee said quietly and everyone turned to look at him. He looked down at the floor without speaking.

"You've been there haven't you buddy?" Nef asked and Manlee nodded. "In the dark time?" Another nod. "What's it like there?"

"It's going to be a tough place to survive in," Manlee explained. "It's only inhabitants are scientists. I say its only inhabitants but I mean its only humanoid inhabitants." He looked around at them and sighed.

"What?" Jake asked.

"It's home to all sorts of creatures," he replied. "And not all of them are benign."

"What exactly do you mean buddy?" Ace asked. "What are we dealing with here? Come on we need to know."

"Fearsome predators, some of them huge and all of them hungry."

"Oh shit," Jake exclaimed. "Talk about going from the frying pan into the fire. What's Tellizon 3 like?"

"I've no idea," Manlee replied. "I've never been there."

Nef took off the backpack he was wearing. "Good idea I thought to bring these along then wasn't it?" he said as he removed three of the daggers from the wall of his quarters.

"And there's bound to be some guns around here," Ace said as he jumped up and headed to the back of the shuttle to rummage around in some lockers he had seen there.

"Hey guys, look what we have here," he grinned as he brought out three laser rifles and five boxes of power packs. He headed to the next locker and found a box of fire kits.

"And we got plenty of camp fires here," he said as he handed them back to Nef. The last locker revealed another two laser rifles and three laser pistols with twenty spare fuel clips.

"We've got plenty of hardware and enough power packs to last us so we stand a good chance of surviving. We're gonna get through this guys. Now, who's good with a gun?" He looked right at Jake as he asked the question and Jake went red as he realised they expected him to be an expert.

"Hey guys I'm an actor remember?"

"But you've played plenty of guys who've had guns," Ace replied. "I've seen all your movies man; you must know how to use a gun."

"The guns in the movies aren't real Ace," Jake replied. "I can wave a gun around with the best of them but I've never fired one."

"Well you're nine tenths the way there if you can wave it about," Nef said with a grin. "All you gotta do is pull the trigger while waving and it's goodbye asshole." Everyone laughed and Jake nodded.

"Well okay," he grinned. "I guess you're right when you put it like that."

"Just make sure you're not waving it in my direction eh buddy?" Crib said and everyone roared with laughter.

Lew steered the Mayan Queen shuttle out of the shuttle bay and headed towards the Barclay. Halfway across, the engines died and the shuttle stalled to a halt.

"What the fuck?" Ilyas yelled. "What's going on Lew? Come on talk to me buddy."

"It seems we've lost power Captain."

"Well I managed to work that out for myself," he replied. "Why we've lost power is what I want to know."

"I don't know," Lew replied as he frantically scanned the console. "It's fully fuelled but somehow the fuel isn't getting through."

"That bastard sabotaged it when he fuelled it," Ilyas hissed. "I thought he was taking a bit too long to check the fuel level. Damn that asshole."

"We'll have to get Kreeve to come and give us a blow job," Lew replied.

"Yeah I guess that's our only option." Ilyas opened a comms channel. "Kreeve? Kreeve, where the fuck are you?"

"Captain? I'm here Sir."

"The shuttle is fucked. You'll have to come give us a blowjob buddy."

"Okay, on my way." Kreeve leapt into the pilot's seat and manoeuvred the Barclay towards the becalmed shuttle. When he was within a hundred metres, he turned through one hundred and eighty degrees and engaged the reverse thrusters. The open loading bay doors of the Barclay loomed towards the shuttle like a huge open mouth and Captain Nagle suddenly realised why this manoeuvre was known as a blowjob. Kreeve gently guided the Barclay backwards towards the shuttle until it was suspended in mid-air just inside the loading bay.

"Now just a touch of vertical thrust," he muttered to himself as he deftly fingered the controls. The Barclay slowly lifted vertically until the occupants of the shuttle felt a distinct thud, followed by a horrendous groaning squeak that put Arsh Baglin's teeth on edge. Once the loading bay doors shut, Kreeve pressed the recompression switch and the shuttle's passengers listened to the familiar hiss.

"Okay people," Ilyas grinned. "We would like to thank you for flying Barclay Airlines. We hope you've enjoyed your flight and look forward to having you aboard again. Your hosts will now show you to the first class accommodations." The pirates roared with laughter and Captain Nagle groaned inwardly.

"Okay," Ilyas continued. "Ink, get our friends here to their quarters and fix em something to eat."

"Yes Captain," Ink replied as he ordered Moody and Johnson to undo their restraints.

Ilyas raced up the steps and into the cockpit. "After them Kreeve. Can you follow their trail?"

"Yeah, I can follow the Uniax particles left behind by the shuttle engines."

"Good, do it."

"There's only one problem though."

"And what would that be?"

"We can only match the shuttle's speed. We can't outrun it, which means we won't be able to catch them up."

"Shit," Ilyas replied. "But it's gonna run out of power sooner or later and then we'll have em. How long will it take till the shuttle runs dry?"

"At top speed, twenty three hours and a few minutes."

"Okay then so we just have to follow for now and in just over a day we'll have em and boy am I gonna enjoy finally meeting the great Jake Elloway."

Jake and his friends spent the day talking over their combined knowledge and experience of surviving in the wilds amongst fearsome man eating predators, which amounted to practically zero apart from Manlee 18 who had visited Tellizon 4 once before. He didn't seem too keen to give him much information about why he was there and Jake got the distinct impression that everyone but him knew what he was on about. He felt annoyed that he was the only one who didn't know.

"So you've been to this planet before then Manlee?" he asked and Manlee nodded. "Oh, okay," he replied, suddenly unsure of what his next question should be. He didn't want to demand they let him in on the secret so he faltered.

"It was ten years ago Jake," Nef said as he shot a look at Manlee, who nodded. "Is it okay Manlee? Should I tell him or would you rather?"

Manlee hesitated for a second and then looked at Jake. "Jake, I am from Zylom 2. We are very different to most other races in that we don't have different genders like you do."

"Yeah I know," Jake replied. "Shib told me."

"Twenty years ago I was First Officer aboard a scientific research vessel. We stopped at Tellizon 4 to liaise with the various science outposts there, to check on their research and bring them some much needed supplies. While we were there, a small time freight hauler got into difficulty as it passed by the nearby shipping lane and we went to offer assistance. To cut a long story short, they were what you might call a rather uncultured bunch. Their language was crude and their manners, cruder still. Two of the women on board my vessel were raped, our ship was almost blown apart and I was captured and taken down to Tellizon 4, where they beat me and left me to die."

"Shit," Jake sighed. "I'm sorry buddy, I had no idea."

"They did a job on him Jake," Nef said. "They beat him almost to death, tied him to a tree and left him for the creatures."

"I have vague memories of sounds; creatures nearby and the wind through the trees. It was cold and I remember shivering. Then it just went black and I woke up seven months later in a medical facility back on Zylom 2."

"My god," Jake exclaimed. "How the fuck did you survive?"

"What he didn't know," Nef explained, "was that some of the crew from his vessel chased after him in one of their own shuttles and found him after twenty four hours unconscious and near to death. Their ship was so badly damaged that they couldn't leave orbit, so they took him to the nearest scientific outpost and called for help. It took a month for someone to arrive and all that time he hung on to his life by no more than a thread as the scientists at the outpost treated his wounds and tried to bring him back. He was in a coma for seven months before he woke up."

"You were obviously not meant to die at that moment Manlee," Jake said.

"Nope, he wasn't," Nef smiled.

"When I regained full physical health," Manlee continued, "I was changed."

"How changed?" Jake asked.

Manlee looked at Jake, then dropped his eyes to the floor as he hesitated to find the words.

"I was afraid."

"Hell who wouldn't be?" Jake replied and the others nodded in agreement. "I can't imagine how I'd react if I had to experience that."

"For three years I was too scared even to try to work amongst other races again, but then I heard about the Mayan Queen and they offered me a position as cargo hand. I was prepared to refuse but then I heard they already had another Zylomian on board and they let me spend some time talking with him. He convinced me that the crew were nice people; he told me he'd been very happy amongst them and so I decided to try it and see how it went for a few months. I've been there ever since and although I'm happy there, I've never been able to find the person I was before. He's gone forever."

"And he's the most awesome dude I know," Ace replied and everyone grunted in agreement.

"Well for what it's worth," Jake said as he suddenly remembered a line from his most recent movie, "I feel a lot safer knowing you're here and on my side."

"When I realised the situation you were in, I was suddenly transported back ten years to that day and I realised I couldn't sit back and not do something. It's ironic but probably right that we find ourselves heading back to Tellizon 4 again. I wished I had someone to fight for me back then, so I knew I had to come with you today and maybe when we go back there I might even find him again?"

"Him?" Jake asked.

"Me."

"We'll all help you look for him buddy," Crib declared and the shuttle was filled with yells of 'yeah' and 'damn right.'

"Absolutely," Jake smiled.

They spent the next few hours swapping life stories and Jake regaled them all with some of the funnier moments of his film career and gave them some of the more shocking open secrets about one or two of his rival celebrities. He was in his element holding court to fans about his movies and the folks he mixes with and he began to relax into his comfort zone. When everyone started to yawn, Shib suggested that they try to get some sleep.

"We still have around fifteen hours before we reach Tellizon gentlemen. I would recommend you get some sleep for as Manlee has told us, it's not going to be exactly a picnic down there and it would be wise for you to be as fresh as possible."

"But what about you?" Jake asked. "You're gonna be dead on your feet. Doesn't this thing have auto pilot or something?" The group snickered and he looked at them.

"What?"

"You forget Jake," Shib replied. "I'm an android and as such, sleep is not necessary for me."

"Shit, I forgot," Jake laughed. "Sorry."

"Don't apologise," Shib said. "I take your forgetting as a compliment and I thank you for it."

The group tried their best to get comfortable in the shuttle and managed to get seven hours of reasonable sleep before stiff necks and aching backs forced them awake. They spent the first hour alternately stretching and wincing in pain and snickering at each other before Nef went in search of any emergency ration packs.

"Okay boys what do we have here? We have several packs of vegetable stew, a few oatmeal's and a whole bunch of Enershakes." The group groaned in response and Nef grinned.

"If I may make a recommendation gentlemen," Shib cut in and everyone looked around. "The Enershakes would be the best option here. Heating the other options would take valuable power from the engine and I seem to remember that Earth people aren't that keen on stone cold oatmeal without sugar."

"Good thinking buddy," Nef replied and handed out the Enershakes. These high calorie milkshake type drinks contain all of the nutritional requirements for Basic Humanoid - Earth Types. This means that those races similar in anatomy to Earth humanoids can rely on getting the necessary nutrition from them in the absence of their normal fare.

"Here ya go Manlee; you get two cos you're special."

"Aww papa I want another one too," Crib called and everyone laughed.

Jake read the label and frowned. "Nutritionally balanced for Basic Humanoid - Earth Types? Huh?"

"That means those races basically the same as us will get the right nutrition from them. Guys like Manlee and Titch and a couple of the other crew members have different requirements. Manlee here needs two to our one. Titch needs four to our one and others like Faline for instance only need a half of one at a time."

"Oh I see," Jake nodded and took a tentative sip and grimaced. "Holy shit, you sure you don't want three instead of two Manlee?" Guffaws of laughter filled the shuttle as it raced towards its rendezvous with Tellizon 4.

Several hours behind, Ilyas Da Costa and his men managed to keep pace with them. The room that Captain Nagle and the bridge crew were in was a meeting room refitted into a cell. It had a bathroom and a few bunks and nothing else. Ilyas ordered their restraints be left on, which made things a little uncomfortable for them, but they were happy that at least they were all together and as yet unharmed.

"Any ideas where we're headed? Captain Nagle asked.

"The nearest system is the Tellizon system, if my memory serves me correctly," Arsh Baglin replied.

"What do we know about it?"

"Zip."

"Actually Sir I do know something about it," Hefton 24 said.

"Good, then tell us what you know."

"It's where Manlee 18 had his terrible experience ten years ago."

"You mean it's the place where those thugs beat him and left him to die? The place he told us about where huge creatures live?"

"Yes Sir," Hefton nodded.

"Fuck," Captain Nagle replied and the others nodded. "That's all we need."

"I've heard his story about it and if it's true then we're toast," Stella Bodecki said and Arsh nodded.

"So have I," Captain Nagle agreed. "Elloway won't last five minutes down there and if we get there and find he's been something's dinner, how are these morons going to react? What will they do to us then?"

"That's what I'm wondering Sir," Hefton replied.

"We have to try to formulate something resembling a plan of action guys. Ideas?"

"Well there's only one thing we can do as far as I can see," Stella Bodecki replied. "We over power them, take their guns, find Jake and get back to one of the shuttles and get back to the Mayan Queen."

"Hmm," Captain Nagle sighed. "Better still, we over power them and steal their guns, then dump them there and take off in this shuttle back to the Mayan Queen and forget Jake fucking Elloway altogether."

"Sir?" Hefton 24 replied.

"Never mind, just thinking aloud."

"Would it be unwise for us to ask why you hate the guy so much Captain?" Arsh bravely asked.

"Umm, yeah it would," Captain Nagle replied. "Let's just say I'm not a fan of celebrities and leave it at that huh?" Arsh nodded and stole a look at Stella, who looked back at him and raised her eyebrows. He raised his own and shrugged in response.

"I wasn't aware that Jake could pilot a shuttle," Hefton said.

"Neither was I actually," Captain Nagel replied. "But wait, he can't pilot. I had to send Shib to pick him up from Earth. He's got company."

"I wonder who?" Stella said.

"Who do we know can pilot?" Hefton asked.

"The only qualified pilot on board apart from me and Arsh, is Shib," Captain Nagle replied. "So he's gone and nicked my android too. Nice. Fucking nice one Elloway."

"Maybe he didn't steal him Sir," Hefton replied. "Shib may have gone voluntarily."

"Shib knows exactly how I feel about Jake Elloway," Captain Nagle argued, "and he wouldn't take his side against me, his Captain."

"But Sir," Hefton continued. "Shib is incapable of taking anyone's side. He cannot react emotionally to any situation. All he is capable of is weighing up the facts of the situation and formulating the most logical reaction that adheres to his programming. It stands to reason that the information he had influenced him in such a way as to decide that helping Jake escape was, in his opinion, the best course of action."

"Your point being?" Captain Nagle replied.

"My point being that Shib decided the course of action he took was the only course of action he could take. This infers that at the moment at least, he regards Jake's safety as a priority and will act to safeguard it whenever he feels it necessary."

"So as I said, he's taken Jake's side against me."

"You misunderstand me Captain," Hefton explained. "What I mean is that Shib has decided that Jake's safety is his top priority right now. In order for Shib to make such a decision, he needs information that specifically puts Jake's safety in danger. As we all know, Shib has access to all parts of the ship and hears everyone's conversations and we all confide in him from time to time knowing he won't gossip. His actions now are a direct indication that he knows something we don't."

"And what would that be?" Arsh asked.

"That he knows someone is out to put Jake's safety in danger. Remember that Shib's programming contains an extremely important point, that he cannot knowingly or willingly cause harm to any humanoid unless to not do so causes danger to another humanoid within his programmed circle, which as we know is a way of saying his family. His programmed circle is everyone who lives and works on board the Mayan Queen, even temporarily. The moment Jake came aboard, he became one of Shib's family, which means he will not only regard his safety as a priority but that he will also defend him with aggression if necessary, even if the danger to Jake comes from within that same family circle."

"Oh fuck," Stella exclaimed as she got Hefton's point at last. "You mean it's an inside job?"

"Oh surely not," Arsh replied, "that's crazy. Isn't it?"

"Emotionally it must sound crazy," Hefton continued, "but if you put the emotion aside and look at the facts, it's the only logical explanation and the fact that you find it hard to think of any of your work colleagues as capable of aiding such an event as that which has just occurred to us is of little consequence. However you feel about it emotionally it would be wise to remember that it is the most likely explanation."

"But who would do such a thing?" Stella said.

"Who indeed," Arsh replied. "It could even be one of us here now."

"Now you are being crazy," Captain Nagle snickered.

"Not necessarily," Hefton cut in. "If one of the crew were indeed in league with the pirates to bring about Jake's abduction or death, it would make sense that he, or she," he said as he looked at Stella, who blushed, "would be brought along here to avoid suspicion. Or even to further assist in tracking him down by gaining his trust, only to betray him again."

"Look, this is just going to make us all suspicious of each other, which isn't going to help us survive on Tellizon," Captain Nagle commanded. "Whilst what you say unfortunately makes perfect sense Hefton, if we allow it to influence the way we four work together, we could wind up as dog meat down there."

"That is also true Sir," Hefton nodded, "and it would seem that these two truths are in conflict with one another, wouldn't it?"

No one knew what to say so everyone sat in silence and thought about Hefton's unarguable logic. The brains of Zylomians like Hefton 24 and Manlee 18 are wired very differently from those of other humanoids. Although they have very similar emotions, the logical, reasoning parts of their brains are hard wired to take control over the emotional parts. They have the benefit of total understanding of humanoid emotions, without being controlled by them as other races are. This makes them invaluable in times of crisis and experts at logical deduction. The four lay on their bunks and tried to get comfortable and each wondered which of the other three is the inside man and each came to the same conclusion. There was only one person who continually made it plain that Jake's presence on board the Mayan Queen was not welcome. They had all heard Captain Nagle ranting about Jake ever since he came aboard and when Arsh questioned him about it, he had clammed up like a Virgin in a sausage factory.

Stella Bodecki breathed deep and tried not to cry. She didn't want to think Captain Nagle was capable of being the inside man in league with pirates. It changed her view of him, which upset her greatly and she didn't know how to cope with the feelings she was now experiencing. She had carried her secret love for her captain ever since she came to work for him four years ago. From that first day on the job she had tried to catch his eye, smiled at him all the time, laughed at his jokes and understood when he was in a bad mood and all because she hoped one day he would look at her and decide he loved her back. Even though throughout her four-year career on the Mayan Queen, he had never given her a single reason to believe he cared for her, she never stopped loving him and she never gave up hope. For him to turn out to be in league with the pirates who put everyone's life on board in danger and abducted the entire bridge crew, leaving the rest of the workforce stranded without a pilot, was like standing there watching the love of her life die in front of her eyes. She could not be in love with someone who would do such a thing and so she mourned for her broken heart and her lost love, those wasted years, pointless tears, and all the joy and fun she had missed while waiting for a love that now could never be. She cried herself to sleep in silence and with each tear, she laid a stone around her heart and as she slept and dreamed of loss and abandonment, she built a wall. When she awoke six hours later, a new Stella Bodecki stretched herself and rolled her neck around to get the knots out of her muscles. The old Stella was gone, along with the old Captain Nagle and she would mourn no more for either of them.

CHAPTER EIGHT

Shib looked at the sensor readout and nodded. He was pleased that his calculations were correct and the shuttle did have enough power to get them to Tellizon 4 but he was a little worried about how his companions would survive the landing. He wondered whether to tell them or not and decided that honesty is always the best policy.

"Gentlemen?" he called.

"Yeah buddy," Nef replied.

"We're approaching the Tellizon system now and we do have enough power in the cells to reach the fourth planet."

"That's fantastic." The group sighed with relief and grinned at each other.

"However," Shib continued, "we don't have enough to control our landing."

"Oh shit," Crib hissed.

"What?" Jake exclaimed. "You mean we're gonna crash after coming all this way? What the fuck?"

"Our power will run out approximately two thirds the way into our landing manoeuvre, which will mean we have to glide our way in and our landing won't be the most comfortable."

"How long do we have?" Manlee asked.

"Forty six minutes," Shib replied.

"Okay everyone, lock down," Nef yelled and the group leapt up, leaving Jake sitting there wondering what was going on.

"What can I do?"

"We have to lock down everything that isn't already bolted down," Crib called. "Anything loose could take off your head when we touch down so either tie it down, lock it up, stuff it somewhere or sit on it. Whatever works for ya buddy, just use your initiative."

"Oh shit," Jake hissed as he too, leapt up. "Okay, yeah." He looked around and saw several boxes at the back of the shuttle, stacked together. He ran over, grabbed one, and looked around for somewhere to put it. He was about to despair when he saw the door to the toilet standing open. He stacked the boxes in the toilet cubicle, along with the ten emergency space suits he found stuffed into a corner, the boxes of emergency ration packs and a toolbox full of tools. He checked and double checked the rear section for anything loose and found nothing more so he shut the toilet cubicle door and went to join the others.

"Everything clear down the back Jake?" Ace asked and he nodded.

"Yeah, I stuffed everything into the toilet so y'all are gonna have to piss ya pants," he replied. Everyone looked round at him and one by one, started to laugh.

Manlee came rushing over and handed everyone a small package.

"Here ya go guys; I found these under a seat."

Jake took one and turned it over in his hands. It was roughly six inches square and wrapped in some kind of clear film.

"What;s this?" he asked.

"It's a crash collar," Nef replied. "Open it up and unfold it." Jake found what looked like a twelve-inch-by-twelve-inch inflatable cushion three inches thick, with two stiff, three-inch wide bands attached to one side.

"You blow it up by pulling out that plug there," he said as he pointed to a small nipple in one corner, which Jake pulled and watched as the cushion immediately inflated.

"Then you put the two bands around your neck," Nef continued as he demonstrated, "with the cushion at the back of your head. Once we're strapped into our seats, these will ensure that your head and neck are stabilised so that the movement of the crashing shuttle doesn't cause your head to rock back and forth enough to damage your neck."

"Oh I see," he nodded. "Neat, thanks. I may have two broken legs and a shattered pelvis but at least I won't have a crick in my neck." Guffaws once again filled the shuttle and this time, Manlee was amongst them.

"I would urge you all to buckle up now gentlemen," Shib called and the group leapt back into their seats and strapped themselves in. Jake struggled with his until Nef came to his aid, before strapping his backpack to a bulkhead and jumping back into his own seat.

"I'm trying to ensure we land as near as possible to one of the scientific outposts but as we will be gliding in, I cannot be accurate as to exactly how far away we will be."

"We trust you buddy," Ace yelled as the shuttle gave a lurch and Jake went white.

"It's okay Jake," Manlee said from the next seat. "It's just the natural turbulence of re-entry. Once we're through the outer atmosphere things will calm down."

Jake looked at Manlee as much as the crash collar would allow and tried to smile but he was terrified and it showed.

"It didn't jump around this much when Shib flew me up to the Mayan Queen," he remarked.

"We are going a hundred times the speed now Jake," Shib called. "And it is essential that I lower our speed considerably if we are to have a chance of survival. To do this I have to turn the ship's nose up slightly so that we're effectively in the belly flop posture. This is extremely un-aerodynamic which is the cause of the turbulence. Once we're down further I can get the nose down a little and things will calm down, trust me."

"Okay," Jake hissed. "I choose to trust you buddy."

The shuttle shot down through the outer atmosphere of Tellizon 4, the belly of the craft soon becoming white-hot and the turbulence rougher with each passing second. Jake was convinced that they were going to break up any second and although not a religious man in any sense of the word, he prayed for deliverance. All at once, they broke through the cloud layer and into the bluest sky any of them had ever seen and as Shib brought the nose down and the turbulence disappeared, the engines died. The shuttle glided silently down and those in the nearest seats to the cockpit craned their necks to see out of the windows. Thick forest met their eyes and Ace wished he had not bothered to look. He turned away and gulped.

"What?" Jake asked when he noticed him pale. "What did you see?"

"It's thick forest down there," he replied.

"Oh shit," Nef exclaimed and closed his eyes."

"So I guess that's a bad thing huh?" Jake asked, his eyes darting from Ace to Nef and back again.

"It's certainly not the best thing we could've hoped for," Nef replied.

"Why not? Won't the trees help to break our fall or something?"

"Unfortunately not," Manlee cut in. "The first moment we hit a tree, the momentum will flip us over and we'll end up cartwheeling down through the trees. This is probably gonna hurt guys."

"But won't they just break under our weight?"

"This shuttle is too small and at the speed we're travelling, any sudden change of balance will have a massive effect on the whole craft."

"For fuck's sake," Jake hissed. "This movie better break the box office records or I'm gonna be seriously pissed."

"What's the movie called Jake?" Manlee asked. "You never told us."

"Acts of Life," he replied. "It's a play on words y'see. Facts of life to acts of life. It's about this man going through a traumatic experience, but it's also about him facing up to his life and how he gets to know himself, the real guy within and how that changes him into a better person. Up to then he's been something he's not, hiding behind a mask designed to keep the real person hidden away from sight and it's all about how he finds himself again, the real person. So instead of acting someone he's not, he becomes his true self. Y'see? Acts of Life."

"That's a nice title," Ace said and Crib nodded. "Clever."

"Thanks," Jake smiled. "Actually I thought of it myself."

"That shows insight Jake," Manlee said. Before Jake could reply, there was an almighty bang, the shuttle lurched violently up at the rear, and everyone found themselves momentarily upside down as the craft cartwheeled twice through the air. Shib fought with the emergency glide controls and managed to right the shuttle moments before it hit the ground belly down with a bone wrenching crunch and slid several hundred yards; coming to rest facing back the way they'd come.

Several moments of complete silence ensued before the first groans and swear words. Jake didn't know whether he was alive or dead, conscious or unconscious. All he knew was that his body felt like it was several seconds behind his brain and as he waited for it to catch up, nausea welled up within him like a volcano. He opened his eyes and took a deep breath as he fought with his guts but within seconds, he knew he was losing the battle. He didn't want to puke in front of his friends but he wanted to puke into his lap even less.

"Oh shit I'm gonna puke," he moaned as he aimlessly fought with the harness control. He felt a thump to his belly and the harness holding him fell away with a clatter. He lunged from his seat and made it almost to the rear wall before bringing his guts up. A body appeared beside him and he looked up to find Nef holding out a bottle of water.

"Here ya go, have a swill and you'll feel better."

"Thanks. Sorry."

"No need to be. You're not exactly experienced in this kind of thing."

"Is anyone?"

"Well no but the rest of us are used to life aboard a space ship. We train and drill for this kind of emergency all the time. You did good buddy. Come on, let's get ourselves armed and out of here huh? Those pirates are not gonna be far behind us y'know."

"Is everyone in one piece?" Nef called and everyone nodded. Some nods were accompanied by a grunt and others, by a sigh but everyone had survived.

"Okay great. Now let's get ourselves armed and get moving. The pirates are not far behind us so the more distance we can put between them and us, the better. It's gonna be hard enough with whatever lives out there, without having those assholes on our tail too. Shib, which way and how far to the science outpost?"

"Approximately eighty three point seven miles north east of here."

"Okay so allowing for twenty miles a day give or take, that means it's four day's hike. I've brought along a few ration packs to see us through a day or two but we'll have to try to find our own food or just go without. It won't kill us to fast for a day or two."

"I fast every month for three days," Jake replied. "Lack of food for a couple of days isn't a problem for me at all."

"Me neither," Manlee responded. "Zylomians can go without solid food for up to three months before serious detriment to our health."

"Good, then so long as we can find water, we'll be okay," Nef nodded. "Let's go."

Shib blew the emergency bolts on the side hatch, which fell to the ground and they got their first breath of Tellizon air.

He looked outside before jumping down and indicating for the others to follow. They found themselves at the very edge of a large flat open area several miles across.

"You did a good job Shib," Nef remarked. "We made it past the trees."

"Almost," Shib replied. "I just clipped the very edge of the tree line but I think we got off lucky. It could've been a lot worse."

"Which way is north east?"

"That way," Shib replied pointing directly ahead into the forest.

"Okay guys," Nef said. "Everyone ready?"

"As much as we'll ever be," Ace replied.

"Keep together and keep your eyes open. Remember we don't know what the animal life is like here so even though it may look cute and cuddly, don't assume it will be. Anyone sees anything bigger than a house cat, let us know immediately."

"It would be wise to try not to leave too obvious a trail," Shib said. "We don't want to make it too easy for the pirates to catch up with us do we?"

"Good thinking," Nef nodded. "Come on." He led the way and the group approached the tree line cautiously. The ancient living monoliths soared into the sky, all at once graceful and yet sinister, inviting them closer like a spider waiting in her web.

"Is it too late to admit that I'm scared of bugs?" Jake asked.

"Umm yep," Crib replied at once. "Far too late buddy."

"I thought so."

The temperature dropped considerably as soon they stepped through the tree line into the cool gloom and Jake felt goose bumps rise on his arms. They stopped and allowed their eyes to adjust to the dark and the forest came into full focus all around them. It was beautiful yet at the same time, it exuded a tangible sense of danger.

"Wow," Ace gasped as he looked at the lush greenery, "I ain't seen nothing like this back home."

"I made a movie once," Jake replied, "where one of the locations was the Amazon jungle but even that was nothing compared to this."

"Remember this has never had any interference or management by humanoids of any kind," Shib said "and as such it has been able to grow unchecked for millions of years. It is unlikely that you'll see anything like this on any planet where humanoids live."

"It's beautiful sure," Crib remarked, "but why the hell do I feel creeped out?"

"I know what you mean," Manlee nodded. "Oh boy do I ever know what you mean."

"Hey I'm sorry man." Nef suddenly turned and looked at Manlee. "I forgot you've been here before and it was a real bad time for you. Are you gonna be okay?"

Manlee looked about him before taking a deep breath in.

"Yeah I'll be fine. I have my friends around me this time. It might even be a way to lay the ghosts of the past to rest huh?"

"We're with you all the way buddy," Crib put a hand on Manlee's shoulder and gave it a squeeze.

"Okay guys, let's go." Nef stepped forward cautiously, picking his way through the undergrowth. "Look where you're putting your feet, we don't want anyone stepping on something that might object to being stepped on."

"Oh shit," Jake hissed under his breath and Crib smiled at him.

"Don't worry Jake. You never know, it's not beyond the realms of possibility that this place doesn't have spiders as big as your head after all." He snickered and Ace grinned.

"Thanks buddy," Jake replied as he glared at Crib, "that's a real comfort." Crib grinned back at him and then Jake noticed his expression change. His eyes moved slightly to his left as if he were looking over his shoulder instead of into his eyes and they widened ever so slightly as his mouth opened. He went cold to the bone as the breath left his lungs. He tried to turn around but fear rooted him to the spot and he could not tear his gaze from Crib's shocked expression. All of a sudden, something whizzed past his ear and he heard a dull thunk behind. Nef suddenly appeared beside him and yanked him forward, snapping him out of his trance. He blinked and gasped for breath as he turned and found himself looking at a pair of jaws lined with wickedly sharp teeth, the pink tongue lolling from one side as the life left its orange eyes. Nef's dagger pinned it to the tree trunk through its neck and Jake was mesmerised to see its hands were almost human like. Grey brown fur made it impossible to see against the bark of the tree and it wasn't until it had reached out for Jake's neck and shoulder that Crib had seen it. Luckily, Nef had seen it too.

Jake spluttered at the realisation of what almost happened.

"Oh shit. Oh fuck. It was gonna bite me. Oh fuck I gotta get out of here. I can't do this guys, I can't."

Nef stepped towards him and slapped him hard across the face.

"Feel the fear Jake," he hissed. "Feel it, acknowledge it and then let it go. Don't try to deny it but don't let it control you. It's a part of you but it doesn't have to define you." He reached up and retrieved his dagger, his eyes never leaving Jake's. The body of the creature fell to the forest floor at his feet.

Jake breathed deeply and nodded. "Okay. Thanks for saving my dick. I owe ya." He wiped a hand across his brow and sighed. "Okay, let's go. Onto the next excitement huh?"

Crib clapped him on the back. "Sorry buddy, I didn't see it until a split second before Nef got it. I was vaguely aware of movement on the tree behind you but I couldn't make out what it was until it reached out and opened those jaws. When I saw those teeth I realised what was happening and was gonna grab you but Nef was quicker and thank god for him. It was like everything was happening in slow motion y'know?"

"Do not feel bad gentlemen," Shib cut in. "You're not trained soldiers so you will be at the mercy of your fears and it will take some time to learn to react instantly. This is what I believe they call a baptism of fire back on earth."

"Ain't that the truth," Jake replied.

"It would be wise," Nef suggested, "for two of us to focus attention in front, two keep watch to the left and two watch to the right. It does mean our rear is unguarded but there's only six of us and we have to choose the safest course of action. Does anyone disagree?" The group set off again, their recent close encounter helping to sharpen their focus as they scanned the trees and undergrowth for movement. The forest was alive with sounds and some of them reminded Jake of sounds he heard on Earth. One sound was very much like a cricket, another like a cicada and once they all heard what sounded just like a frog. There were buzzes, whines, clicks and taps of all kinds and apart from insects flying around everywhere and movement in the deeper undergrowth when they passed nearby, they didn't see another creature for over an hour.

After carefully picking their way through the undergrowth, the group were beginning to relax a little. No man-eating creatures set upon them and they thought perhaps this place might not be so bad after all. Nef suddenly stopped and looked down at his feet. Crib, following behind, almost bumped into him.

"What's up Nef?" he asked. "What do you see?"

"Can you feel that?"

"Feel what? I don't feel any, hey what is that?"

"What's going on," Manlee called from further back.

"Can you feel something in the ground?" Crib asked and the group concentrated. One by one, they all became aware of the slight rumble coming up through their feet and they nodded.

"Feels like an earth tremor," Jake said. "We get them all the time on Earth."

"Maybe," Nef replied.

"It would make sense," Shib replied. "Plate tectonics is the natural process by which landmasses are formed and earth tremors are to be found on all planets with landmasses. Tellizon 4 won't be any different."

"Yeah I guess," Nef said. "Something about this is just not right though."

"What do you mean?" Ace asked.

"In an earthquake the rumbling increases and then stops. This rumbling is the same all the time. Y'know what it reminds me of? The Orgnal mining back on Damiklon. It feels just like the tunnelling torpedo they use in the mines. If you stand on the ground above a mine you can feel the slight rumbling and it's just like this."

"And it feels like it's coming from our right too," Shib remarked. "It's stronger under my right foot than it is under my left." Jake was just about to comment when everyone heard the sound of branches breaking and undergrowth being trampled from their right. They all looked up in time to see hundreds of creatures stream from the undergrowth all around them and race off to their left, oblivious to the invaders' presence in their world. Every size, shape, colour and form of creature imaginable raced through the trees and away into the depths of the forest to their left.

"What the fuck is going on?" Jake hissed.

"What are they running from?" Manlee asked.

"Maybe we should run with them?" Ace offered.

"I think that's a good," Shib began but the growls cut him off mid-sentence. Before them stood a pack of five creatures that resembled slightly over large dogs from Earth. The pack, led by a huge male with long jet black fur stood facing them, their lips pulled back to reveal jaws designed for ripping and tearing flesh. The sight of these strangers temporarily distracted them from their flight. As the two groups stood facing each other, the huge male advanced towards them, followed by his duller grey companions.

"Oh shit," Jake hissed. "Wolves. That's all we need."

"Take aim guys," Nef ordered quietly but firmly, "and please make sure you miss each other's heads huh?" The group spread out and Jake automatically aimed like so many times during his movie career. This move was easy for him, he had played characters with guns many times and he could wave a gun around like a pro but as he stood there facing the pack, he was not sure he would be able to hit one of them if he fired. It was just like being back on set; look angry, lift your gun and aim whilst issuing some pithy put down, then jerk back a little to simulate the kickback and on to the next bad guy. He had never fired a real gun even though he knew his way around most of the standard ones. One of his stunt guys taught him to strip, clean and put a laser rifle back together in a decent time and he used the skill to great effect when he played Sergeant Millfoy in Return of the Joyrider. There was never any real gunfire on set and the health and safety rules meant he had always been discouraged from learning. He guessed now was as good a time as any to learn something new.

He aimed as best he could and began to squeeze the trigger. Suddenly the animal's hindquarters dropped and he let out a loud squeal of alarm. The rest of the pack backed off in fear and hesitated as they watched their leader scrabbling his forelegs and squealing in terror. Jake watched, mesmerised as the animal's body sunk lower into the ground leaving just his head, which thrashed and squealed. He lowered his weapon as the head suddenly disappeared from view and the rest of the pack ran off squealing in fright.

"Umm, what the fuck just happened?" Jake asked as he looked around at his companions. Vacant stares and shrugs informed him that they knew as little as he did so they stood there looking at the spot where the animal had been just seconds ago, ready to pounce on them; a slight depression in the ground the only visible clue that something had happened.

"The rumbling has stopped," Nef said and everyone concentrated before nodding in agreement.

"Let's go huh?" Crib said. "This place is creeping me out." He took a step forward and the rumbling began again, this time right underneath them.

"Stop," Nef hissed. "Don't move a muscle, anyone." Everyone froze and waited but for what they didn't know. The rumbling grew steadily until the undergrowth around them began to tremble. Suddenly the forest floor in front of them exploded in a giant spray of dirt and plant roots that sprayed through the trees in all directions and showered down upon the group of friends. When the dust began to clear they heard what sounded like a loud belch emanate from the hole and the dismembered head of the wolf like pack leader flew up and landed ten yards from Nef's boot. Everyone jumped back in alarm and from the hole came a creature the like of which none of them had seen before, nor would again. A worm, but on an enormous scale with a pulsating, segmented body loomed from the hole. Each segment sported three or four long bristles that stuck out and wavered around in the air. Twenty feet of it soared out of the hole and stood ramrod straight as it pulsed, the bristles wavering. The top three feet curved down toward them and they saw its huge circular mouth ringed with several rows of triangular teeth. They could not see any eyes but somehow it knew they were there and it suddenly reared its head back as if preparing to strike.

A loud bang made Jake nearly jump out of his skin and he turned to see Crib firing his laser rifle right at the horrific looking mouthpart. Ace joined in and added his gunfire to Crib's and Jake saw the laser bullets tear holes through the creature's soft body. Gouts of blue substance flew out from the top of its head as the laser bullets found their mark and Jake took aim. He aimed for just under that circle of dreadful looking teeth and squeezed the trigger. The kickback hurt his shoulder and he winced in pain.

"Pull it in tight to your shoulder Jake," a voice said so he squeezed the rifle in closer and fired again. This improved things and he was able to get a couple of shots in before the group's combined effort succeeded in blowing the top three feet clean off the rest of the body, which fell to the ground spraying blue gunk everywhere.

"What the fuck was that?" Jake hissed as he stood there shaking with adrenaline, his gun held limply by his side.

"I haven't the first fucking clue but whatever it was, it's dead now," Ace replied.

"Come on," Nef sighed as he wiped his brow with a hand. "Let's get going and if anyone feels that rumbling again, yell." They took off at a jog, Shib ensuring they headed northeast at all times and headed deep into the ancient forest.

"Stop," Manlee shouted.

Nef turned and went to his friend. "What's up buddy? Can you feel the rumbling again?" he asked as he looked at the forest floor and concentrated.

"No it's not that," Manlee replied. "It's something else."

"What?" Crib asked.

"I sense another Zylomian nearby."

Nef was taken aback and frowned. "Oh," was all he could think of to say.

"How do you know?" Jake asked.

"We can sense another of our own kind," Manlee replied. "It's a kind of telepathic connection if you like. I can't describe it any other way but I know without a doubt that I'm not the only Zylomian here."

"The only other one it could be is Hefton 24 but he's back on the Mayan Queen," Ace said. "Unless there's Zylomians here somewhere doing research or something."

Nef shrugged and was about to suggest they continue when they all heard the sound of something clambering through the undergrowth. They all took aim and waited for whatever it was to appear from the brush and lunge at them. Nef almost fired when something suddenly leapt from behind a tree.

"Whoa, hey calm down," Stella Bodecki exclaimed as she raised both hands and panted with the effort of running.

"Stella?" Nef said. "What are you doing here?"

"They took the bridge crew as hostages after you guys stole their shuttle," she told them just as Arsh, Hefton and Captain Nagle joined them. They stood, hands on their knees as they panted with the exertion.

"So they're here too?" Crib asked and she nodded.

"Yeah they're a couple of hours behind and several guys short now thanks to the creatures. We were attacked as soon as we landed and in the confusion, we managed to make a run for it and leave them to it. Hefton realised Manlee was here so he tracked you guys and we've been trying to catch you up."

"You saw the worm things too?" Crib asked.

"Oh jeez did we ever," Arsh replied. "I'm gonna be having nightmares for months, I just know it."

"Captain," Nef said. "I guess now that you're here you are the senior officer. We're headed to the nearest science outpost, roughly eighty miles northeast. It seems the obvious thing to do."

"Nef," Captain Nagle replied. "Damiklonians are amongst the finest warriors of any race I know of. That makes you far more worthy of being in charge buddy."

"If you say so Sir. Right then let's go guys and keep your eyes open all around and your senses ready for that rumbling okay?"

"Rumbling?" Hefton asked.

"Those worm things," Ace replied. "You know they're coming cos the ground rumbles and all the creatures start running away in terror. If you feel even a slight rumbling under your feet, yell immediately."

"Okay," he replied. He went over to Manlee and exchanged the standard Zylomian greeting. They each placed their right hand on the shoulder of the other and said some words no one could understand.

"It would be wise not to get too close to the trees themselves either," Jake said suddenly and Crib started to laugh. Jake glared at him then grinned. "There's a creature that would love to make a meal out of our necks that lives in them and they're so well camouflaged that you won't see them until it's too late."

"Okay, thanks," Arsh nodded and the group set off once again. Ahead lay eighty miles of thick forest filled with unknown horrors whilst behind them, a raggle taggle band of pirates chased them; the money no longer of interest. Now there was just one thing that they wanted and which they were determined to have. Revenge.

CHAPTER NINE

Kreeve managed to track the shuttle all the way to Tellizon 4 and landed a mile from where it lay, battered by the emergency landing but still in one piece surrounded by smashed tree trunks and snapped branches, a deep gouge in the earth giving away its trajectory. Ink and Johnson escorted the bridge crew out and into the afternoon sun whilst Kreeve shut down the ship. Ilyas made sure his men were more than adequately armed before approaching the hostages.

"Well my friends. We've arrived at last and will soon be meeting up with our friend Jake and what a happy reunion that will be. Unfortunately, this is not the most hospitable of planets so it seems unlikely that all of you will live through the next few hours. Oh well, but it saves me having to kill you myself." He turned to go, unaware of the feint rumble beneath his feet and then turned back. "By the way, if any of you run away, we won't be chasing after you okay? The indigenous life here will sort you out." He turned and walked back towards his companions who were getting themselves ready for a long hike through the forest. The rumbling grew in intensity and Ink looked at the ground.

"Earthquake? he muttered to Johnson who shrugged.

"Probably."

"Jeez, what a place."

Suddenly a scream rang out and everyone turned to see one of the pirates buried waist deep into the ground. He yelled and screamed for help and two of his friends rushed over, grabbed his arms, and pulled. Without warning he was suddenly yanked out of their grasp and disappeared into the ground, leaving everyone staring with disbelief at the slight depression where seconds before, their comrade was standing. Twenty feet away the ground suddenly burst into the air like a geyser, the dust and stones falling down upon the group. Something landed at Ink's feet with a thud and he bent to look. He reached out with his boot and touched it and it rolled away to leave him staring into the dead eyes of his colleague. As comprehension swept over him, he yelled in terror and lurched away, bumping into Johnson and sending him sprawling to the ground. The terrified pirate scrabbled to get up but disappeared head first into the ground before he could even scream for help. The pirates went crazy, firing their guns at the ground and three more of them disappeared before the first of the creatures lunged out of the ground and bore down on them. Its huge pulsating body stood ramrod straight as the bristles that stuck out from its segments wavered around in the air. The ground shook and more of them appeared; four in all standing like sentinels around the band of horrified pirates. As if linked by some unknown force, all four of them lunged down towards the group, who ran around in all directions screaming in terror and firing their guns like mad men. Two of them were injured by the bullets of their colleagues and in the melee, five of them ran off across the flat plain of the clearing.

Captain Nagle saw his chance and nudged Arsh and Hefton. "This is our chance guys. C'mon, let's get some of those guns they stacked over there and make a run for the trees huh?" They dashed to the ship and helped themselves to a rifle apiece and a sack of extra power cells and ran for all they were worth for the tree line. The cool dark of the forest swallowed them up and they ran for five hundred yards before stopping to catch their breath. A short burst from a laser pistol Hefton had picked up from the pirate's stash brought them freedom from their restraints and they took a minute to get their breath back.

Hefton suddenly looked up. "Captain? I sense another Zylomian nearby. I think it's Manlee 18."

Captain Nagle looked surprised. "Are you sure? Manlee is with him?"

130

"It would seem so Sir." The group looked at each other and then at Captain Nagle and all wondered what he was thinking.

Captain Nagle saw them looking and knew what was on their minds. "Okay, can you track him and lead us to them? If we hook up with them, we'll be a stronger group than have us all split up. Besides, I don't feel comfortable knowing Manlee is back here again, after what he went through last time he was here. He'll feel more comfortable with more friends around him."

"I agree," Hefton nodded. "Yes I can track him but they are a couple of hours ahead of us. We will need to travel swiftly."

"Okay," Captain Nagle said. "Everyone up for an afternoon jog?"

Ilyas Da Costa was transfixed at the sight of his friend and colleague buried up to his waist in the ground; his screams filling the air as panic took hold of the group. By the time the creatures had gone, he had lost eight of his men and all the hostages. He was not sure whether the hostages had succumbed to the creatures or whether they had managed to run off in the chaos but he was incensed with rage and swore loudly as he thumped the side of the ship.

"Captain?" Ink puffed as he came running up. "Are you okay?"

"Yeah I'm fine, you?"

"I'm okay Sir but we've lost a lot of men and the hostages too."

"I know. Fuck it. Did the creatures get em?"

"I don't know."

"Who do we still have?"

"Kreeve, Cady, Moody, Lew and Patch. With me and you that makes seven of us."

"Well at least we'll be able to get off this rock. Thank god Kreeve is still with us. Are they all okay?"

"Cady took a bullet in the shoulder but everyone else is fine Sir. Shall I get everyone into the ship?"

"What?" Ilyas looked shocked. "No way Ink. We're going after Jake. That's why we came and I ain't about to back out now because of some giant worms. Get everyone together and armed up." Ink nodded and ran off to gather what remained of the pirate crew.

Ilyas passed around bottles of water and approached his Navigator. "Maria? How are ya feeling Hun?"

"I'll survive Sir. What were those things?"

"Fuck knows but now we know what to expect we will be ready for em next time. Are you right handed or left?"

Maria Cady looked at him and frowned. "Right."

Ilyas looked at the wound in her right shoulder and knew she would not be able to fire a weapon. She would be more of a burden to them than a help so he had no choice but to leave her behind.

He sighed. "You can't fire a gun with that shoulder wound and it could get infected or who knows what else. You're gonna have to stay behind in the ship and wait for us?"

She sighed sadly and nodded. "Yeah okay."

"You'll be safe inside the ship and there's plenty of supplies and medicines in there. Just keep the doors locked and you'll be okay."

"Yes Sir," she said as she struggled to her feet and headed towards the open rear hatch.

"And don't come out for anything except us?" Ilyas called after her.

"I won't. Be safe guys."

"We love you Cady," Kreeve called and winked at her when she turned and smiled at him.

"And get the kettle on," Patch called. Maria answered with one finger and the group laughed.

"Okay guys let's go," Ilyas said. "We'll head north. There's a scientific station that way if my memory serves me correctly, they're bound to head for that. Any questions?" Ilyas Da Costa led his now small band of pirate comrades towards the tree line. There was now just one thing occupying his mind and he would happily sacrifice every one of his crew to achieve it. He was mad for revenge and as he entered the cool of the trees, he meant to have it.

Jake looked at Stella Bodecki's backside as she ran ahead of him and he liked what he saw. She obviously worked out and although she was clearly Hispanic, she was attractive and that backside was sexy enough for him to overlook her flaws. She reminded him of some of the actresses he had worked with, a pretty girl but tough and sexy. He hoped their current situation would give him an opportunity to attempt to get into her panties. They jogged for a couple of hours until exhaustion forced them to take a rest. The going began to get steeper too and soon the sound of water came to their ears and they eventually emerged from the tree line to find themselves at the edge of a gorge looking down at a wide river a hundred feet below, the white water plunging furiously away to their right and into the far distance. Above them, an enormous waterfall thundered and drenched them in spray. The mist was icy cold and a shock to the system after their exertions.

"Shit," Captain Nagle gasped. "Where the hell do we go from here? Anyone fancy jumping?"

"After you Captain," Stella smiled.

"Ladies first Bodecki."

"Think I'll pass," she replied, "but thanks all the same."

"We have no alternative but to climb Sir," Shib said as he gazed upwards. "If you look up, there is a clearly defined path that will take us right to the top of this plateau."

"Yeah," Captain Nagle nodded. "I guess that's our only option. I'm not a great lover of heights myself but since there's no alternative I vote we get on with it before I chicken out."

"It is the only way forward," Nef agreed. "Okay guys let's get this over with. Slow and steady, it's not a race okay? If anyone gets into difficulty, yell."

Jake looked up and saw the ragged rocky path leading up the steep sided plateau. He was not a huge lover of heights either and he always wore a secure harness when doing high work in his movies. He gulped and tried to imagine he had his safety harness on; pulling the belt of his pants a notch tighter to make the image seem more real. The going was not as bad as it looked and with regular stops to catch their breath, they made slow but steady progress up the side of the plateau.

"Hey Jake," Stella called from behind him. "This reminds me of that movie of yours, oh what was it called? The one where you chase the escaped prisoner through the mountains and have to get the deadly virus off him before he infects the whole planet.

He grinned as he remembered. "Population Zero," he said and she nodded.

"Yeah, that's the one. One thing I never understood though," she asked. "Why Population Zero? The guy never did get to release the virus so no one was killed."

"The nickname of the virus was population zero," he told her.

"Oh I see, thanks," she replied.

"No problem," he said and turned to give her his best celebrity smile. As he did so, something caught his attention, a tiny movement out of the corner of his eye. He snapped his head up and saw the huge boulder hurtling towards them. Instinctively he grabbed her by the shoulders and yanked her into his arms as the boulder hit the rock wall, shattering into several pieces and continuing its journey to the forest floor below.

"Shit," Stella gasped when Jake let her go. "Fuck. I didn't see that coming," she sighed, trembling with fear at how close a shave she had just experienced.

"Is everyone all right," Nef yelled from the front.

"Yeah, we're fine," Jake yelled back. "You okay?" he asked Stella, taking the opportunity to give her arm a squeeze.

"Yeah I'm okay. Thanks buddy."

"Anytime," he beamed, confident he had just taken a step nearer those panties.

With one last push, the group reached the top of the plateau and found themselves looking at another tree line, another dense forest stretching out before them. By now, it was beginning to get dark and Jake looked at the forest ahead of him. He didn't fancy negotiating his way through there in the pitch dark.

"It's getting dark guys," Nef called. "I vote we make camp for the night." No one disagreed and within thirty minutes a decent campfire was burning and Nef was handing round the ration packs.

"There's more of us now so these won't last more than one more meal for each of us," he said. "So after tomorrow night we're gonna have to find food or do without."

"We need to organise a watch rota," Captain Nagle suggested. "There's enough of us now for a pair of us to do two hours each, that way we all get the chance of enough sleep. I'll volunteer to be part of the first watch."

"I'll join you," Crib offered.

"I might suggest that I take the watch," Shib suggested. "After all, I don't sleep and there's no likelihood of me dozing off. You are all exhausted and the sleep would be beneficial."

"Okay buddy," Captain Nagle smiled. "It just seems a bit bad making you do all the work all the time."

"Isn't that what I'm for Sir?"

"Yeah but you're a person to us Shib not just a machine. You're a friend."

"Thank you Sir, that is great compliment."

"It's gonna be pretty chilly overnight guys so I suggest we all put aside our personal spaces and snuggle up all cosy like," Ace said. "Shib? There's a pile of wood there to keep the fire going to keep off the worst of the chill."

The group lay down side by side and Jake managed to engineer it so that he was spooning with Stella Bodecki and her cute ass. It was uncomfortable on the ground but exhaustion claimed them all within thirty minutes. Shib kept watch, stoked the fire, and listened as the night creatures called. Four times he chased off inquisitive animals and he even managed to catch breakfast. By the time the group began to awaken, he had skinned and cleaned the carcass and was roasting it over the still roaring fire. The smell of roasting meat reached the nostrils of the sleeping group and forced them awake.

The group yawned, stretched themselves, and sniffed.

"Something smells wonderful," Ace remarked.

"No wonder I was just dreaming of Thanksgiving dinner," Jake grinned.

"I thought you'd all like something substantial for breakfast," Shib replied. "The protein will help your bodies cope with the demands of our current situation."

"Is it safe to eat?" Manlee asked.

Shib cut off a small piece, put it into his mouth, and chewed. He closed his eyes while his android brain tested and analysed the substance. Finally he nodded and spat out the sample and smiled.

"It is quite safe, although my analysis shows that it probably won't taste too wonderful. It's rather strong, a bit like

136

rather ripe game from Earth or the Catlinale from Zylom 2. Nef, you might find it a little tasteless but all of you should endeavour to eat as much as you can."

"I can't stand game," Captain Nagle remarked and Jake nodded.

"Neither can I but since our lives depend on it I guess I'm man enough to give it a go. I had to eat a huge slug like bug thing once for a movie and if I can eat that, I can eat anything."

"I remember that movie," Ace smiled. "That thing was the real deal? I assumed it was fake."

"It was a bet from the producer. He said if I used the real thing instead of a fake one then he'd donate a huge bunch of cash to my charity. I was determined to part that miser from his money but it almost killed me. This thing can't be that bad, it just can't."

"Hefton 24 looked at Manlee 18 and grinned. "Have you ever eaten Catlinale?"

"No, but I've heard about it," Manlee replied. "Is it really as bad as they say?"

"Worse."

"Shit."

"Looks like I got the best end of this deal then," Nef smiled as he cut off a large slice and stuffed it into his mouth. "Doesn't really taste of anything," he mumbled.

Captain Nagle tried a small piece and immediately spat it out, to the amusement of the rest of the group.

He looked around at them. "Well you try it and see what you think," he hissed as he took a deep breath and stuffed the rest into his mouth and swallowed it without chewing. Crib took a slice, bit off a small piece, and chewed slowly. He raised his eyebrows appreciatively and nodded.

"I gotta pee first," Stella Bodecki said as she turned and headed towards the tree line.

"Be careful," Ace called after her. "Don't go too far." She nodded and headed into the trees. The group ate their breakfast, albeit reluctantly and encouraged by Shib who found the whole procedure fascinating. Rustling behind them made them all turn around to see Stella stumbling out from the trees, her hand to her neck and her eyes wide in shock. She held out her other arm to them and they leapt towards her but before they could reach her, her eyes rolled back and she fell to the ground.

"Let me through please," Shib said as he elbowed his way through the throng gathered around Stella's prone body. He crouched by her side, held a finger to her neck and then looked up at Captain Nagle. "She's dead Sir. It seems something either bit her or stung her, look." He pointed to a small mark on her neck, right under her earlobe. It was tiny, no more than a pinprick. "I will attempt to analyse the substance if you'll give me a few minutes."

Captain Nagle nodded and Shib pressed a switch on the inside of his right wrist. The top of his middle finger flipped back and a tiny needle emerged. He inserted it into her carotid artery and took a blood sample, then sat down, closed his eyes and waited for his brain to work out what it was.

"Shit," Captain Nagle yelled. "Shit, shit." He grabbed his temples and closed his eyes as he fought with his anger and frustration.

"Damn you Elloway," he yelled as he rounded on Jake. "This is all your fault you asshole."

"Sir," Hefton 24 said as he stood and faced his Captain. "This isn't his fault. It's those damn pirates' fault if anyone is to blame. Or more accurately whoever the inside man is on the Mayan Queen." He gazed into Captain Nagle's eyes and the two men stared each other down.

Captain Nagle sighed and looked at the ground. "You're right Hefton and I'm sorry. She was a good friend and an exemplary employee."

Jake stood; his eyes wide with shock at what had just happened and didn't know how to react or whether to react at all. He looked at Hefton and raised his eyebrows questioningly.

"Inside man?" he asked.

"On the way here we were discussing what happened and we came to the conclusion that there had to be an inside man on the Mayan Queen. Pirates almost never target freightliners unless they ship arms or currency and all of those who don't, make sure to advertise the fact as widely and plainly as possible. It just seemed too strange that we should suddenly be targeted four days after you arrived and we surmised that we must have an inside man on board."

"Well when and if we find out who it is, I can assure everyone here that he's gonna have to answer to me," Nef announced and several of the others nodded.

"Sir?" Shib called and everyone turned and looked. "I've been able to analyse one substance from Stella's bloodstream that is the most likely cause of her death. It's a type of neurotoxin and an extremely potent one. The single entry wound on her neck tends to infer that it was delivered by means of a sting."

"It could've been a bite too though don't you think?" Ace said but Shib shook his head.

"I would say not. Animals with poisonous bites deliver their venom through a pair of long fangs, such as Nef has. If Stella were bitten, there would be two entry wounds but her body shows only one. Therefore, I surmise that she was stung by something, but what is anyone's guess. It could be anything but by the size of the mark on her neck, whatever it is, is tiny."

"Chances are that it's a bug though, don't you think?" Jake suggested.

"Bugs aren't the only things that sting Jake," Shib replied. "On Earth there are many creatures and even plants that sting but yes, the vast majority of stinging creatures that we know of, are bugs. It would be wise to avoid contact with any bugs if at all possible."

"Aww jeez," Jake sighed as he ran a hand through his hair. "I hate bugs."

"Everyone cover up as much as possible," Captain Nagle ordered as he began taking off his shirt. "Try not to have any exposed skin if possible. Tuck your pants into your boots or socks and if anyone is wearing a vest, take it off and use it to wrap around your head and neck." Jake took off his shirt and removed his vest. After carefully tucking his pant legs into his socks and doing up his boots tightly, he tucked his shirt into his pants and did all the buttons up. He wrapped his vest around his head and neck and then lifted his shirt collar up as an added barrier. Three of the men had no vests or extra layers with which to cover their heads, so Shib removed his shirt and tore it into two pieces.

"I cannot be stung and nor am I affected by temperature so you may use my shirt gentlemen," he said as he handed two of them a piece each. They thanked him and wrapped their heads.

"Now we just have to find something for Ace. Does anyone have anything at all?"

"What about Stella's shirt?" Jake suggested.

"A good idea Jake," Shib nodded and walked over to where her body lay. He removed her shirt and handed it to Ace, who thanked him and got to work wrapping up his head and neck.

"If we're all ready gentlemen, I suggest we get moving. The pirates won't be far behind us and hopefully won't know about the poisonous bugs."

They set off through the trees and kept to where the undergrowth was fairly open as much as they could. With their bodies wrapped up, they soon began to sweat, which attracted clouds of flying insects. Jake yelled in terror when he found a huge many-legged creature crawling up his leg and only stopped when Crib slapped it away.

"Can't you scream quietly Elloway?" Nagle muttered a little louder than he had intended.

Jake heard him and shot him a glare. "I'm sorry Captain," he countered aggressively. "I'm sorry to have ruined your comfortable schedule but I didn't exactly get into this willingly either. I would much rather be back on board hauling crates and chatting up the nurse but y'know what? I can't cos I'm stuck here with you and I'm just gonna have to make the best of it and I suggest you do too."

Captain Nagle looked at the big muscular actor who now towered over him. He raised both hands in a placating gesture.

"Okay, okay, let's take a breath and try to get along enough to survive huh?" Jake held his gaze for another couple of seconds just to prove his dominance before turning away and catching up with the others. They slogged on for a couple of hours until they found themselves climbing up a fairly steep and rocky incline. The trees thinned out a little as they climbed and Nef suggested they stop for a rest.

"Thank heavens," Arsh puffed. "You read my mind Nef." He leant against a large boulder and wiped a hand across his brow before reaching for his water bottle. As he enjoyed a long cool swig, he felt the rumble under his feet.

"Hey what the?" he muttered.

"Oh shit not again," Crib hissed. "Quick everyone, onto the rocks and keep still."

"What's going on?" Hefton asked as everyone scrabbled onto boulders.

"It's the worm things," Manlee said. "That rumbling is them coming this way. They seem to be able to feel us walking on the ground so hopefully they won't feel us through these rocks."

"Ready your weapons guys," Captain Nagle ordered. Everyone waited in silence, scanning the ground all around, ready to open fire at the first sign of disturbance. None came and after a few minutes, everyone started looking at each other, wondering what they should do.

Shib put a foot gently down on the ground. "The rumbling has gone. My guess is that the creature has passed us by this time."

Everyone sighed with relief and clambered down from their perches amongst the boulders. All of a sudden, the sounds of distant gunfire rang out from somewhere behind and everyone looked at each other in shock.

"The pirates," Jake and Ace said together.

"Now we know where the worm thing went," Crib hissed. Shib took a step forward and stopped, looking intently back the way they'd come, back towards the sounds of gunfire that still rang out through the trees.

"Shib," Captain Nagle said.

"Yes Captain?"

"They're not in your circle buddy."

"I'm aware of that Sir and do not worry about my allegiance. I'm just trying to ascertain how far back they are and by my calculations, I'd say they're approximately six point seven miles behind us. I suggest we get moving immediately and try to put some more distance between us."

"Agreed," Captain Nagle said. "Sorry Shib, I didn't mean to question you."

"No need to apologise Sir. I am aware that humans are not yet able to fully trust Androids. I am unable to be offended by that fact but I do understand it. I am bound by my programming and cannot deviate from it."

The group set off and continued their climb. Twice they encountered the tree climbing creature that tried to reach for

Jake's neck the day before and once more they had to scrabble up onto the rocks as the rumbling came through the ground to their feet. They listened for gunfire but none came and all of them wondered whether that meant the pirates had all perished or they had learned to tread carefully.

"Do you reckon all the pirates are dead?" Manlee asked.

"Fuck knows," Crib shrugged. "Could be I guess."

"Or maybe they've learned to be careful," Arsh replied. "It only took us one experience with them to learn to be careful where we trod so I guess they've sussed it out too."

"And it would make sense to assume they're still alive and after us," Hefton replied.

"Come on guys," Nef said. "We're in sight of the top now." They set off and climbed the last five hundred yards without incident. The view from the top of what was clearly a fairly high mountain was stunning. They could just make out the open plain where two dark dots indicated where the shuttle and the pirate ship still stood.

"We've come a long way," Hefton said.

"What a view," Jake sighed as he looked around. "Wow you don't get a view like this back on Earth."

"At least not for the last several million years anyhow," Arsh agreed.

Ahead of them lay a gentle descent through sparsely forested and rocky terrain beyond which they could see another deep forest bounded on the left by a wide open plain that meandered vaguely north east for many miles before glancing off almost at right angles north west.

"Oh look guys, another forest," Arsh said, "yippee."

"I have an idea that might help us gain the upper hand over our stalkers back there," Shib said. "What if we head for the plain, leaving a clear trail but when we reach the tree line, head back and go into the forest? They'll think we've wimped out of going through another forest and its creatures. If they take the bait, it'll make them slip further behind us and give us some more elbow room."

"I've an idea too," Crib said. "How about we head down to the forest, again making sure we leave a clear trail but when we reach the tree line, we head off to the left and follow the edge of the trees alongside the flat plain? It might fool the pirates into believing we've headed into the trees, especially as it is more directly in line with where we wish to go."

"That is also a good idea Crib," Shib nodded. "Either plan has a good chance of success. Which should we take?"

Captain Nagle thought about it and then looked at Nef. "I seem to remember saying you're the boss for this trip Nef. It's up to you buddy."

"Who votes for Shib's idea?" Nef asked and counted the hands. "And who votes for Crib's idea?" He sighed as he realised it was an even split.

"Okay well it looks like I have the controlling vote so I vote for Shib's idea. We'll make it look like we're heading for the easy way around but then double back and keep to a direct line as we've been doing. It gives us the best chance of putting a little more distance between us and them. Is everyone okay with that?"

They set off down the incline towards the flat plain that bordered the thick forest and made sure to leave a clear trail. Broken branches, scrapes in the earth and even a discarded ration pack wrapper all indicating clearly which way the group had headed. They hoped their followers would take the bait.

CHAPTER TEN

Ilyas Da Costa set out north with Ink, Kreeve, Moody, Lew and Patch and all were more than a little unsettled from their encounter with those giant worm-like creatures. They entered the tree line and welcomed the drop in temperature and shade from the sun. It was very dark, the undergrowth extremely thick and lush, the going slow and arduous.

"We don't know what other kinds of creatures are waiting for us in here guys so if anything moves, shoot it."

"Oh yes Sir," Ink replied as he looked about nervously, convinced something was watching them, maybe even stalking them. They trudged for an hour before stopping to rest their legs and get their breath. Ilyas took a drink from his water bottle and wiped a hand across his brow. As he lifted the bottle to take another drink he found himself staring into the eyes of what looked like a huge wolf. It was chestnut brown and its orange eyes bored into his as it curled back its lips and gave a low growl.

"Guys," he whispered. "Guys."

"What's up? Oh shit," Kreeve said as he turned to find out what the Captain wanted, automatically shouldering his gun and taking aim. The creature took a step towards the group and Ilyas was relieved to hear the others ready their guns.

Moody, at the rear of the group was terror-stricken.

"Holy shit," he exclaimed as he began to tremble in fright. The creature took a second step towards them, his eyes locked on Ilyas'. A third step towards them and they all opened fire. The animal dropped to the ground and everyone breathed a sigh of relief.

Kreeve wiped his brow and turned to grin at the others. "Moody?" he called. "Moody," he yelled a bit louder. Everyone turned to look and Ilyas noticed drag marks in the soft earth of the forest floor. They followed the marks until they saw a boot sticking out from under a tree root.

"Moody," Kreeve called as he ran towards it, leaping over the root and immediately leaping back in horror, his hand going instinctively to his mouth before he turned away and vomited into the undergrowth. Ilyas peered gingerly over the root and saw what remained of Moody's lower right leg; the sharply split finger of bone standing slightly proud of the torn and bleeding flesh around it. The once white sock was now bright red and already, tiny insects were making their way to this fresh new feast.

He leapt back in alarm, turned away, and breathed deeply. "Oh shit."   His chest heaved as he fought to control the adrenaline that now coursed through his body, urging him to flee back to the ship and away into the safety of space.

"Come on," he ordered, "let's get moving." He marched onwards, not caring if the others were following or not, his mind holding fast to the one thing that kept him going, revenge. Most of his men had been lost during the past few hours and all because of Jake fucking Elloway and if it was the last thing he did, he would have his revenge. It had taken him ten years to find a group of people he could rely on and although they were a motley bunch at times, they knew their job and did as they were told and he respected them for that. Everyone knew he was a fair man; many pirate captains ruled by fear but he had always been different, preferring to be friends with his group as well as their Captain. He had a good reputation and he knew it.

They continued their walk without incident and it was quite dark before they realised they would have to stop for the night. After climbing a low plateau, they found a place amongst the rocks to settle down for the night and agreed to keep watch on a two-hour rota. Kreeve won the draw for the first watch and climbed onto a large boulder to sit it out. Halfway through he climbed down and took a walk around to stretch his legs and get the blood flowing into his cold backside. A hundred yards around the gentle curving edge of the plateau, he saw the faint glow several miles away, halfway up a further and much higher peak. For a moment he wondered whether to wake Ilyas but he knew that the Captain would demand they set out right away to close the distance between them and he was too tired to walk any more today. It was so dark in the forest and with who knows what kind of creatures lurking in there; it would be foolhardy to venture in there at night. Besides, he concluded, the fact they had a fire going proved they had stopped for the night too so if they got up at first light and set off, they would be no further behind. Aching with fatigue, he turned back, resumed the last forty-five minutes of his watch, and hoped that none of the others decided to take a stroll this way and see the campfire in the distance.

Ilyas took the last two-hour watch of the night and was more than a little relieved to be able to get off the ground and walk around. He had not slept much; it was far too cold and the noises from the nearby forest creeped him out. His dreams had been plagued with all sorts of horrors creeping up on him as he lay there and more than once he started awake, convinced he had heard something right behind him and snapped his head around, only to see one or other of his companions snoring and snuffling in their own fitful sleep. Stiff and cold, he decided to take a walk to get the blood flowing and warm his chilly muscles and it was just as dawn broke that he spied the still glowing campfire halfway up the neighbouring peak. He rushed back to where his companions lay and yelled at them to wake up.

"Guys," he yelled, "guys wake up." He nudged a snoring Patch with the toe of his boot. "Come on guys, wake up."

"What's up Captain?" Ink yawned, having only just laid down after his own watch. "It can't be two hours already, I only just came off watch myself."

"They're just over there," Ilyas pointed. "I can see their camp fire. They're halfway up that mountain over there. Come on, we've been going in the wrong direction. They must be going northeast so we have to get over there and close up the gap. Come on." The tired and chilly men hauled themselves up and gathered their guns and Kreeve was very glad he had not woken Ilyas when he had spied the campfire the evening before.

"Can't we even make some coffee first?" Patch asked.

Ilyas gave him a dark look. "No. Stop being such a pussy and get moving."

"Can I take a pee first Captain?" Ink asked and the others all nodded.

"Okay," Ilyas nodded. "I need one myself actually," he said as he unzipped himself."

They started out and Ilyas showed them where he had seen their campfire.

"See it?" he asked as he pointed it out. In the rapidly brightening dawn it was less easy to see but the plume of lightly coiling smoke was just visible and they nodded. They began their descent into the valley between the two neighbouring peaks and found the forest strangely quiet. It was still early, the night creatures had returned to the safety of their dens and the day creatures did not yet dare to venture out and they made the valley floor in less than an hour without incident. The sun was burning off the last of the morning chill as they started up the neighbouring peak and they became more aware of noises from the first of the day creatures getting up and moving around. It was still too early for the relentless clouds of insects that followed them the day before and they were glad of the respite from the constant need to swat them away.

They found a trail leading up the side of the mountain and decided to follow it instead of making their own way through. It would be easier on their legs to follow a well-worn animal trail and they didn't want to make more work for themselves when it was not necessary. Half way up they passed underneath a tree that bore bright yellow fruits the size of man's fist, hundreds of which lay around them on the forest floor. Patch stopped and picked one up and wondered if it was safe to eat.

"I wouldn't if I were you," Ink said. "But he might," he grinned and indicated behind Patch, who swung around and saw a small furry creature clinging to the bark of the tree; his forelegs reaching towards his hand that held the bright yellow fruit.

"Hey there buddy," Patch remarked and grinned at the critter who leaned even further towards him, front legs reaching as far as they could. "You want this?" he asked as he held out the fruit. The creature looked at it, and then looked right into his eyes before taking hold of the fruit. Patch could feel its little hands around his fingers and he grinned.

"Aww ain't it cute?" he snickered as the creature continued looking into his eyes. A few seconds later, it opened its mouth and Patch just had time to register its wicked looking teeth before it bit his finger down to the bone, snatched the fruit and ran up the tree out of sight. He yelled in pain as blood trickled down his finger and hand and dripped from his wrist. Kreeve came running up and tied a handkerchief around his finger, telling him to stop being a baby and grinning at his stupidity.

"Can we please get going now?" Ilyas asked sarcastically.

"Sorry Captain," Patch replied.

"And please can everyone remember this isn't a petting zoo?"

"Sure thing Boss," Ink nodded as he glared at Patch. They set off again and within another hour Patch's finger was throbbing and had swollen so much he could not bend it. He was in agony and had already swallowed a couple of painkillers he always carried with him, which seemed to have done him no good whatsoever. It was still bleeding too and nothing they did stopped it. The wound was not gushing or anything, just a steady drip every second or so and the handkerchief Kreeve had wrapped around it was now soaked and useless. They hopped over a small stream, so Ink washed the blood soaked handkerchief in the freezing water and re-wrapped Patch's finger. The icy water was a shock but it did seem to take the pain away temporarily, until the temperature rose once again.

As they continued their climb, Patch found the going harder and harder as the pain in his finger spread through his hand and began to climb up his arm. His finger was now beginning to turn black and everyone was getting worried. The pain in his head was excruciating and soon he was having trouble negotiating his way over fallen trees and boulders. He fell over constantly, his companions having to support and half drag him along.

"Boss," Kreeve called. "Can we stop for a couple of minutes? Patch is in a bad way."

Ilyas stopped and looked at Patch who was by now sweating and trembling and not fully conscious. "Okay let's take ten minutes," he nodded and Ink and Kreeve laid Patch down. It was heavy going hauling him along when they had to climb up the steep trail and both of them secretly cursed him for his stupidity.

Ilyas went over to Kreeve. "Are you thinking what I'm thinking?" he asked as he nodded towards Patch, who lay trembling and rambling on the ground.

"I think so Sir," Kreeve nodded.

"It's poison isn't it?"

"I reckon so."

"We don't have anything like antidotes or any shit like that with us. We don't even know if that poison is gonna kill him or if he'll recover."

"It's only been a couple of hours since he was bitten and already he's almost unconscious," Kreeve replied. "His arm is black up to the shoulder and he's burning up. I doubt if it's something he can expect to recover from."

"So what do we do?" Ilyas asked as he looked from one to the other. "Do we all agree it looks like whatever it is will kill him?" Everyone nodded. "Then we either leave him here or we sit with him until he dies. Which is it to be?"

"We can't just leave him here Sir," Lew said. "He'll be attacked and eaten by creatures and we don't know how aware he is. I wouldn't like to leave a buddy to be eaten alive by creatures. It's not right. On the other hand, we could be sitting here for days. It might take ages for him to die and in the meantime, we could run out of ammo and get eaten ourselves. I don't like the idea of just leaving him but there are dangers with staying here with him."

"There is another option Sir," Kreeve whispered and everyone fell silent. They all knew what he meant.

"I don't like that option," Ilyas replied.

"Neither do I," Kreeve said, "but what I do know is if I was in his situation, I wouldn't want to be left behind to be eaten alive and I wouldn't want to be the cause of my buddies being eaten alive either. I would hope my buddies could end my suffering and maybe say a few words over me; say something nice about me y'know?" Everyone fell silent as they thought about Kreeve's words.

"I agree," Ink said. "I would hope for the same if it was me."

"Yeah," Ilyas nodded and sighed, "me too."

"Who's gonna do it?" Lew asked.

"I'm the Captain so I guess it has to be me," Ilyas said. He approached the now unconscious Patch, knelt down and laid a hand on his shoulder. "You've been a good friend buddy, thank you. I'll make sure your Mom and Pop know you died a hero okay?" He stood up and looked around at his companions.

"Does anyone want to say a few words? I'm not a religious guy and don't know the right words."

"Patch wasn't religious Captain," Ink said, "but he told me once he does believe that you go somewhere when you die. Like you have another life y'know? I used to tease him about it."

"Okay, ahh let me think," Ilyas replied as he tried to think of appropriate words to say before shooting his friend through the temple. "Umm if there is a God out there we ask that our friend Patch be taken to the new life he always believed was waiting for him. We ask that all his sins be forgiven and we ask forgiveness for what we are about to do. Amen." He retrieved his laser piston, held it to Patch's left temple and fired. "Bon voyage buddy."

After laying him out and covering him with some branches, they started off once more. Ink wiped his eyes and set off after Ilyas and Kreeve with Lew bringing up the rear. They walked in silence, each lost in memories of moments shared with Patch.

"Hey, do you remember the time Patch fell into that swamp on Marlangue 3?" Kreeve said suddenly.

Ink snickered. "Yeah. Man he stunk worse than anything I've ever smelled and it took days for it to wash off. He must've had more showers in those three days than at any other time in his life."

"And how about the time he organised a whore for my birthday?" Ilyas said and the others roared with laughter. "Trouble was it wasn't my birthday and he kept the whore for himself and ended up with the clap." By the time they reached the camp now long abandoned by Captain Nagle and the others, they had re-lived many poignant and funny moments in Patch's life. It was the only way they knew to celebrate his life and they felt better for it.

Kreeve went over and examined the remains of the campfire. "It's been out for several hours Captain," he announced. "They must've left at dawn."

"Hey Boss," Ink yelled from the tree line. Everyone ran over to see what the fuss was about. "They've had a casualty," he said as he turned the body of Stella Bodecki over. "She's a beauty," he hissed as he ran a hand over her generous breasts and down her belly.

"Ink, you're a sick man," Ilyas snickered as he turned away. "Let's take a few minutes to catch a breath and decide which way to go." He wandered back to the remains of the campfire and sat down. "We've got no choice but to head through the trees again. I can't see any other way they could've gone."

"I agree Sir," Kreeve said and turned as a grunt from behind them caught their attention. They turned and saw the body of Stella Bodecki, her pants now around her knees and her pink lacy bra lying across her left boot. Ink knelt by her side, his own pants around his knees, his pink ass cheeks clenching as he grunted and shuddered. Kreeve turned back.

"That is one sick fuck," he remarked and Ilyas snickered.

"Yep," Ilyas nodded. "He's a damn good pirate though and that's what matters."

"Remind me never to introduce him to my wife."

"How is Carla these days?"

"She's fine."

"Give her my regards next time you go home huh?"

"I'll do that."

Ink re-joined them and they set off through the trees. It was now approaching mid-day, the sun was at its height, and the clouds of insects became more of a nuisance. Without warning a large animal leapt out of the undergrowth to their right and ran across in front of them, their presence ignored. More followed the first and within a minute, creatures of all shapes, sizes and colours surrounded them and all were running in the same direction.

"What the fuck?" Ilyas yelled and leapt back as a huge creature with horns leapt passed him and almost knocked him to the ground.

"Where are they going?" Ink asked as he gazed wide eyed at the stampede.

"More importantly," Kreeve hissed, "why are they running?"

"And what is that rumbling?" Ilyas said as he looked at the ground. "Can you feel it?" The others concentrated before nodding. Loud squealing up ahead made them jump and they turned to see another of the huge creatures with horns buried up to its forelegs in the ground. Its squeals split the air as it scrabbled with its front legs.

"It's fallen into a hole or something," Kreeve said as he raised his gun. "It looks like a deer from Earth. It might taste nice." He was just about to fire when the creature suddenly disappeared from view.

He looked up. "Where did it go?"

"Oh shit," Ilyas whispered in fright as the realisation of what was happening began to dawn on him. "It went into the ground. Just like our buddies did back at the ship."

Kreeve went white. "Oh no. Get ready to shoot guys." Everyone fell silent and waited. After several agonising seconds of silence, the earth in front of them suddenly exploded as a plume of dirt and dust rose high into the air. A loud thud to Ilyas' left caught him by surprise and he let out a yell and jumped away as the severed head of the horned animal gazed up at him lifelessly. Another plume of dirt and dust from behind made them spin around to see a deep depression in the earth from which a loud belch emanated. Lew, closest to the hole, grimaced and took a step forward. Without warning the huge worm like creature rose from the hole and stood ramrod straight as the bristles on its body wavered in the air. He was terrified and started inching his way to the right in an attempt to get away.

The top three feet of the worm suddenly bent over and they looked at the circular mouthpart ringed by hundreds of triangular teeth. Lew shook his head and continued inching away.

"Lew," Kreeve hissed. "For fuck's sake stand still you asshole." Before he could obey, the worm-like creature suddenly lunged and Lew disappeared into its mouth down to his waist. Everyone could hear him screaming from within its mouth. As one, they raised their guns. Laser rifles are noisy firearms and the quiet calm of the forest was split painfully with the din but they kept firing, blue gunk spraying everywhere from the many holes that appeared in its soft, pulsating body. Lew was still screaming as the creature suddenly bit down and his lower half fell to the ground as the huge monster slithered back into the hole and disappeared. The pirate group stood, breathing hard and silent for several minutes before realising that the rumbling had gone, which meant the creature either had moved away or was dead.

"Run," Ilyas commanded and all three remaining pirates took off as fast as their legs could carry them and ran for a mile before they stopped to get their breath. Once they set off again, they walked in silence, each feeling for the rumbling that would signify another worm thing was approaching. As the going became steeper and the trees thinned out to reveal a more rocky terrain Ilyas sighed with relief.

"If those things come back, jump up onto these boulders," he ordered.

"How will that help us?" Ink puffed.

"They obviously tunnel through the earth," Kreeve replied. "So it stands to reason that they're gonna stick to soft ground. They can't tunnel through solid rock. At least I hope they can't."

"Right, yeah that makes sense," Ink nodded. "By way Captain. Even if we do catch up with Jake and you get your revenge. We're gonna have to haul our asses all the way back to the ship before we can get off this rock."

Kreeve nodded slowly. "The thought doesn't exactly delight me either Boss."

"I know and I've been thinking about that," Ilyas replied. "I reckon the scientists who work here will have some sort of transportation. They must have to go out into the field to collect samples or whatever shit they do so it makes sense they'll have something, even if it's just a hover buggy. We'll ask them to give us a lift back to the ship and if they refuse, we'll take it anyway."

Kreeve and Ink nodded and they set off up the incline, which was getting rapidly steeper. The trail zigzagged up and around and after three more brief stops to get their breath and rest their legs, they reached the top and got a fabulous view for miles in all directions.

"Y'know guys," Ilyas remarked. "If I never see another tree so long as I live, I'll be a happy man." Kreeve and Ink both nodded in agreement. "Now, it looks like we have two options," he said as he looked ahead and saw another deeply forested area bordered by a wide flat plain to the left.

"I vote we stay out of the trees as much as we can," Ink said.

"Me too," Kreeve agreed.

"Okay," Ilyas nodded. "I'm inclined to agree with you. If you look into the distance you can see the plain heads off west a few miles ahead so we will have to take to the trees at some point or we'll end up going in the wrong direction."

"There's just one thing troubling me though," Kreeve said. "That flat plain looks the same as where we landed."

"Yeah, so what?" Ink asked.

"Well I remember the ground was soft, like a rather firm sandy beach, which is gonna be real easy for those worm things to tunnel through. Out in that flat area we'll have nowhere to hide if they appear. At least in the forest we can hide behind a tree if all else fails."

"He's got a point Boss," Ink reluctantly agreed.

Ilyas pondered the two options. "Okay, here's what we'll do. We stick right to the very edge of the trees, where it joins the flat plain. That way we won't have to wonder what's lurking in the bushes all around us but we can still use the trees for cover if necessary. It'll make the going a bit easier and faster if we don't have to fight our way through the undergrowth all the time. What d'ya say?"

"Okay," Kreeve nodded. "It sounds like the best option to me.

"Yeah okay," Ink nodded.

"Great," Ilyas sighed. "Let's go." They set off down the incline towards the border between the forest and the flat plain and found the gentle descent a lot easier to manage than the climb up had been. The view was wonderful and although Ilyas was not a cultured man, it pleased him.

"Hey boss." Kreeve's call made his musings vanish away. "Look here."

"What's up?" Ilyas asked as he went to look. He saw the broken stems and branches and clear drag marks in the ground.

"Well what do we have here? Looks like some idiot lost their footing and slipped. We're on the right track guys, keep your eyes peeled for anything else."

A little further on Ink found a discarded ration pack wrapper. "Hey Captain? Looks like someone didn't like their oatmeal this morning."

"They're headed right for the flat plain," Kreeve said. "Looks like they had the same idea as us. We may even bump into them."

"Something is bothering me about all this," Ilyas said as he fingered the ration pack wrapper."

"What's up?" Kreeve asked with a frown.

"Well umm," Ilyas sighed as he looked into the distance towards the flat plain. "We've been chasing them now for twenty four hours and not once have they left so much as a footprint and now suddenly they're leaving the most obvious clues," he said as he waved the wrapper from side to side. "It just seems a little too convenient to me."

Ink sighed loudly and swore. "Shit. That's a valid point Boss."

"They must've guessed we'd choose the easy way if at all possible, so they wanted to make us think they did too," Kreeve remarked. "And meanwhile, they're still headed directly north east. Clever."

"But not clever enough," Ilyas replied. "Come on, let's make for the trees."

"Could we maybe catch something decent to eat and maybe take a while for some lunch?" Ink asked. "I'm getting awful tired of the ration packs myself and some real meat would be nice."

Kreeve nodded. "Hell yeah that would be nice Boss."

"Okay," Ilyas nodded. "Some real meat would be very welcome. Kreeve, you go catch us a meal, you're the best at hunting. Ink and I will make a fire."

"Yes, Sir," Kreeve grinned and set off. Twenty minutes later, he returned with something the size of a large house cat with pale yellow fur and enormous ears. He skinned and cleaned it and set it over the fire to roast. There was not a lot of meat on the bones, so it cooked within thirty minutes and the three were overjoyed to find it tasted delicious, if just a little fatty.

"That was the most delicious meat I've had in years," Ilyas smiled and belched loudly. "Thanks Kreeve, you did us proud buddy."

"Yeah thanks buddy," Ink grinned as he picked at his teeth. "I'm gonna feel so much better for that."

"Okay we'd better be off," Ilyas said as he dragged himself to his feet and began kicking the fire out. "We may have all sorts of things to worry about while we're on this rock, but at least for the moment, hunger isn't one of them."

They set off towards the tree line, the food in their bellies helping to relax them and they entered the cool gloom of the trees confident that they could face whatever awaited them. They headed directly northeast, clambering through undergrowth and avoiding creatures when necessary. Once, they felt the rumbling beneath their feet and all three clambered up trees like schoolboys on a summer afternoon. At one point halfway through the afternoon, just before the shadows began to lengthen, they rounded a clump of huge tree trunks to find themselves staring into the face of a pack of four of the same huge wolf-like creatures they had seen before. They wasted no time and the one in the front of the pack fell dead, its skull blown apart from their laser rifles whilst its three companions turned on their heels and ran off into the depths of the forest. Hours later, they came upon a stream and decided to follow it while its course took it northeast. It was only a few inches deep and made the going much easier and by the time the gloom made it difficult to continue, they found a suitable place to make camp for the night. They agreed on a two-hour watch rota and Ilyas agreed to watch first. He sat and listened to his companions snoring and was very glad to see that this planet had two bright moons that lit up the night and kept the suffocating darkness a little further back.

CHAPTER ELEVEN

Nef led the group down the gentle incline, making sure everyone knew to leave a clear trail for their pirate stalkers to see and, he hoped, follow. He led them straight towards the edge of the flat plain that bordered the deep forest and separated it from another identical forest a mile to the west. Once they reached the tree line, they turned northeast again and headed into the trees.

"It would be wise to try to keep at least several feet from the trees themselves wherever possible," Shib reminded them. "We want to try to avoid any close encounters with the indigenous animal life, since we don't whether they are dangerous or not. And please remember not to let any flying insects land on you."

"Sure thing buddy," Captain Nagle replied. They trudged through the undergrowth, being as careful as they could and all worried about where they were putting their feet.

"Hey guys," Jake called out, "look at these. Aren't they beautiful?" Everyone looked at the delicate white blooms that Jake was admiring; the slender five petalled stars massed above a bloated stem as thick as a man's wrist. He bent down to smell them and failed to notice the nearest flower slowly bend its delicate white head towards him. Shib leapt forwards, bundling him out of the way roughly so that he almost fell to the ground.

"What the fuck?" Jake exclaimed as he stumbled. "What's your problem buddy?" Shib stood and turned to face him and everyone saw the tiny needles embedded into his cheek and neck and watched as they withered and fell away within seconds. Everyone gaped.

"Holy shit," Crib hissed. "What is that?"

"I think we've most likely found what killed Stella Bodecki," Shib replied.

"Oh man I'm sorry," Jake said, eyes wide with shock.

"Do not apologise Jake," Shib smiled. "Now we know where the poison that killed her came from, we know what to avoid."

"But how did you know?" Manlee asked.

"I saw the head of the flower bend towards Jake as he bent to smell it," Shib replied, "and it occurred to me that it seemed almost as if it knew he was getting close."

"Is there anything on this rock that doesn't want to kill us?" Ace remarked as they set off once again.

"Well I don't," Arsh replied.

"Thank god for that," Captain Nagle said.

They walked for a couple of hours without incident until they came to a small stream and decided to stop to refill their water bottles and take a rest. Shib tested the water and found it to be drinkable so they drank plenty and filled their bottles. Jake took off his shirt and the vest he had wrapped around his head and had as decent a wash as he was able. The water was icy cold but he felt sticky and dirty and didn't mind. His jet-black hair so beloved of his millions of fans was covered in a film of dust and he hated the way his scalp itched. He ran a hand over his chin and jaw and wished he could have a shave as well. After rinsing his shirt and vest, he laid them out on a boulder to dry. Everyone watched in envy and within minutes, the little stream filled with men, stripped to the waist and braving the icy chill to wash the sweat and dust from their bodies and hair.

"That feels mighty nice," Manlee said as he sat down beside Jake. "I hate being sweaty and sticky."

"Same here," Jake nodded. "If I turned up anywhere looking like that on Earth I'd drop ten places on the ranking board within a day."

"It must be a pain having to be so obsessional about the way you look all the time."

"I'm used to it. I've been in the movie business for twenty years and the way you look is a huge part of that. You have to take care of yourself and keep yourself looking good, at least if you want any decent roles. It's hard work keeping in shape and I've been lucky with good genetics but I work hard at it so I enjoy the rewards."

"It's not exactly work though is it?" Captain Nagle said as he sat down beside Manlee. "I mean not in the proper sense. Anyone can stand, smile, and kiss young girls. Jeez I'd love to do that for a living and earn your money."

"Do you smoke Captain?" Jake asked.

"Occasionally yeah, why?"

"Do you drink alcohol?"

"Sure, socially."

"Do you take drugs of any kind?"

"Hell no."

"What about painkillers, cold remedies, sleeping pills?"

"Well of course, sometimes. What the fuck has that got to do with it?"

"I can't smoke. I can't drink alcohol, take painkillers or a cold remedy. Nice things like doughnuts or cookies are not allowed because I have to watch my weight and keep in shape. I have to work out three hours every single day. It's impossible for me to go to the store, my folks and I can't go out to a restaurant and walking down the street is simply out of the question. The only people I ever have proper conversations with are my parents and my staff. If I want to keep my job, I have to smile all the time, to everyone, no matter how low I may be feeling. People ask me the same old questions in every single interview and I have to look happy to answer them every time. Learning lines takes weeks and we have to do scenes over and over again. I have to be gracious and deal with the paternity suits, death threats and petulant wannabe actors who hate me because I'm good at what I do. At any moment, I know that I could be murdered or kidnapped and sent to some prehistoric hell hole with some guy who obviously hates me and everything I stand for, and I'm not allowed to punch him in the face because I'd never work again. So it's not real work? You try it for a month buddy." He glared at Captain Nagle, trembling with anger.

The Captain didn't know how to reply. He hated to admit that he'd never thought about what life for celebrities was actually like or what the downsides of such a life might be and he knew without a shadow of a doubt that he wouldn't last a day with such restrictions.

"I'm sorry," he said as he got up and went to speak with Shib.

"What the fuck is that asshole's problem?" Jake hissed.

"I've no idea Jake," Manlee whispered, "but if it's any consolation, we've all begun to wonder the same ourselves."

"You have?"

"Yeah. It seems our Captain really doesn't like you at all and he's not made any secret of the fact ever since you came aboard. Hefton 24 told me he asked Shib to keep an eye on you and report to him if you made any mistakes or upset anyone and he saw him talking to two guys about you the other day, just a few hours before Titch almost went berserk on you."

Jake was horrified. "Are you saying what I think you're saying?"

"I don't know what you're thinking Jake."

"Someone said yesterday about an inside man."

"Ahh," Manlee said. "That."

"Yeah, that."

"Well it has crossed our minds, since he so obviously hates you. It may be that he just doesn't like celebrities though. It could be just coincidence; you can't act on supposition. Although it looks likely, it might not be him."

"Well it has to be someone," Jake replied. "No one knew which ship I was going to be working on. We all deliberately kept that a secret and it was part of the deal signed by Mayan Freightlines that they keep it a secret because of this kind of risk."

"I don't know what to say Jake," Manlee said, "apart from it isn't me and whatever happens, you can trust me okay? I'm your buddy."

"Thanks man. That means a lot. By the way, can I ask a personal question?"

"Of course."

"Why do you and Hefton have a number after your name?"

"It's what we call the Generational Indicator. In our society, families only have one name, not two like on Earth. You're Jake Elloway; your father will have a different name, your mother a different name again, and so on."

"Yeah, my dad is Leonard Elloway and my mom is Jacqueline Elloway."

"We don't have different genders, as you already know and we pass down not only our genetics to our children but also our names. My parent is Manlee 17 and their parent was Manlee 16 and so on. It's the same with Hefton's line."

"Oh I get it, okay. So you can't change your kid's name if you want to?"

"Yes we can if we wish and some do."

"Do you have a child?"

"Not yet."

"Do you mind if I ask um," Jake hesitated.

"How we reproduce?" Manlee smiled.

"Sorry, it's none of my business," Jake blushed. "It's just that a single gender is very strange to us."

"Of course it is, and I don't mind at all. We do it in a very similar way that you do, only with us it's not one side impregnating the other. With us we both impregnate each other simultaneously."

"Wow, that's umm. So you have um?" Jake blushed again as he indicated towards his own crotch.

Manlee laughed aloud. "We do, but ours are inside the body and we only use them to reproduce, not for fun like you do."

"Only to reproduce?" Jake was astonished. "My god I'm so glad I'm not from Zylom buddy." Manlee roared with laughter and Jake could not help but join in. "So do you have umm, y'know, like relationships and stuff? Do you fall in love, get married and raise kids together or what?"

"No we don't. We choose someone with whom we wish to share our genetics and spend time getting to know them, which I suppose is a bit like a relationship in the sense that you know it but there is no monogamy or binding emotional contract although there will always be an emotional bond. Emotions don't really play a part in our life Jake. Our brains are wired very differently to yours. The logic and reasoning parts of our brains are hard wired to control the emotional parts, so although we have emotions and understand them, they seldom control our actions. We choose someone based on who they are as a person in the same way you do but it's mostly because of their genetics that we choose them. We have to keep our gene pool as varied as possible in the same way you do, so records are kept as to who reproduces with who, to avoid different generations reproducing with the same person and risking genetic faults."

"Wow that sounds um," Jake struggled to find the right words.

"Clinical?"

"Well yeah, a little. I hope that doesn't offend you."

"Not at all. I'm not in the least offended by your race's emotional need for sexual gratification at every possible opportunity." There was a pause before both men burst out laughing.

An hour later, they set off and decided to follow the stream while it seemed to be heading northeast. When it veered off suddenly directly eastwards, they headed back into the forest to keep to their intended northeasterly direction. It was early afternoon as they once again struggled through the thick undergrowth and the clouds of insects began their relentless onslaught. Jake let his mind wander to Captain Nagle and the prospect of him being the inside man and what he should, or even could, do about it if it were found to be true. He was so far inside himself that he didn't notice his companions had stopped and he bumped into Arsh.

"Oops sorry buddy I was, oh shit," he said as he saw the huge wolf like creature staring at them from twenty yards ahead. It curled back its lips and growled at them; its head held low as its eyes bored into them. Grey furry hindquarters began to sink low to the ground as it readied itself to spring but before the men could fire, it fell to the ground, apparently dead. Everyone looked at each other and shrugged.

"What the fuck happened to it?" Nef said.

"I do not know," Shib replied.

"Do not worry, it cannot harm you now," a voice called.

Nef raised his rifle. "Who's there?"

"Have no fear my friends. My name is Professor Greg Hunt." A man stepped into view in front of them and reached down to the prone animal. He retrieved something embedded in its flank and put it into a box he carried strapped to his hip.

"It will be asleep for at least an hour and will wake with no ill effects."

"You must be one of the scientists working here," Captain Nagle said.

"That's correct. My colleagues and I are on a sample collection mission today. And who might you be and what the devil are you doing here?"

"Forgive me Professor. I'm Captain Alex Nagle of the Mayan Queen Freighter. Pirates boarded us and brought here but we managed to escape when those giant worm things attacked us when we landed. We headed for your outpost in the hope of calling for help to get us out of here and back to my ship. Oh, and the pirates, or at least what's left of them, are still after us and not far behind either."

"Why did they bring you here?"

"Well to cut a long story short, they boarded my vessel with the intention of kidnapping Jake here," he indicated Jake who smiled and nodded. "Jake managed to escape with a few of my crew by stealing the pirates' own shuttle craft and headed here because it was the nearest system to our position. The pirates then took my bridge crew and myself as hostages and chased after them. We know they've lost a few of their men and we unfortunately lost one of our crew too, a woman. We had to leave her body behind."

"Come with me," Professor Hunt replied as he turned and walked away.

They followed him to where a group of men were busy digging up roots and taking samples of earth. After the introductions, the Professor brought his colleagues up to speed on the group's situation and offered to give them a lift back to the outpost in their hover buggy. Within four hours they were sitting in the warm of the outpost drinking hot coffee and eating a decent hot meal. Shib gave them the co-ordinates of Stella Bodecki's body and two of the scientists promised to go and retrieve it first thing in the morning.

"You can relax here," Professor Hunt told them. "It will take the pirates another two days to hike all the way here and by then you will be long gone."

"Gone? How?" Captain Nagle asked.

"At first light, our pilot and co-pilot will take you back to your ship in one of our shuttles. We have two but one is out of action at the moment so even when the pirates get here they will have to wait until our pilot returns before they can give chase. That will be another two days, by which time the law enforcement authorities will have been informed and will no doubt be on their way to keep you safe and apprehend them."

"We can't thank you enough Professor," Nef said. "You're putting yourselves out for us in a big way and we're extremely grateful."

"Not at all," he smiled. "This is the most excitement we've had in six months. Now let's get that emergency call out shall we?" Professor Hunt took Captain Nagle into the side room where the scientists kept their comms equipment. A young brunette smiled at Jake.

"Don't I know you from somewhere?" she asked.

He gave her his best celebrity smile. "Hi, I'm Jake Elloway," he said as he extended a hand and grinned as a look of shock spread over her face.

"The actor?"

"The same," he smiled. She shook his hand and blushed.

"Wow it's great to meet you," she said. "I love your movies."

"Thank you very much, it's a real pleasure to meet you," he said as he eyed her rather disappointingly small breasts.

Professor Hunt arranged some sleeping quarters for them and after a meal and a wonderful hot shower, they all managed to get a decent night's sleep for the first time since they landed. Jake was delighted to be able to have a shave at last and after a good breakfast, they said their goodbyes and thanked their new friends again for their help before following the two pilots out to the shuttle.

"Jake?" a voice behind them called.

He turned and saw the brunette running up to him. "Hi honey."

"Could I get a picture with you?" she asked shyly as she handed one of her colleagues her camera.

"Sure," he smiled. "Come on over here and gimme a hug huh?" She melted into his arms and grinned at the camera.

"Thank you so much," she smiled as she stood and watched them walk to the shuttle. Jake waved to her before entering the shuttle and allowing the smile to drop from his lips. He took a seat, fastened the safety harness, and heard Captain Nagle sigh and shake his head.

"What's the problem Captain?" Jake demanded.

"It just seems weird to be doing all the celebrity stuff while we're in this situation that's all. Photo calls and autographs?" he snickered and shook his head again.

"Well it may seem weird to you Captain but y'know what? She pays my wages. Every time she pays to watch my movie, she's buying my cars and paying my mortgage and my staff's salary and if I can repay her by giving her a tiny moment of my time and make her year into the bargain, then I feel I've done a good job."

Captain Nagle tried to think how to reply but could think of nothing appropriate so he shrugged and looked away. He had not thought of that but he would sooner die than admit it to Jake fucking Elloway.

The pilots introduced themselves as Haze and Pug and the journey back to the Mayan Queen began. Once they were safely off Tellizon 4 Captain Nagle called the Mayan Queen on the comms and informed an extremely relieved Head of Security that they would be back with them in twenty-four hours or so. Professor hunt had assured them they would retrieve Stella Bodecki's body and hold it until the law enforcement authorities could get there and take charge of it and Captain Nagle informed his Head of Security of her death and asked if he could arrange a service for her when they returned. Several times during their journey, Jake wondered about Captain Nagle and he secretly confided to Nef and Manlee that he was worried he was still in danger.

"Try not to worry Jake," Nef said. "You know you have at least a few friends on board and we'll look after you."

"Thanks buddy."

"Remember too that the pirates lost a lot of their men, so they won't be in a position to do much damage, at least for a while. The law enforcement authorities are going to meet us on Sigma Prime and take statements, and we'll all be confiding our thoughts as to the possibility of an inside man."

Jake nodded. "Yeah okay."

"Remember too that you can always ask them to take you home if you feel you can't stay," Manlee reminded him.

Jake thought about it but shook his head. "There's nothing I'd like more than to go home but y'know what? I'm damned if I'm gonna let that asshole make me run away. I'm gonna stick around and find out the truth and enjoy it when he's found out."

"Good for you buddy," Nef grinned, "and we'll do plenty more practice with the daggers when we get back too, so at least you'll be able to look after yourself with something more than just those pretty blue eyes and that superstar smile."

Jake threw his pillow at him and the three laughed aloud.

Twenty-six hours after they left Tellizon 4, the scientist's shuttle set down on the pad inside the shuttle bay of the Mayan Queen and everyone stepped out to a welcoming committee.

Titch grinned when he saw Jake and shook his hand vigorously. "Oh man it's so good to see you back in one piece. I was worried about you Jake."

"Titch you'll never know how good it is to see you again," Jake grinned.

"Let's all go and have a drink in my quarters and we'll tell you all about it," Nef said. "Ace, Crib, Manlee you boys coming too?"

"Hell yeah," Crib said as the other two nodded.

When they were safely within the confines of Nef's quarters, they told Titch everything that had happened on Tellizon 4 and how it seemed likely that the Mayan Queen was host to an inside man. Titch was even more shocked when they told him it seemed likely it was Captain Nagle himself.

"We're gonna have to be careful what we say to Shib from now on guys," Ace said. "We can't expect him to lie to the Captain and I wouldn't know if he is capable of being trusted not to tell him something."

"I agree," Manlee replied. "We know he can be relied upon to save a life when necessary but when the danger comes from within his programmed circle, I don't feel confident he would be on our side. It would be safer to assume that he'd obey Nagle before us."

"And at least one of us must be with Jake at all times," Nef said. "Whenever we are outside of my quarters, we don't talk about this in case anyone is listening. If anyone wants to talk about it, we do it in here and nowhere else okay?"

"Then we need a code word," Crib said, "just like in that movie of yours Jake. I can't remember what it was called but you and this other Cop fella thought one of your buddies was a double agent so whenever you wanted to discuss your plans you said 'let's go get some ice cream' and both of you knew what that meant."

Jake grinned at the memory of that movie. "We had a lot of fun making that movie. Okay so what's our code word to be?"

"How about, 'let's go write that movie' or something like that?" Ace offered. "If anyone asks we can say we're writing down an idea for a movie based on what happened to us."

"Sounds good to me," Manlee grinned. "It's so stupid no one would think it meant anything else and it's just the kind of thing they'd think us idiot movie fans would do."

"Actually it's not such a bad idea," Jake grinned, "and I might just pitch it to my producer when I get back. If I get back."

"You'll get through this Jake," Nef said.

"I hope so. If I do then you can all have starring roles," he laughed.

"We just have to survive until we reach Sigma Prime and hopefully the law enforcement people will do something constructive about it."

"By the way," Jake said quietly. "Thank you guys, you're awesome. I probably wouldn't have survived this without you."

"Aww this is the most excitement I've had in years," Crib laughed and the others nodded in agreement.

"I feel bad that Stella had to die because of me though. I feel responsible for that and I'll make sure her family is secure financially if there's a need. It's the only thing I can do. I can't bring her back or make it not have happened but at least I can make sure none of her family struggles for money now she's gone."

"I'm sure they'd appreciate that," Manlee smiled. "Now how about some dinner?"

"Oh man, proper food," Crib said.

"That meat Shib caught wasn't bad," Nef grinned, "although it didn't taste of anything much."

"It was disgusting Nef," Ace exclaimed. "You need your taste buds looked at buddy."

"It was awful," Jake laughed.

The group went in to dinner, to find the two pilots entertaining everyone with stories of the indigenous life of Tellizon 4. Everyone listened intently, shocked when they told them all about the huge man eating worm things. They found a table and sat and listened and were intrigued when the two pilots described what they assumed was the furry creature on the tree that almost got Jake in the neck. When they found out it has an extremely poisonous bite, Jake went cold and the group looked at each other in shock.

"That was a near miss to beat all near misses buddy," Crib said.

"Jeez," Jake replied and shivered.

"What'll it be gentlemen?" a voice to the side said. They turned to see Aamy ready to take their orders.

"Hey Aamy, are you feeling better now," Crib asked.

"Fine now thanks Crib. What'll you be having this evening?"

"I'm sorry if I did anything to upset you honey," Jake said.

"Not at all," she replied without even looking at him. "No problem at all. Now who's for the fish option tonight?" She wrote down their orders and left without acknowledging Jake at all.

"Man whatever it was you did Jake, it sure did some damage," Crib remarked. "Did you see it?"

"See what?"

"The look."

"What look?"

"Exactly. It's not there anymore, didn't you notice?"

"Oh that. Yeah I did notice. She wouldn't even look at me. I wish she'd tell me so I can try to make it right. Zeke warned me off so I couldn't get close to her or anything, but now it seems I'm the bad guy anyway. All I can do is apologise but I don't even know what I'm apologising for."

"Maybe she's confided in Zeke by now," Nef said. "Why not catch him when he's alone and ask him. At least that way you'll know what it was and can avoid doing it again or explain to her or something."

Jake nodded and sighed. Sometimes his celebrity status was a huge drag and he found himself wishing he were just another ordinary Joe. Aamy was not his type and he was not interested anyway but he didn't want to openly hurt her or upset her, especially as she is a fan who pays his wages. He knew he had to find out, even if he could not put it right he had to know just to settle his own mind.

Zeke brought their food and Jake noticed he seemed a little distant with him, although he was friendly enough and asked him how he was after his ordeal.

"I'm fine thanks Zeke. It was a nightmare for all of us but we got through it and we're grateful. Is Aamy okay? She doesn't seem like her old self."

"She's umm," Zeke struggled. "She'll be fine. She has her friends around her and that's what's important."

"I tried to apologise to her for whatever it was that I did but she kinda blew me off and I don't wanna push."

"Well Jake, it's probably best you leave her be. She's not that experienced in the ways of other races than her own and some lessons are harder to learn than others."

"Why can't you just tell me what I did? How can I make it right if I don't know?"

"You can't make this one right now Jake. I gave her my word I wouldn't betray her confidence. All I will say is ask you to remember that even though a fan maybe just a fan, to them their feelings are very real and very strong and when their feelings are hurt or they feel betrayed after giving so much love for so long, the damage is just as severe as if they were a family member. Just be aware that what you do and say affects those who decide you're important to them okay?"

"So I've hurt her feelings?" Jake asked. "How? Please tell me."

"No Jake. Just leave it and her, alone." He walked back to the kitchen and Jake sighed with frustration.

"Hey buddy," Titch said. "I'll have a word with Rosa and see if she knows anything. They're friendly and she may have confided in her."

"Thanks Titch," Jake nodded. "I'd be grateful. I hate not knowing what I'm supposed to have done wrong. See what I mean about the celebrity life not being so wonderful all the time? Every single thing you say and do can be scrutinised and no matter how careful you are, you always upset somebody and have to carry the guilt for it."

"Let it pass now Jake," Nef said. "Eat your meal and push that to the back of your mind for now. There'll be time and opportunity later to visit that again but for now, eat and relax and keep your mind on the situation here okay?" He smiled at Jake but gave him a stern glare at the same time; a gentle reminder that it was most likely that he was still in danger for his life and that someone aboard the Mayan Queen and maybe someone in this very room, at the next table, was still out for his blood.

Jake got the point and nodded. "You're right," he sighed. "Let's not allow anything to spoil the first decent meal in a week huh?"

CHAPTER TWELVE

It took Ilyas, Kreeve and Ink a further two days to reach the scientific outpost, during which, they nearly fell victim to the giant worms seven times. They did however, manage to kill two of them and a further huge wolf like creature and they saw several of the cute but deadly tree dwelling furry things that poisoned Patch so expertly. Each evening they hunted down their meal easily enough but all three lost several pounds in weight, all three stunk badly and all three had beards.

The scientists greeted them warmly, invited them in and after hearing their sad tale of how they were trying to catch up with some friends of theirs who had landed here after their shuttle ran out of power, commiserated with them at not having found them.

"We haven't seen anyone at all for over six months," Professor Hunt told them, "and it seems likely that they will have succumbed to the various creatures that live here. It is a very dangerous place here as you've found out. You are welcome to remain here with us until you decide what you must do next and we can offer you food and shelter. Let me show you where you can take a shower and I'll rustle up some overalls to change into so we can get your clothes washed and dried."

"That's mighty nice of you Professor," Ilyas said as they followed him out of the room.

"Not at all gentlemen," Professor Hunt smiled as he showed them to the shower room and left them alone. Over a delicious meal that evening Ilyas broached the subject of transportation.

"Is there any possibility of giving us a lift back to our ship in the morning Professor? Our Navigator is there alone and will be worried. She was injured when we arrived and were attacked by the worms and we had to leave her behind. We'd like to get back to her as quickly as we can."

"I'm afraid our remaining shuttle is out of action at the moment," the Professor replied, "as is our hover buggy. Our pilot and co-pilot have gone for supplies to effect repairs but they won't be back for a couple of days. I wouldn't recommend you try to hike back through the forest, it's just too dangerous and with just the three of you, you wouldn't be able to protect yourselves if the creatures target you again. You're welcome to stay as long as you need to."

Ilyas sighed and swore inwardly at this news and looked at Ink and Kreeve, both of whom looked dead on their feet and totally incapable of make the journey back the way they'd come. He was angry that Jake was getting away from them and even angrier that circumstances forced them to sit on their backsides and wait while he got further and further away.

Professor Hunt showed Ilyas and his friends where they could sleep and re-joined his colleagues. "What a bunch," he hissed.

"How long can we stall them do you think?" Doctor Pope asked quietly.

"I've no idea but every minute helps the others get away and allows time for the law enforcement authorities to get here."

"We must make sure they don't get into the cold storage locker and discover the woman's body or they'll know we've been lying to them."

"I wonder which one of them violated her," Pope said sadly as he thought of the woman who was obviously a nice looker when she was alive.

"I hope we don't find out until after they've gone," Hunt replied, "or I'm likely to find it hard to be nice to them." Pope nodded and looked into his cup of coffee.

Next morning Ilyas and his friends felt rested and after a good breakfast, Kreeve asked if he might go and look at the hover buggy. Professor Hunt could not think of a reason he could refuse without it looking suspicious so he nodded and showed him to the small hangar where they kept the two shuttles and the buggy. Kreeve examined the buggy and the remaining shuttle and poked about for nearly an hour before returning with a smile on his face.

"Professor. I've looked at both the shuttle and the buggy and if I take some parts from the shuttle, I can get the buggy working. Then we could get back to our ship and be out of your hair. The shuttle parts won't be damaged and you can easily be remove them and return them to the shuttle when your pilots return. Come with me and I'll show you."

Professor Hunt hoped his smile looked genuine as he stood and followed Kreeve to the hangar. His heart sank as he realised this man was a very talented engineer and would have no problem at all getting the buggy working again within a couple of hours.

"Well that sounds wonderful Mr Kreeve. We will ensure you have a decent lunch inside you before you leave. Just shout if you need any help out here." He turned and left him to it. Within three hours, Kreeve had the buggy running better than it had been in a year and Professor Hunt could not think of anything more he could do to stall them. After a hefty lunch, they took him back to his ship in the newly repaired buggy and graciously accepted their thanks. They watched the ugly pirate ship take off and breathed a sigh of relief.

"I thought you sabotaged the buggy?" Professor Hunt said to his colleague Doctor Pope.

"I did," Pope shrugged.

"Not well enough. That pirate Kreeve is one hell of an engineer."

"We did what we could and we have given Jake three day's head start. They said it would take them a day to get back to their ship and another four to Sigma Prime where they're meeting with the Law Enforcement Agency people, so that means they just have another two days to go until they get there. The pirates will have to get a move on to catch them before they get to Sigma."

"Their ship looks pretty powerful to me," Hunt said. "Anyway, as you so rightly said, we've done everything we can do. Let's get back huh?"

Back on board the Mayan Queen, Captain Nagle led a service of remembrance for Stella Bodecki. It was a simple affair, non-religious and a celebration of that part of her life she had shared with them whilst a member of the crew. Captain Nagle accepted pledges towards a fund for her family and Jake announced that Elloway Enterprises would be funding the setting up of a new award for bravery by civilians, which he would call The Bodecki Award. Everyone thought that was a wonderful idea and Jake was pleased to be able to do something to honour her as he felt genuinely bad for her loss. He also decided to ask Adam Maydell to dedicate the up-coming movie to her memory and he felt confident he would agree.

Life aboard the Mayan Queen got back to something resembling normality, although Jake was never allowed to be left alone for more than the time it took to take a shit and although grateful for his friends' attention to his safety, he wondered if they would ever allow him enough privacy for another liaison with the nurse. He decided to go and pay her a visit and headed up to the medical bay with a grin on his face as he remembered their mind-blowing sex session just a few days previously. The door to the medical bay was standing open so he entered but found it empty and assumed Faline was away on an emergency. As he turned to leave he noticed the door to the examination room was open a crack and he could see movement from within. Creeping up to the door he peered through the crack and was rather taken aback to see a naked Faline astride an equally naked Captain Nagle, both of whom looked near to an amazing orgasm. Jake wasn't into watching so he crept away, shocked that Faline should choose to have sex with Captain Nagle and if he was truly honest with himself, a little put out that she could move onto someone else so quickly after such a wonderful experience with him just days before.

He met Nef and spent a couple of hours with him in his quarters, learning the Damiklonian Martial Art and quickly began to get a feel for the movements. Nef was a good teacher and he, an eager pupil and both felt sure Jake would be competent in the basics before too long. He found it both exhilarating and calming and again pressed Nef about his offer to come and work with him as his personal trainer and reminded him of the possibility of opening his own studio, which he would be happy to finance in payment for his teaching. He fully expected Nef to turn him down but to his complete surprise, he didn't.

"I will think about it Jake. I am tempted to accept but give me time huh? It's a big move y'know?"

"Sure thing buddy, take the time you need. I just didn't want you to think I'd changed my mind about it or anything."

"Okay, thanks. I really do appreciate the offer by the way. Now let's go and get some dinner."

They found Crib, Titch, Manlee and Ace already there and wandered over to join them. Ace noticed Jake looked tired and they listened as he told them how he was enjoying learning the Damiklonian Martial Art and how he fully intended to use it in future movies whenever possible. From his early teens, he had been obsessive about learning anything that helped him keep his body healthy and improved his fitness and this new martial art had really piqued his interest. A few years previously, he had a personal trainer who was an expert in aikido and studied with him for several months before losing interest. Although it helped his fitness, it didn't afford him any of the expected mental or emotional benefits and soon became a chore. He knew right away that the Damiklonian Martial Art was completely different and gave him something he had not even realised was missing from his life. The sense of calm and mental balance he experienced when working out with Nef was very new to Jake and very addictive.

"What'll it be tonight gentlemen?"

The small voice brought Jake back from his musings and he turned to see Aamy waiting to take their orders. He ordered the meat option without questioning her and turned away to continue listening to Ace, who was telling them all about a time in his past when he had tried to learn Kung Fu. For some reason, the awkward situation with Aamy was of no interest to him anymore and he felt no need to think about her. Crib noticed Jake's lack of interest and frowned.

"What's up Jake? Giving her the cold shoulder now huh?"

"What?"

"Aamy."

"What about her?"

"Not going to ask her what's wrong or what the problem was?"

"Huh? Oh no. She said she doesn't want to talk about it so fine."

"Man you can switch off easily buddy."

"Yeah, it's a gift of which I'm very proud."

"So how did it go with the nurse today?" Crib asked with a grin. Everyone on the table went silent as all faces turned towards Jake.

"It didn't."

"Why not?"

"She was umm," he struggled to find the words. "She was busy with someone when I called in." Everyone at the table snickered and grinned and he joined them.

"Well you'll have to the join the queue Jake," Ace grinned. "You're not the only guy on board y'know."

"Yeah well, maybe I've lost interest," he replied.

"But you said she was the most perfect looking female you'd ever seen," Crib said.

"Yeah she is," Jake agreed, "but I umm, I'm not really into having anyone's leftovers, especially not his leftovers. If I ever reach a point in my life where I have to lower my standards then maybe, but I'm not there yet."

"Who was she with?" Manlee asked.

"Captain Asshole," Jake whispered. His friends looked shocked at this news.

"No, really?" Ace hissed and Jake nodded. "I didn't know he visited her."

"Well you do now and it's put me right off her. A decent rack she may have, but now he's had his paws all over it, I couldn't. I just couldn't."

"You know Jake," Manlee said. "Her people have a very different way of looking at sex than a lot of other races do."

"I know," Jake nodded, "Shib told me about her when I first came aboard."

"You can't really equate her cultural beliefs with any lack of morality, especially since she's not from Earth."

"I know, and I wouldn't disrespect her racial or cultural habits or beliefs but I can't disrespect my own either. I can't go there again, not now."

"But you have many sexual encounters," Nef said quietly. "You've told us about some of them. You surely don't believe you're the first man they've ever been with."

"No of course not, but I don't have to see them at it and I don't know the guys or have to work with them and join a queue with them for her time." He raised his eyebrows to emphasise his point and Nef nodded.

What he didn't tell him was that the sight of Faline having sex with Captain Nagle had upset him more than he would have anticipated. Jake had always been blessed with a high self-esteem but to know that a beautiful woman would make the choice against him was a knock to his ego and it unsettled him more than he liked. On the one hand, he felt like punching the captain but on the other hand, he felt used and tossed aside.

"Y'know Jake," Nef said. "Some of the most valuable lessons are wrapped up in painful experiences."

Jake knew he spoke the truth but didn't quite know how to respond so he just nodded and shrugged his shoulders. Aamy brought their food and Jake thanked her dismissively without looking at her before tucking straight in and enjoying it immensely. His extra workout sessions with Nef allowed him to be more generous to himself with food and he enjoyed the rich dark meat dish.

After dinner, he spent an hour with Ace learning a little more about Tapshots and had begun to understand the basic concepts well enough to take an actual role in a couple of games. Although he lost them both, he didn't lose so badly that he embarrassed himself and he was pleased at his performance as he and Nef left to do another couple of hours practice in the Damiklonian Martial Art. Manlee accompanied them and took several photographs of Jake as he followed Nef's movements.

"Your fans will love these shots Jake," he laughed. "Try to get a little bit sweatier and take off your shirt. That'll get the girls drooling."

"Are you sure you wouldn't like to be my publicity consultant Manlee?" Jake grinned. "You have a natural flair for it y'know."

"Manlee laughed. "Well I could do it while you're on board at least," he said as he continued snapping. "And I've some wonderful shots of you working in the cargo hold, just to show the fans that you did actually do some work while you were here."

"You mean you've been spying on me buddy?" Jake laughed and Manlee nodded.

"Well umm, yeah," he laughed.

Crib joined them later that evening and they sat around in Nef's quarters and discussed possible scenarios for the next day's planned arrival at Sigma Prime and their intended meeting with a representative of the Inter Galactic Law Enforcement Agency. Nef produced his bottle of Limagian Nasra juice and Jake proposed a toast.

"Guys," he said as he stood and raised his glass. "I would like to propose a toast to you guys, for your friendship and loyalty. I haven't felt like just another guy in years and you've really helped me to settle in here. Thank you. To friendship," he said and downed his drink.

"To friendship," they chorused and drained their glasses.

One by one they each made a toast and by the time they all began to yawn and think of sleep, much male bonding had taken place and Jake felt a little less scared at this new situation in which he'd found himself. Since their return from Tellizon, Jake's bunk had been moved into Nef's quarters so he would not be alone and the two of them settled down and talked late into the night. Jake realised that Nef was, in many ways, the kind of man he would love to be and realised with some trepidation that he was more inexperienced and insecure than he felt comfortable being. As he drifted off to sleep he realised that he was learning stuff about himself that he would really rather not know.

Ilyas Da Costa, Kreeve and Ink were happy to see Maria Cady again and were pleased to see that her shoulder wound was healing nicely. They thanked the scientists and left the surface of Tellizon 4, delighted to be leaving behind the terrors that lurked there and all secure in the knowledge that they would never willingly return.

"So do you reckon Jake and his crew are dead down there?" Ink asked.

"Come on Ink," Kreeve laughed, "you can't be that thick buddy."

"What?"

"Of course they didn't die down there. Those scientists met them and helped them get away and they're now at least two days ahead of us."

"How the fuck do you know that?" Maria Cady asked.

"Because that hover buggy had been tampered with to make it look like it was damaged."

"Are you sure?" Ilyas asked, knowing Kreeve was telling the truth. He was the best engineer he had ever met and if he said the hover buggy had been sabotaged, then it had been.

"Hell yeah," Kreeve answered. "They were obviously trying to keep us there for longer and you have to ask yourself why would they do that?"

"The only possible reason could be to allow time for Jake to get further away," Ilyas said and Kreeve nodded.

"And they may even have called the Law Enforcement Agency onto us and were hoping we'd stick around long enough for them to arrive and arrest us."

"So where do we go now?" Ink asked.

"The Mayan Queen's manifest said they were headed for Sigma Prime," Kreeve replied. "So that's where we should go. Even though they've got a head start on us, our ship is way faster than their old crate, so we should arrive at Sigma ahead of them."

"And we can have a welcome party waiting for them," Ilyas smiled. "Let's get going huh?"

"Sure thing Boss," Kreeve smiled as he set course for Sigma Prime and engaged the Barclay's engines into top speed. "We should be there within thirty hours. What's the plan?"

"When we reach orbit, we wait for them to shuttle down and then we follow their trail. Elloway will no doubt do some celebrity stuff, signing autographs and shit like that so we can take him then. We'll have to use our initiative and take the first opportunity that comes up, so no fuck ups guys."

"Absolutely Boss," Ink nodded. "Are you still planning to ransom Elloway?"

"Yeah that's the plan," Ilyas nodded, "but if things go wrong I'll be satisfied with just killing the asshole."

"It would be kinda cool to take him back to Tellizon and dump him there wouldn't it?" Ink asked and Kreeve snickered and nodded.

"That's another option," Ilyas grinned. "Good idea buddy."

Jake awoke early and found Nef already up.

"Hey buddy, you sleep okay?" Nef asked.

"Yeah, not bad actually. I'm getting used to these bunks now. How about you?"

"Actually no. I feel really unsettled and I don't know why. Something about this whole thing is playing on my mind."

"How do you mean?" Jake asked as he sat up, swung his legs to the floor, and stretched.

"It's difficult to explain. It's like something is nagging me or there's something that we've missed. I sense danger up ahead but I also sense a link from something nearby, to that danger. Does that make any sense?"

"Sort of," Jake nodded. "We guessed there's an inside man on board somewhere but we don't know who it is. Maybe whoever it is will be trying something when we get to Sigma."

"We must be vigilant Jake. Let's go take a shower and get some breakfast and then get back here with Ace, Crib and Manlee and talk it over." The two men left Nef's quarters to head to the shower room next door. When they entered the corridor, they saw the nurse, Faline standing outside the door to Jake's quarters.

He was surprised to see her and it showed. "Hello nurse, what can I do for you?"

"Hello Jake," she smiled as she looked him up and down, which this time didn't turn him on and, he noticed, actually disgusted him a little. "You are going down to the surface of Sigma today?"

"Yep."

"I was wondering if you'd thought about what we talked about during the treatment for your allergy, about the further healing I suggested." She looked at Nef, who chose not to disappear discreetly and remained by Jake's side.

"I have thought about it," Jake nodded, "and I've decided not to pursue it, but thanks for the offer."

"Perhaps you would like to talk?"

"About what?" he asked, despite knowing what she was getting at.

"Anything at all," she said as she looked him up and down once again. He didn't react and her surprise showed.

"I don't think there's anything I need to talk about at the moment," he said as he scratched his chin. "And besides, I have my buddies to talk to about stuff. Thanks for the offer though," he smiled and began to move away towards the shower room with Nef.

He didn't look back and she remained in the corridor for nearly a minute wondering about the change in his manner towards her. Just days ago he had been more than willing to enjoy sex with her but today he seemed to find it difficult even to talk to her.

"Wow Jake," Nef snickered. "That's the first time I've ever seen anyone give nurse Faline the brush off. Most other guys would've had their pants in their hands within seconds."

"Yeah well I guess I've lost interest."

"It really bothers you that she is as willing with others as she is with you?"

"Well yeah, I guess it does."

"Even though it's a bit of a double standard on your part?"

"I know I know," he grinned. "I can't just suddenly change my own standards though can I? I'm a product of my own culture, however flawed that might be and although it's been a revelation, I'm not yet ready to evolve that far in one leap. Gimme time huh?"

They showered and dressed before heading to the dining hall for breakfast. They joined Ace, Crib and Manlee and saw Captain Nagle at a nearby table talking to a man they had never met before.

"Who's the guy?" he hissed.

"That's the law enforcement man apparently," Crib hissed back. "He came aboard a couple of hours ago and is to come down to the surface with us to meet with the Law Enforcement Agency people."

"Okay," Jake shrugged as he looked at the man and tried to get a handle on him. He looked nice enough but as he'd found out to his cost recently, you never can tell about people. He decided to reserve judgement.

Over breakfast they talked about how there were going to try to make sure Jake was never left alone or in danger and they warned him not to get involved with crowds of fans.

"There's bound to be some and if they see me, I can't just ignore them," he remarked. "My career would take a knock if I was seen to be rude to the fans that pay my wages. I'll have to at least acknowledge them and do an autograph or two."

"Okay but don't go mad," Manlee said and Jake nodded. "And it will give me a chance to take a few more shots of you meeting more off world fans."

"You're really getting into this photography lark," Crib grinned and everyone laughed.

"Yeah well maybe I've found a new vocation," Manlee countered.

"Excuse me guys," a voice from beside them called and they all looked round to see Captain Nagle standing beside their table with the law enforcement man.

Jake looked Captain Nagle right in the eyes without smiling. "Yes Captain, how can we help?"

"After breakfast would you and the guys who were with us on Tellizon, report to the security room for a chat before we head down to the surface? Say in one hour?"

"Sure thing Boss," Ace smiled.

"Thanks," Captain Nagle smiled, turned, and left the room, his new companion following behind.

"He looks okay don't you think?" Nef said and everyone nodded.

"Yeah but we've learned over the past few days not to judge a book by its cover," Jake replied. "I'll reserve judgement until I've spoken to him."

"Good point," Crib nodded. "He may not be actually crooked but that doesn't mean he'll be able to sort this out properly or find the inside man."

"True," Manlee agreed, "so we keep to our plan no matter what he decides."

The friends ate their breakfast and discussed the coming trip down to the surface of Sigma Prime and the outcome they all hoped would be the result. Behind them, safely hidden behind its covert stealth optimiser, Captain Ilyas Da Costa and his three remaining pirates shadowed the Mayan Queen's every move. They watched as the Law Enforcement ship docked with the hulk and guessed that the officer within would be accompanying them to the surface and they were confident that one lone law enforcer would not scupper their plans for a reunion with Jake Elloway.

"Taking out the law enforcement guy will be a priority," Ilyas told them, "as will getting everyone away to somewhere quiet. As soon as we track where they've landed, we go down there and hide out somewhere nearby but quiet that we can use as a base. We then secure Elloway and get him back to base as quickly as possible so I can decide what I want to do with him."

"What if the law enforcement guy becomes a problem?" Ink asked.

"Then we take him too and deal with him back at base."

"Okay," Kreeve nodded. "I'll go and check the power cells for the rifles."

Jake was laughing with his friends when he noticed Aamy out of the corner of his eye approach his table with their food. They were talking about what it might be like down on Sigma Prime and how they hoped there were no creatures like the ones on Tellizon 4. Jake decided to let Aamy know he was not going to worry about whatever her problem was anymore and, he hoped, regain the upper hand in their little power game.

"Hey guys, do you reckon there'll be some cute ass down there?" he grinned.

"I sure hope so buddy," Crib replied. "It's been a damn long time."

"I'm sure you'll find at least a few movie fans down there buddy," Ace said.

"And I'm sure you can put those pretty blue eyes to good use," Nef smiled and everyone laughed.

"Hey buddy, you're just jealous," Jake laughed, "but yeah I will use them to their full potential. They've never failed me."

He laughed along with them and was glad to see Aamy leave without saying anything. He hoped that what she heard would teach her that holding out on him was not without consequences. Deep inside of himself he knew it was silly to be playing power games with a girl but she had annoyed him by coming on to him and then saying she hated him without giving him a chance to explain or just apologise. She needs to grow up, he decided and he was happy to start that process by letting her know he wasn't going to race around after her, begging forgiveness, until she paid him the courtesy of telling him what he'd done wrong.

When the friends finished their breakfast, they made their way up to the top deck of the Mayan Queen and approached the security room. Nef knocked on the door and a voice Jake didn't recognise bade them enter. He followed Nef inside to find Captain Nagle, along with his bridge crew, the law enforcement man he had seen in the dining room and another man he had not met before who introduced himself as Bayle Lannex, Head of Security for the Mayan Queen.

"Thanks for coming gentlemen. Jake, my name is Bayle Lannex and I'm Head of Security on board. We've not met before and I'm sorry I haven't had a chance to welcome you on board." He held out his hand, which Jake shook. "We'll be heading down to Sigma Prime shortly to give official statements to the Law Enforcement Agency. Just tell them everything you know, no matter how insignificant it may seem to you. We know who the pirates are; we just have to give the law enforcement guys enough information so they can catch them and put them away. I'd like to introduce you to a representative of the Law Enforcement Agency who will be accompanying us down to the surface and will be sitting in on all our interviews. He has been given the task of locating the pirates so that they can be taken into custody."

He nodded to the man Jake had seen briefly in the dining room and sat down. The Law Enforcer stood and Jake looked at him. He looked like he kept himself well enough. His hair was dark with blonde tips, his skin was fresh and clean, and Jake knew he had a vain streak that he recognised in himself. He was obviously familiar with a dermal optimiser and had regular skin treatments from it, as he himself does on a regular basis. He reckoned he liked him, at least from his first impression of him, so he smiled as he introduced himself.

"Hi there folks. My name is Sam Sinclair. I'm a freelance law enforcer. My tag code is Sinclair 27593-4/167AZP and I'll be accompanying you during the next couple of days, to help you through the process and to gain as much information as I can to help me track down the pirates that did this to you. Now, what will happen is this."

Acts of Life

CHAPTER THIRTEEN

Jake looked at Sam Sinclair and tried to work him out. He seemed like a straight down the line sort of man on first impression but recent circumstances made it hard for him to trust his first opinions as easily as he usually did. True, he was law enforcement and his tagged status obviously made him an official rather than a Merc, so he guessed he should be able to trust him. Jake recognised a certain vanity in him; he was good looking and obviously cared about his appearance but he was the same so he could not mark that against him. Within a minute, he made the choice to trust him until he proved himself untrustworthy and he tried to relax.

Sam Sinclair looked around the room and tried to get a handle on the men he saw sitting around the table. The Captain was obviously harbouring a not so secret hatred of the celebrity but he put that down to either jealousy or a secret history connected with him that he had yet to divulge. The rest consisted of two other bridge crew, the celebrity Jake Elloway, four of his co-workers and an android. The two bridge crew seemed to Sam to be trying to be neutral, which worried him a little as he would have expected everyone to back each other up and be a tight unit. This told him that there was some kind of division within this group and he decided he wanted to know what it was. The android was obviously going to be truthful so he was not a worry and Sam didn't spend too long thinking about him. The celebrity, Jake Elloway and the four friends that sat with him gave off an obvious feeling of being a unit and he liked what he saw. Sam took one look at Jake and immediately christened him Pretty Boy. He had known about him from his movies and he was something of a fan of his but the man he saw sitting before him now was not what he had expected to see.

It was obvious that Jake had been through something that had completely changed him as a person, something that had shaken him to the core and if it were not for the four friends sitting with him, he would probably have cracked under the strain. He didn't mark this against Jake; he was a celebrity and the nearest he got to real danger was probably on a movie set where everything is safe and controlled. From the look of him, Jake had obviously been through real danger for the first time in his privileged life and although Sam was sure it would be character building later on, he was struggling with it now. The four friends who were sitting with him gave Sam that same feeling of a divide between themselves and the bridge crew and especially the Captain and he again promised himself he would find out what it was about Nagle that worried the rest of them so much.

"I will be taking you all down to the surface of Sigma Prime to meet with the Law Enforcement Agency at their Sigma Headquarters. You will be interviewed separately and the interviews will be recorded. I will sit in on them but I won't be questioning you, that isn't my job. I'm not a detective as such but I can ask for further information if I feel it necessary in order for me to do my job, which is to find and apprehend the pirates and bring them to justice. You may, if you wish, speak with me alone after your interview but I would advise you not to withhold any information from the interviewing panel. Anything you say to me will be off the record. I am here to be your liaison with the Law Enforcement Agency and you can come to me with any questions or queries concerning the process and I will endeavour to answer them. The main thing to remember is that although the process may seem to be slow moving, everything has to be done in the right way to avoid anyone getting off because of a silly mistake on our part. Are there any questions?"

"How long will the interviews take Mr Sinclair?" Captain Nagle said.

"Well naturally I can't give you an exact time frame but from what I know of the events, I'd say a couple of hours apiece should cover it. You will be given secure accommodations within the Law Enforcement Agency Headquarters but if you wish to return here to your vessel, you can do."

"I'd like to take up the offer of a bed down there," Jake said immediately and looked at his four friends who all nodded their agreement.

"Then you're welcome to do so," Sam smiled. He could see Jake was scared to death of something and the speed at which he had accepted the offer of alternative sleeping arrangements told him what he feared was on board this ship.

"Has Stella Bodecki's body been recovered from Tellizon yet?" Arsh asked.

"The Law Enforcement Agency representatives are doing that now," Sam replied, "and in fact they're probably starting their journey back with her around now."

He continued looking around the table and noticed Jake seemed to want to say something but was holding back. He guessed it was because he didn't feel comfortable talking in the presence of the bridge crew and especially Captain Nagle so he decided Jake and his friends would be getting a lift to the surface in his ship, which would suddenly be too small to accommodate the Captain and bridge crew as well. Besides, if the Captain would rather return to the Mayan Queen for the night, then taking his own shuttle was the only way.

"So when do we start?" Captain Nagle asked.

"As soon as you get yourselves ready," Sam replied. "Mr Elloway, if you and your friends who wish to sleep in the Agency HQ overnight would pack an overnight bag, we can be off. You and your four friends will come with me in my ship and the Captain and bridge crew can come in one of the Mayan Queen's shuttles so they can return here as soon as they wish to. Shall we meet in the shuttle bay in say, thirty minutes?"

Jake and his friends met in Nef's quarters when they had packed their bags. Nef decided impulsively to take along a couple of his daggers and Jake raised his eyebrows when he saw him packing them.

"Just in case," Nef smiled. "You never know."

"What do you think of Sinclair?" Jake asked him.

"He seems okay to me."

"Yeah, I agree."

"I like him," Manlee said. "I'd lay money on him being someone we can trust and confide in."

"I hope you're right," Jake replied.

"He's seldom wrong," Ace said. "He's an excellent judge of character."

"That's good to know," Jake smiled. "Okay let's go shall we?"

They entered the shuttle bay to find Sam Sinclair, Captain Nagle and the bridge crew waiting for them. Sam smiled as they approached and showed them into his ship.

"It's not the height of luxury I'm afraid but it's my home as well as my transportation. Make yourselves comfortable. There's lockers at the rear for your bags."

Captain Nagle, Arsh, Hefton 24 and Shib entered the Mayan Queen shuttle to their left and they prepared to leave. Sam lifted his ship off the pad and headed out, followed by the Mayan Queen shuttle and steered the craft towards the huge green planet below them.

"Okay Mr Elloway," Sam said, "now what is you're not telling me?"

Jake looked at Nef and his friends and raised his eyebrows questioningly. "Huh?"

"Come on Jake," Sam said. "I've been doing this a long time and I'm an excellent judge of people. I know you're holding out on me and I also know you didn't feel like confiding in me with Nagle around, so what is it? Off the record unless you wish otherwise."

"Am I really so bad an actor," Jake hissed and Nef grinned. "We firmly believe there's an inside man somewhere on board the Mayan Queen Mr Sinclair, and it seems likely that it's the Captain."

"Ahh, so that's it," Sam smiled. "I knew there was a divide amongst the two groups. Okay, tell me how you come to this conclusion."

"Firstly," Nef cut in. "The fact that Jake was to spend his time aboard the Mayan Queen was kept a strict secret for safety reasons. Secondly, pirates almost never hit freighters unless they ship arms or currency and Mayan Freightlines never carry such stuff. Thirdly, the pirates hit us four days after Jake arrived and told us right off that they were after him. Another thing is that Captain Nagle makes no secret of the fact that he obviously hates Jake but won't tell anyone why. Lastly, it's Shib."

"Shib?" Sam said.

"The android," Nef replied. "His programming is very specific. He is programmed to respond to what is known as his circle, which means those whom he is programmed to regard as his family, which in Shib's case is everyone aboard the Mayan Queen. He is also programmed in such a way that he cannot cause harm to anyone within his circle. Another point is that he must do everything he can to keep those in his circle safe and free from danger. He will not harm anyone within his circle and he will keep those in his circle safe. The only time he can cause harm is if someone within his circle is in danger from someone else and then his programming is set so that keeping the one in danger safe is his first priority."

"Okay," Sam nodded. "I follow you so far."

"This means," Nef continued, "that he can and will react with aggression if one of his circle is in danger, even if that danger comes from another within his circle. He made the choice to come with us and help us when we asked him. It was his choice to abandon the rest of his circle to keep Jake safe. He could've chosen to remain with the rest and obey his captain, but he didn't. He made the conscious choice to leave his captain and come with us, which might infer that he sensed the danger to Jake lay within his programmed circle. He could've just stayed and reacted aggressively to the pirates but he didn't and that tells me that he reckons something else is happening here."

"I get your point," Sam replied. "What about the other two bridge crew? Where do they stand on this?"

"We don't know but we can't take risks. The four of us have pledged to keep Jake safe and that is what we fully intend to do."

"If it's any consolation," Sam replied, "I sensed a divide between you five and the other four right away. Taking all of the information you've just given me, it does seem likely that there is an inside man aboard somewhere."

"Yeah but who?" Jake said.

"Don't worry Jake," Sam said. "We'll find out. By the way, make sure you tell the interview board everything you just told me. Don't hold back on them okay? They are impartial and everything you say is confidential and won't be passed on to anyone else other than those security force personnel who need to know."

"Okay, thanks," Jake said.

"Now I understand why you were so keen to take up the offer of accommodation."

"Yeah," Jake smiled. "It will help me sleep better."

"I'll see to it you all get a room together if that would help," Sam offered.

"Thanks." Nef replied. "That would be great."

"By the way," Sam said. "The news of the pirate hit on the Mayan Queen has got out so we've arranged a small and easily controlled bit of media coverage of your arrival at the Agency HQ so that anyone who may be worried can see you're okay."

"Oh shit," Jake exclaimed. "My mom must be worried sick."

"You can contact her as soon as we land and get you settled in. I'll set you up with a secure Unicom channel and you can put her mind at rest. I would advise you not tell her any information though. Just keep it to assuring her that you're fine and that you're talking to the Law Enforcement Agency to get this all sorted out. Although it's unlikely, she may talk to someone who could be involved in all of this and the fact that you gave out information could end up meaning someone gets off on a technicality, and I don't happen to like technicalities."

"Sure, don't worry," Jake replied. "I'll be spending most of the conversation trying to stop her crying anyway."

"We've allowed a small crowd of your fans to gather outside the Agency HQ building so you can sign some autographs and have some photos taken to assure everyone who needs to know, that you're fine and still doing what you do."

"Sure, no problem," Jake nodded.

Ilyas Da Costa and his crew watched the two shuttles descend towards the surface of Sigma Prime.

"Okay Kreeve, keep scanning and once you know where they land, find the nearest quiet area for us to lie low without being discovered."

"Sure thing Boss," Kreeve replied as he watched the scanner display. Forty minutes later the Barclay, still hidden behind its covert stealth optimiser that made it invisible to the Sigma authorities, headed for a remote area just ten miles from the Law Enforcement Agency Headquarters building. Surrounded by woodland, with a large lake and mountains in the distance, it was beautiful.

"Okay guys, let's get the shuttle going," Ilyas said. "There should be a parking lot in the city and with our shuttle being ex Mayan Freightlines, we shouldn't be questioned."

"What's the plan?" Maria Cady asked.

"He's bound to come out and meet fans some time," Ilyas replied, "so we join the crowd and wait. Kreeve, you remain in the shuttle and when I call, get to us quickly and back to base. Maria, you will be acting as an Elloway fan. You'll be wearing a wire so get yourself to the front of the crowd and when he appears, tell us. Ink and I will keep to the back and as soon as you tell us he's near you, we'll be there."

"What if things don't go to plan?" Kreeve said, remembering the last time he was left guarding the ship.

"We don't have the privilege of knowing exactly what is going to happen this time," Ilyas replied. "We're gonna have to be flexible and be ready to use our initiative okay?"

"Sure boss."

"Good. Maria, you got the wire on?"

"Yep, good to go."

"Let's go."

Kreeve lifted the shuttle and headed towards the city and easily found the public parking lot, which was by now almost filled with shuttlecraft of various sizes, colours and designs. After checking Maria's wire was working properly, she headed off to join the throng of fans waiting outside the Law Enforcement Agency Headquarters whilst Ilyas and Ink stood to the rear of the crowd within easy reach of Maria's position and not too far from easy access to the shuttle in the parking lot.

Sam Sinclair settled his ship on the roof of the Law Enforcement Agency building and escorted Jake and his friends down to meet with his bosses and law enforcement colleagues.

"Hello Mr Elloway," a tall dark haired man smiled as they shook hands. "I'm Tinnias Vaylo, Head of Law Enforcement here on Sigma Prime. I'm very happy to meet you, although I would rather it was a result of different circumstances. My daughter is a huge fan of yours and I will admit to having been forced to sit through most of your movies, some of which I've enjoyed very much."

"Glad to meet you Sir," Jake smiled back. "Say hi to her for me."

"I will, thank you." He introduced Jake to his colleagues and gave him a brief overview of what he could expect during the interview.

"Now since Captain Nagle and the bridge crew wish to return to the Mayan Queen, they will be having their interviews first so you and your friends have time to relax. Sam here will show you to your accommodation and then he will be sitting in on the interviews. There is quite a crowd of fans outside and we all felt it would be good PR for you to do a little meet and greet to let the outside world know that you're safe and well and that the Law Enforcement Agency is taking care of things."

"That's fine," Jake smiled. "Sam said I'd be able to call my parents sometime. My mother will be worried sick."

"Absolutely," Tinnias replied. "Come with me, I'll show you where you can make that call now." He led Jake into an adjoining room and showed him how to use the Unicom setup.

"Put this headset on like this and then dial 50 to call outside Sigma, then 460551 for Earth, followed by your parents' normal number. Take as long as you need and don't worry, the line is completely secure. No one will be listening in but please don't tell them anything about who the pirates are, where they might be or anything else. We don't want to cause any problems that could let someone get away with this later on. Best to keep your conversation to assuring them that you're okay."

"Sure, no problem. I'm really grateful for this."

"Not at all. Just come back through when you're done and I'll get Sinclair to show you to your room."

Jake dialled the number and waited. Nothing happened for several seconds and he was just about to wonder if he should redial when he heard his father's unmistakeable voice.

"Hey Pop, it's Jake."

"Son?" his father let out an audible sigh of relief. "Jeez it's good to hear your voice Jake. Are you okay?"

"Yeah I'm fine, still in one piece."

"What happened? All we know is that the ship was targeted by pirates and that you and some others had been taken hostage."

"Yeah that's basically right," Jake replied. "I'm not allowed to give you more details though. It was a horrendous experience and one I shall never forget."

"Where are you now? Have you sorted everything out? What about the authorities?"

"I'm in the care of the Law Enforcement Agency at the moment on Sigma Prime. We're about to be interviewed officially. They're doing everything by the book Dad, don't worry. I'm about to go and meet some fans and the media will be there so keep an eye on the news and you'll no doubt see me."

"I wish I was there with you Son."

"I know but I'm fine really. I've got some real good buddies here with me so I'm not on my own."

"When will you be coming home?"

"Well I've decided to stick the three months out when this is done. I did wonder about cutting it off and coming home but after talking with my friends here, I want to stay. I'm actually enjoying it now I've got to know folks."

"Okay, whatever you feel is right but if you want to come home, you just call and we'll arrange it right away okay?"

"Sure thing Dad."

"Your mother is here tugging at my ear. Stay strong Son, I love you."

"Love you too Dad."

"Jake? Honey?" His mother's trembling voice came on the line accompanied by quiet sobs.

"Hey Mom, don't cry."

"I was so worried about you. Are you all right? What did they do to you?"

"I'm fine, don't worry and stop crying. Everything is okay and I have good friends with me. I'm unharmed and just waiting to speak to the Law Enforcement Agency and tell them everything so they can put all the necessary wheels in motion."

"I'm so relieved. Are you coming home after this is done?"

"No I'm gonna do the three months."

"But why? It's dangerous."

"Life is dangerous Mom. I've made some great buddies and I don't wanna just up and leave them now. Everything will be fine now the Law Enforcement guys are onto it. Stop worrying please huh?"

"Well if you insist I won't nag."

"Good girl. Now you keep an eye on the news okay? I'm going out soon to do a meet and greet with some fans here on Sigma and the media is here so you'll see for yourself that I'm okay and unharmed."

"Oh good, I'll get Hank to record it for me."

"You do that. Now I gotta go and get ready. You take care of Dad."

"I miss you Jake."

"I miss you too Mom. I love you."

"Goodbye honey."

"Bye Mom."

He hung up and went back through to find Captain Nagle, Shib, Arsh and Hefton 24 had arrived and were being introduced to Tinnias Vaylo. A small man was handing coffee around and Captain Nagle accepted a cup gratefully.

Shib went over to where Jake and his friends were standing.

"Jake, I've asked to remain here for the night with you. I hope you don't mind."

Jake hesitated, a little taken aback by this. "Sure buddy, if you feel you want to."

"I do feel it necessary that I add my own observations to those of you five, since I was with you during the first part of our experience."

"Yeah that's probably a good idea," Nef nodded.

Jake was a little annoyed that Shib's presence meant they would not be able to talk openly about the problem of the inside man.

"You have something on your mind Jake," Shib said. "Does my presence here cause a problem for you?"

"No Shib," Manlee replied. "It's just that we have thoughts and views that we don't wish Captain Nagle to be aware of and we don't know whether you would feel comfortable keeping things from him, should he ask you."

"I understand your quandary," Shib nodded, "but you needn't worry. It is not beyond the realms of possibility that my own observations and deductions may mirror your own." He looked into Jake's eyes for several seconds before looking away and Jake looked at Nef and raised his eyebrows. Nef raised his own in response.

"Right then Jake," Sam Sinclair said as he approached the group. "I see there are six of you to stay the night. Follow me and I'll show you to your accommodation. We have a suite of rooms on the fourth floor that you can use." He led them up and showed them into a very comfortable suite of rooms overlooking the market square in front, which was by now filled with a crowd of fans eager to see Jake.

"The windows are all made from an especially toughened Cosmiplex alloy and can withstand everything except the most powerful pulse laser weaponry and pulse bombs. Oh, and they probably wouldn't stand up to the Hellfire Pulse Laser Canon either but now those Transmortals are history, we don't have to worry about that weapon. There are two armed guards outside the door but they aren't to keep you in so no need to get suspicious. They are there to help protect you. There is a surveillance camera here in the main sitting room, but not in the bedrooms and bathroom. Oh, and there is no microphone, it's just a visual recording so you may speak freely with each other. Again, this is just for your safety. We sometimes have to keep witnesses here who are in very great danger so the precautions are necessary and if something did happen to you, we would be at fault if we didn't do all we could to keep you safe."

"Thanks Sam," Jake said.

"No problem. You settle in and Tinnias Vaylo will come and escort you through your meet and greet in thirty minutes. I have to go and sit in on the interviews of the Captain and Bridge crew now so I won't see you until later this evening. I'll join you for dinner if I may?"

"Sure thing," Jake smiled as he shook Sam's proffered hand.

The crowd's chants echoed around the market square as Tinnias Vaylo and his two armed guards escorted Jake towards the main entrance of the Law Enforcement Agency Headquarters. He stopped at the door and turned to face Jake.

"Now don't let time get away with you Mr Elloway. We feel this is necessary so that everyone will know you're safe and things are being taken care of in the proper manner, but let's keep it brief okay?"

"Absolutely," Jake replied with a nod.

Tinnias nodded to the two men standing at each side of the main entrance and Jake went into automatic celebrity mode. The smile appeared with its legendary speed just as the doors opened and the crowd exploded into cheers. Cameras flashed and arms waved photographs and all manner of bits of paper and from everywhere, Jake's name boomed from hundreds of mouths. After all the hell of Tellizon 4 and the terrors that lurked within its beautiful but deadly forest, this was something Jake knew how to do and he felt right at home. He descended the steps and approached a waiting crowd of media news broadcasters, each of whom held a microphone towards him.

"Thank you for coming friends," he grinned.

"Are you okay Jake?" someone called.

"I'm absolutely fine, thank you."

"Can you tell us what happened?" another voice asked.

"I can't give you details about that at this time. The Law Enforcement Agency have taken complete control of the situation and they will issue statements as and when they feel it right to do so."

"How is life aboard the space ship?" a female voice called.

"I've settled in very well and made some great friends, some of whom I will most definitely keep in contact with in the future."

"Are they working you hard?" another, older female voice enquired.

"It is hard work but I'm enjoying it and the company of my new buddies makes it all the more fun."

"Will this experience make it into a movie Jake?" a man's voice asked.

"You never know," Jake grinned. "Watch this space as they say."

"We're sure glad you're okay Jake," another female called.

"Thank you, I'm glad to be in one piece."

"Have you been in touch with your family?"

"Yes I've called them and assured them I'm well and put their minds at rest. Hi Mom, Pop," he grinned at the nearest news camera and waved. The crowd went nuts and Jake smiled and nodded his thanks as he set off towards the nearest crowd of eager fans to sign a few photos and get a few kisses.

Maria edged her way through the crowd and almost made it right to the front. When Jake appeared, she waved and called along with the others and decided to get to know the woman next to her.

"Oh look, there he is," she said and the woman nodded and almost fainted, her hand over her mouth. Ilyas, listening intently through his earpiece decided Maria deserved a kiss after this for her ingenuity. "Looks like he's gonna speak to the news cameras first though," she continued as her companion looked disappointed. A few minutes later, she smiled and began to back her way out of the crowd towards Ilyas and Ink's position. "He's approaching my position now."

"Okay Ink, this is it. See that woman over there with the little blonde kid?" Ink nodded. "Cover me but keep that trigger finger under control, I'm not into killing kids okay?"

"Sure Boss."

Ilyas ran over to the woman and yanked the little blonde kid out of her arms. Scooping her up into his arms, he put his gun to her temple and started yelling for all he was worth. The crowd parted in horror as the man with the ugly scar down his face made his way through them towards where Jake was still signing autographs, unaware of what was happening. Some of the crowd started screaming, the child's mother amongst them and within seconds the screaming replaced the cheering and Jake and Tinnias looked up. The armed guards stepped in front of Jake and started nudging him back towards the safety of the building.

"Get over here Elloway or this kid gets it," Ilyas yelled as Ink and Maria guarded him from both sides and the rear.

Tinnias turned to the guards. "Get Jake inside quickly."

"Elloway?" Ilyas screamed. "You want this kid getting her head blown off to be seen all over the media? You want everyone to know it was your fault this kid got murdered?" Ink and Maria kept the crowds back and Tinnias found himself in a standoff.   "Get over here Jake and this kid can go back to her Mom and everyone can go about their business all peaceful like. Come on Jake; don't make me do this. Your career couldn't take the heat now could it?"

"Come on now," Tinnias said as calmly as he could. "This isn't going to get us anywhere. Put the kid down and we'll let you get away and off Sigma before we come after you."

Ilyas responded by shoving his gun harder into the temple of the kid who was by now screaming her head off. Ink grinned and looked at Ilyas, who nodded to him slowly. Ink looked into the crowd and picked out a pretty brunette who was standing near to where Jake was hiding behind the two armed guards, his signed picture still in her hands. The shot pierced her heart and blood spattered down the front of Jake's crisp white shirt. Screams filled the square and those nearest to the victim tried to back away.

Jake's mind was racing; he was terrified and just wanted to be at home amongst his family and entourage where he knew he could trust everyone. He bitterly regretted agreeing to make this trip and although Nef, Manlee, Crib, Ace and Titch were his friends, his time on board had not exactly been a picnic. Everything started off okay but he'd almost been beaten senseless by Titch, he'd somehow made Aamy and Zeke hate him, he'd annoyed the cargo bay boss Dredge by damaging several crates of cargo and gotten into trouble once by being late for his shift. Some of the others made it plain they didn't like him just because he was a celebrity and even the gorgeous nurse Faline still wanted sex with other men. People always expected him to be as much of a hero as the characters in his movies and he knew they were disappointed to find he was not. It was embarrassing when he had to admit that he could not even fire a gun and was a burden to them on Tellizon, and Stella Bodecki had lost her life because of him. He felt like a failure and he didn't like the way this past week or so had made him question himself. Circumstances demanded that he try to make it right and he wanted everyone to see him making it right.

He straightened his shoulders and stepped between the two armed guards towards Ilyas, the protestations of Tinnias and the guards ringing in his ears. The media cameras followed his every step and although he felt bad because he knew his parents would be seeing this, he knew he had to do it.

"Okay buddy," he said to Ilyas. "Here I am." He walked towards him with his arms raised. "Let the kid go, she doesn't deserve this shit huh?"

Ink rushed towards him and locked a set of handcuffs onto him and marched him off at gunpoint. Ilyas, with Maria guarding his rear, backed off through the crowd. Kreeve set the shuttle down in the square, sending the crowd rushing away as the dust and debris blew about in turmoil from the engines. Ink steered Jake in through the hatch and locked his cuffs to a bulkhead before returning to help clear a path for Ilyas and Maria. Only when Ilyas was standing at the open hatchway did he drop the kid and rush up the ramp.

Kreeve gunned the engines and lifted off the ground to head back to base. Suddenly the shuttle lurched and everyone fell headlong.

"What the fuck?" Ilyas yelled.

"They've caught our port engine Boss," Kreeve yelled back as he fought with the controls.

"Get us out of here now."

"Hold on folks, this won't be the smoothest ride you've ever had." With smoke billowing from its port engine, the pirates limped the shuttle away from the Law Enforcement Agency Headquarters.

The media cameras caught the whole episode which was streamed around the galaxy and, back on Earth, in the comfort and safety of the Elloway Mansion, Jacqueline Elloway sobbed into her husband's chest as she watched the pirate with the ugly scar down his face steal her son away.

CHAPTER FOURTEEN

Tinnias Vaylo yelled into his communication earpiece for his guards to open fire on the pirate shuttle as it left the square and headed up and away. They managed to catch the port engine, which belched black smoke, causing the craft to list and stumble through the air and almost crash into the trader's sector before their pilot regained a measure of control and limped the craft away and out of their sight. The screaming crowd were dispersed and the media cameras sent away after Tinnias assured them that the Law Enforcement Agency would be doing everything within its power to locate Jake and put his captors into custody.

Nef and his friends were beside themselves with anger at the easy way Ilyas had been able to reach Jake and take him away and decided not to rely on the Law Enforcement Agency alone to find him and bring him safely back to them. Sam Sinclair came rushing into their room once news of what happened reached him, which was seconds after he heard the sounds of gunfire.

"Sam," Nef said as he leapt up and met him eye to eye. "Is this the sort of protection you people are able to offer now?"

"We'll find him Mr umm," he began.

"Asmion Nefulan, but everyone calls me Nef."

"Don't worry Nef," Sam replied, "we'll find him and get him back. The guys are tracking the shuttle's trail now."

"Well don't take this personally but we don't feel comfortable just waiting for you people to sort out this mess. We're going to look for him ourselves."

"I should really advise you against that. That is my job. It's what I do and I know what I'm doing. However, I'm experienced enough to know that even if I did you'd take no notice and go off causing hell knows what kind of trouble, so I guess you'd better tag along with me. That way at least I can keep you from screwing things up further."

"Thanks Sam. Okay let's go."

The five friends stood and looked at him; two Earthmen, an android, a Damiklonian and a Zylomian. Sam realised that whatever Jake may be and however people feel about him, he certainly has some sort of ability to engender affection from all regions of the galaxy. He led them up to the roof of the Agency building, stopping on the way to get the latest update as to the shuttlecraft's last known heading and within ten minutes, they were heading out of the city.

Kreeve wrestled with the shuttle's controls and almost crashed into the ground at one point before managing to regain control and heading out of the city. Within minutes, Law Enforcement Agency sniper drones were chasing them and before they were halfway back to base and the safety of the Barclay, they crash-landed and made a run for it. As luck would have it, they crashed at the very edge of the city and had less than a mile to run before the safety of the forest enveloped them and Jake thought back to Tellizon and hoped that the fauna on Sigma Prime was a lot less hostile. They did the last four miles on foot, with Ink holding a gun on Jake all the time and wishing Ilyas would give him permission to shoot him.

The sniper drones were everywhere and Ilyas knew the moment they fired up the Barclay and tried to leave Sigma, the authorities would be all over them in minutes and with only the three of them, they would not stand a chance. He quickly realised they had no choice but to sit and wait for things to die down a little. They decided to try to make it look like they were campers if anyone should happen to come by, so they made a fire and dragged a couple of logs to sit on. Ink secured Jake to a couple of stout wooden stakes driven into the ground and Kreeve decided to take a stroll and hunt for a meal. The sun was beginning to set as they ate the delicious creature and although Jake was scared for his life, he was hungry and enjoyed the meat.

"So what's the plan?" he asked quietly.

"I haven't decided yet," Ilyas replied without looking at him. "Originally we were going to make a pile of money out of you and your rich Mommy and Daddy but after all the trouble you've caused us, I may just kill you to make myself feel better."

"Then you'll still be stuck here on Sigma and you won't have a bargaining chip," Jake said, remembering his role as Captain Johns in The Game, a movie for which he was nominated for, and gained, yet another EnWatch award.

"True," Ilyas replied, "but y'know, maybe the sheer pleasure will be worth it."

"I have to pee," Jake replied.

He didn't but he wanted to try to get the conversation away from the possibility of them killing him. Ilyas looked at Ink and nodded his head towards Jake. Ink led him at gunpoint to the tree line and waited while he had a pee, then led him back and sat him down again.

"Thanks," Jake said, hoping the simple courtesy would lighten the mood a little.

Maria Cady wandered over and crouched down beside him. She looked him up and down and he met her gaze and held it defiantly. "I used be crazy about your movies Jake," she smiled. "Those blue eyes and that smouldering gaze you do so well, man that always did it for me. What was that movie called where you played the guy who lost an arm?"

"Night Train to Anywhere," he replied and she nodded.

"That's the one," she smiled as she remembered. "I must've watched that damn movie a hundred times."

"I'm glad you enjoyed it," he replied, a little stuck for an appropriate response.

"Oh I did," she nodded, "and it was my dream to meet you one day."

"Well now you have," he hissed. He didn't know where this conversation was going but he didn't trust this apparently innocent small talk.

"Can you guess how many letters I sent to your fan club? Can you guess how many hours I spent waiting in the rain to see you emerge from a movie premier or open yet another kid's hospital? Can you guess how many competitions I went in for where the prize was to meet you?"

"Nope."

"A lot," she replied. "You know Jake, your fans spend many hours of their time devoting their energy to you. They put aside their families, work, hobbies and even their health and give all their focus to you for hours and hours, hoping for just a moment from you to acknowledge their effort, their love and their existence. All those hours they give to you are gone Jake and they can't ever get them back and use them in a more positive way. I gave you hours of my life and I can't get them back and give them to someone else. That's one hell of a big slice of my life I gave to you and you can't give me a couple of seconds to let me know all my efforts and energy and affection were worthy of your acknowledgement."

"I'm always aware how much the fans give me of their time and energy and I always appreciate it," Jake countered defensively. "I know the fans pay my wages and give me my nice lifestyle and I try to let them know that, but if I was to spend time individually with each one I'd never have time to do anything else. I have to work. Making a movie takes time, more time than you know. I have to spend time with my family who have helped me become the success that I am. I have a business to run and a charity to oversee and sometimes it's nice to get a few minutes to myself just to think. It's not that I don't appreciate the fans; it's not that I don't care but there simply aren't enough hours in the day. Thank you for being a fan, even if you're not anymore. People like you have helped me become what I am and I do

216

appreciate your affection and your energy." He looked her in the eyes for several seconds until she sighed deeply and walked off.

Ilyas kicked the sole of Ink's boot and he awoke with a start.

"Your snoring is driving me mad Ink. Get Elloway inside for the night and let's make camp."

Ink yawned, dragged himself to his feet, and reached for his gun. He led Jake into the Barclay and after locking him in the tiny bathroom cubicle so he could pee and have a wash; he restrained him into a bunk and threw a blanket over him.

"Sleep tight asshole," he grinned as he turned to go.

"Hey Ink?" Jake called. "Don't you get tired of him bossing you around so much?" Ink shrugged his shoulders; it never crossed his mind. "How long have you worked with him?"

"Around five years or so."

"I'd have thought he owes you a little more respect after all that time. If I treated my employees like that, I wouldn't last a week in the movie business. Does he pay you well?"

"We split things sixty forty."

"So he gets sixty percent of everything and the rest of you get forty percent between you?"

"Yeah. It's the going rate."

"Man that's slave labour. I make sure I pay my employees way over the standard rate so they stay with me and stay loyal and I treat them like members of the family. You should ask for a raise buddy. Does he give you housing and other benefits?"

"Nope."

"Really? Shit man, that's awful. All of my employees get free housing while they work for me, a handsome pension plan, medical benefits and three months holiday a year on full pay. They work hard and they deserve it. They're people with families, not robots."

"Yeah well maybe I should come and work for you then huh?"

"You'd certainly earn more. I'd have to get outta here first though." Jake looked at Ink, who stared right back at him before turning and leaving him alone.

Sam Sinclair and Jake's friends headed out of the city and landed at the scene of the pirate's shuttle crash.

"Okay guys," he said as he shut down the ship and headed for the hatch, "I have to ask you to remain inside while I go and see what gives out there. It's an official crime scene now. I'd be breaking the rules if I allowed you anywhere near so please don't be awkward with this huh? I'll tell you everything I find out."

"Okay Sam," Nef nodded with frustration, "we understand." He sighed as he watched him leave the ship and walk towards a group of men clad in overalls who were picking over the crashed shuttle.

"I hope Jake survived the crash," Manlee said. "I'm gonna be mighty annoyed if we got him this far, through all that hell on Tellizon, only to have him die from a bump on the head in a shuttle crash."

"It doesn't look too serious," Crib replied as he peered out of the window at the scene ahead. "He may have a few bruises but I'd lay money on it being easily survivable."

"I would estimate their most likely plan would be to head for the trees," Shib said as he looked out of the cockpit window. "There is a forest just a mile from here that stretches for several hundred miles into the mountains and it would seem most likely that they have made their base there. If they remained within the city Jake would be recognised immediately so they are going to want to get him away from people quickly to avoid drawing attention to themselves."

"It would seem the obvious thing to do," Ace nodded.

"So it seems we have another trek through the forest ahead of us," Nef said and sighed.

"At least we know we aren't in danger from the creatures that live in this one," Shib replied.

"Well that's a blessing," Manlee said.

"And once we get within five miles of his position, we will know exactly where he is and could, conceivably be taking him back to safety within hours," Shib added. The others frowned at him and he smiled.

"Do you not remember when I met you in the Law Enforcement Headquarters and asked you if I might join you in remaining here?"

"Yeah," Nef nodded, "so?"

"Do you remember what happened?"

"You asked us if we minded you staying with us," Manlee replied.

"And you asked if it would be a problem," Ace added.

"And we said we'd be happy for you to stay." Nef said.

"And you didn't see me shake hands with Jake and put a hand on his shoulder?" Shib asked with a smile.

"Umm, yeah I think I remember that," Nef said with a frown, "why?"

"Because I placed one of my own axion nodes under his collar."

"One of your what?" Ace asked.

"Axion nodes," Shib explained. "They are components of my android brain network. Each android brain has axion nodes unique to each individual android. The axion nodes from my brain will only work in my brain and not in any other android. They are linked like an extremely complicated network and each one knows where each of the others is and they recognise each other as belonging to their own unique network."

"So this means?" Manlee asked.

"This means that the other seven trillion or so axion nodes still within my brain will recognise the signal given off by the single one attached to Jake's collar. They need to be together as a complete network and will always look for the missing one. As soon as we get within five miles of Jake's position, the axion nodes within my brain will pick up the signal given off by the one under his collar. I can follow that signal and lead us right to him."

"Why did you put it under his collar?" Crib asked.

"Because I guessed that something might happen to Jake once he got out there amongst the crowd and I thought it was a good idea to err on the side of caution, just in case."

"Shib old buddy," Nef said. "Have I ever told you just how much I admire and respect you?"

"Umm, actually no," Shib replied and then frowned as everyone laughed.

Sam was delighted to hear the news when he returned from the crashed shuttle. Everyone was relieved that no blood was evident which meant Jake was more than likely still alive.

"Okay let's head off and cruise over the forest and as soon as you feel something, yell," Sam offered and Shib nodded.

For the next three hours they cruised back and forth covering the forested area in a grid pattern, trying to ensure they covered every inch and not once did Shib utter so much as a word. As the sun was beginning to set, Sam decided he needed to get back to Headquarters to refuel the ship's power cells.

"We need to head back to base fellas. I need to refuel this gal's power cells."

"Okay," Nef sighed with frustration. "Shit, I hate all this fucking around. Why the hell was this allowed to happen anyway? Weren't people aware of just how much danger Jake was in or did they just not care?"

"We'll get him Nef," Crib said as he stood and headed towards the nutri vend machine he spied at the rear of the ship. "Shib will tell us the moment he senses his thingamajig nearby and then we'll know Jake is just five miles away." He pumped a hot drink from the nutri vend and handed it to Nef. "We're all in this together buddy and we feel it too y'know."

Nef slumped down into a seat and rubbed his hands through his hair. "It's just such damn incompetence." He sighed deeply and took the drink from Crib.

"It was just one of those moments when whatever course you choose, something gets fucked up," Sam called. "I've done jobs like this a few times. Celebrities are taken hostage all the time and with them, there is always danger. Their lifestyle means they have to accept a little risk every time they go out in public and judging by the way Jake seems to care about his fans, he accepts the risk. I guess that's part of the payback for leading what seems like a privileged lifestyle. All I know is that if I'd been him and had to choose between running away and letting a little kid get shot in the head and turning myself over to them, I'd want to make the same choice he made."

"Yeah I know," Nef said quietly. "It's just that after everything we've been through during the past week I just wish, oh I don't know."

"Hey buddy, you're beginning to sound like his father," Ace said and everyone laughed.

"Right," Sam said, "let's head back and refuel and we can be back within," he began but Shib cut him off.

"I have him," Shib suddenly yelled.

"Okay let's take a look around," Sam said as he began to circle the area. An hour later Shib informed them that they were getting closer and as they circled an area above a well known spot for campers, Shib yelled again.

"He's below us," he said and everyone looked out of the window.

"I might have known," Sam smiled and shook his head.

"What?" Manlee asked.

"This is Bleane Lake. A very popular spot for off world tourists to come and set up camp. This lake is dotted with ships and craft from many worlds, see all the campfires?"

"Okay so let's go camping," Nef said.

After a quick trip back to refuel, Sam settled the ship down and everyone tried to look like they were setting up camp. No one had eaten since lunch and everyone was hungry so Shib went off to catch a meal, leaving Sam to light a fire. Whilst their dinner was roasting, they discussed what they were to do.

"We're going to have to hike back into the trees and make our way around to their rear and take them from there," Sam said. "There's no way to approach from the front without either getting wet or being seen."

"We'd better wait until first light," Shib said. "It will be so dark in the forest that we will be crashing around and making too much noise. As soon as it's light enough to see we will be able to make our move."

"How many of you guys know your way around a gun?" Sam asked.

"We all became very familiar with them back on Tellizon," Crib replied and everyone nodded.

"Great," Sam said. "I'll get you all armed up and you'll probably just have to aim and look menacing."

"I am an expert shot," Shib replied, "and I am trained in twenty three different martial arts and solo combat techniques."

"And he's as strong as ten men," Ace replied.

"And he's modest too," Nef added and everyone laughed.

Sam grinned. "I'm mighty glad you're here Shib. Now is that meat ready yet cos I'm starving."

They ate in silence and Sam noticed Nef making faces as he ate. "Not enjoying it Nef?"

"It's not exactly to my taste," he said as the others laughed.

"One thing you gotta know about Nef," Crib said. "Anything you like the taste of will be horrible to him and vice versa. I keep telling him he needs to get his taste buds seen to but he won't have it."

"You're Damiklonian aren't you?" Sam asked.

"That's correct," Nef said, "and there is nothing wrong with my taste buds thank you," he glared at Crib with a grin.

"Well just think of this as payback for Tellizon," Manlee said and the others laughed. He saw Sam frowning. "When we were on Tellizon, Shib caught us a meal the first night we were there and it was the most disgusting thing you ever tasted. Of course Nef here loved it and made fun of the rest of us, so we reckon this is payback time."

"Oh I see," Sam said. "I once knew a Damiklonian when I was investigating a scientific research station on Deligon 2. He was a real nice guy. He gave me this," he said as he rummaged down the front of his shirt to reveal a pendant hung on a string around his neck. It was white and smooth as glass and looked like a long pointed fang.

"Then you are a friend of all Damiklon Sam," Nef smiled as he looked at it.

"Really?" Sam asked. "He gave it to me as he was dying from a gunshot wound and he said that it would protect me and bring help when needed."

"He was correct," Nef said. "It is carved from the sacred white stone of the Lavastra Mountain and is a representation of a Damiklonian fang."

"Like the ones you have?" Sam asked.

"Yes," Nef nodded. "That symbol you carry will tell all of Damiklon that you are a friend and none of us will ever harm you and we will always do whatever we can to give you aid if you should call upon us. So your friend told you the truth and I am here."

"That is awesome Nef," Ace said.

"You must've done something unbelievably brave to earn such a display of affection from a Damiklonian Sam," Nef said.

Sam smiled as he remembered the friend who had died in his arms and his eyes welled up at the memory.

"Well I don't know about brave but he was my friend and we'd gone through some weird shit together and I guess that brought us close y'know?"

"Yeah, I know," Nef nodded.

"All I know is, that if Jake has the friendship of one of your people then he must be a nice guy."

"He is," Crib nodded. "Even if he is a celebrity."

"In many ways he has lived a sheltered life," Nef said. "But y'know, there was something in the way he looked at me that told me he was a person wanting to find himself, explore places within himself he hasn't been to before, and become the person he wants to be, even if he doesn't yet know that he wants to be that person. I knew right away that we had to connect, that he needed a friend he could rely on and I knew that person had to be me."

"Are you going to take him up on his offer?" Shib asked.

"You know about that?"

"I heard Captain Nagle talk about it. Are you going to go?"

"Go where?" Sam asked.

"He offered me a job working with him as his personal trainer," Nef said. "I'm teaching him the Damiklonian Martial Art."

"My friend taught me the martial art," Sam smiled. "I still practice every day."

"Then maybe the three of us can practice together when he's safely back with us," Nef replied. "And I have decided to accept his offer, yes."

"You will be the first Damiklonian to live and work on Earth Nef," Shib said. "You may feel very alone and you may suffer some hostility."

"Don't let yourself be bullied like I was," Manlee said. "I'd hate for another of my friends to experience what I did."

"I won't, don't worry," Nef smiled, "and thank you for your concern."

"You were bullied on Earth?" Sam asked.

"Not on Earth no," Manlee replied, "but some of my tormentors were from Earth."

"Because you're Zylomian?"

"Yes."

"I once had to arrest a guy who had tried to murder a Zylomian. He was a sicko. Him and his buddies took this guy from a research vessel and beat him up, then took him to some uninhabited planet and left him for dead. Luckily, they found him and returned him to Zylom where he was cared for but he was comatose and I doubt if he ever regained consciousness. They beat him so bad his skull was split in five places and he'd lost half the blood in his body. I often think of him and wonder if he is still alive or if he's still in a coma. and whenever I wonder if the chase is worth it, I think of that sick fuck and it always keeps me focussed. It was one of those cases that really made me realise why I do what I do. That guy almost eluded me and in the end, I had to take him back in a bag, but I was determined to get him and get that poor guy justice. His carcass is now rotting in Latterways Penitentiary Graveyard."

"Captain Joshua Morgan," Manlee smiled and Sam almost spat out his drink.

"You know of the case?"

"I did survive Sam. It took seven months but I regained consciousness eventually."

Sam didn't know what to say; he stared at Manlee in shock.

"I've never quite gotten back to the person I was before though. Something permanently changed within me, or so I've always believed. It took a few years for me to find the courage to seek work away from Zylom again but when I found another Zylomian working happily aboard the Mayan Queen, I took the chance and I've been very happy there."

"My god, can you believe this?" Crib said. "What are the odds of us meeting someone who was involved in Manlee's trouble?"

"That is some weird shit," Ace nodded.

"I'm so happy to meet you Manlee," Sam said. "I think of you often and it's awesome to know you're alive and healthy and living your life again. That's damn awesome buddy."

"Thank you so much for bringing that man to justice Sam," Manlee said. "It really helps me to put the last few pieces of that painful time behind me. I've always known he was caught and killed but I've always wanted to meet the man who caught him, to say thank you."

"This is the most incredible thing I've ever experienced," Nef said and rubbed a hand through his hair and grinned. "Wow."

The six friends settled down and talked for hours and as the evening wore on, a bond of friendship was born with Sam the law enforcement guy and as they lay down to sleep, they all knew that no matter where his travels took him, nor for how long, he would always be one of their friends. Manlee settled down to sleep and let the last remaining pain from his terrible experience melt away into the night and as it did so, the man he used to be, the man he thought he had lost forever, returned to his side, embraced him and melded back into his soul.

CHAPTER FIFTEEN

Jake awoke, his full bladder ensuring he would not be able to carry on sleeping away the nightmare situation he was in. His back ached from not being able to turn over onto his side, the cuffs on each wrist holding his arms either side of the bunk preventing any change of position. Straining his neck, he looked around but saw no one and wondered what time it was. He listened and thought he heard voices outside so he called out.

"Hey there, anyone home? I need to pee guys. Hey." He was just about to yell louder when the hatch opened and Ink peered in.

"What's up, can't sleep?"

"Funny," Jake replied. "I need to pee." Ink tutted to himself before wandering over and letting him out of his restraints.

"No gun this time? What's wrong? You're not actually beginning to trust me not to run away are ya?"

"The only way out takes you right past the others," Ink replied as he led Jake to the bathroom cubicle. "You'd never make it more than ten yards, unless of course you've suddenly learned to pilot, in which case you could steal the ship and take off, but then of course the local authorities would assume you're one of us trying to escape and shoot you down." He waited while he had a pee and a wash.

When Jake was finished and dressed, Ink led him outside and restrained him with cuffs to his ankles, which he attached to a cable buried in the ground that ran to one of the bulkheads of the ship. This meant he had his arms free and with a carefully placed blanket over his feet, he didn't look obviously restrained should hikers or other campers happen to come past.

"Morning Jake," Ilyas yawned. "I hope you enjoyed the Barclay's first class accommodation. Here, put this on," he ordered as he threw a wide brimmed hat over to him, "and pull it down low. We can't have those famous pretty blue eyes catching folk's attention now can we?"

Jake put the hat on and looked around. It was early morning; the sun having risen a couple of hours ago but had still to burn the mist off the lake. A jetty ran out into the water a few yards to their left, reminding him of a scene from Catching Jack, a movie he made early in his career. Kreeve appeared with a dead creature dangling from his belt, which he immediately set about skinning and cleaning. A fire was already burning and within thirty minutes, the roasting carcass smelt delicious and all their bellies were grumbling. Maria Cady appeared in a red bikini and wandered towards the small jetty, the catcalls and wolf whistles from her companions being met with a single finger. Jake watched her run up the jetty and dive into the icy water.

"Fancy a swim Jake?" Ilyas said. "Or is it the sight of Maria in her skimpies that catches your eye?"

"What? No. I was just thinking I bet that water's as cold as a penguin's asshole."

"Nothing like it to wake you up in the morning," Kreeve laughed.

"I'll stay half asleep, thanks," Jake hissed. "By the way, shouldn't you be issuing demands to the authorities or something? Isn't that what kidnappers do?"

"There's plenty of time for that," Ilyas grinned. "That's what they're expecting us to do so we're just gonna lay low for a while before we do anything and let the fuss die down."

"Anyone would think you don't like our company," Ink said.

"It's not your company that bothers me," Jake replied. "But sitting on my ass all day, chained up, and not being able to walk around or work out is seriously gonna bore my ass off. Couldn't you just let me work out for an hour? You could keep your guns on me."

"Okay," Ilyas nodded and Jake's eyebrows shot up in surprise. "After breakfast has gone down you can have your hour but if you betray my trust, there'll be consequences."

"Thanks man," Jake nodded.

As promised, Ilyas released Jake so he could work out for an hour and had Kreeve and Ink watch him, their guns concealed to avoid alerting passers-by. Jake stood and massaged his numb backside before starting with some stretches. He did some squats, sit-ups and lunges and then practiced the Damiklonian Martial Art movements that Nef had taught him. Even though he was just a beginner, Ilyas and the crew had never seen anything like it before and they were secretly impressed as he ducked, spun and balanced. When he was done, he was breathing hard but felt calm as he sat down and allowed Ink to cuff his ankles once again.

"What was that Jake?" Ilyas asked. "Karate or something?"

"It's the Damiklonian Martial Art," Jake replied proudly.

Ilyas raised his eyebrows. "You've been taught that?"

Jake nodded.

"Wow, they don't usually teach other folks their shit. You must have some influence on Damiklon Prime."

"No, not influence," Jake remarked. "Just a good friend."

"Well I'm going for a swim," Ink said and dropped his pants to reveal his very grey underwear." They watched him go and jump into the icy water and Kreeve laughed.

"I hope he takes the opportunity to have a decent wash," Kreeve said and Ilyas laughed.

Jake was just about to remark when his attention was drawn to the water, and looked to where Ink was splashing around and doing a very amateurish backstroke, but saw nothing out of the ordinary. He was about to look away when he saw it and just stopped himself from shouting out. At once, his eyes widened in shock as he looked at, and then recognised the head that bobbed up out of the water just behind Ink and as the pirate disappeared beneath the surface Jake silently sighed with relief and almost burst into tears.

Sam Sinclair's snoring woke Nef for the fourth time and he sighed as he got up and stretched himself. He crept over to where Sam lay and crouched down beside him.

"Turn over Sam and breathe easy," he whispered into his ear and smiled as Sam turned over and closed his mouth, his sleep undisturbed. Nef crept back to his own bed and lay down.

"Thanks man," Crib hissed. "I was just about to stuff my old sock into his mouth." Nef grinned and tried not laugh. Manlee snickered from his left.

"Can you do something about Ace's farting too?" Manlee asked and Crib laughed.

"Shh," Nef grinned at Crib. "Don't wake him up or he'll turn over onto his back and start snoring again."

"Sorry," Crib snickered as quietly as he could.

They awoke a little later than they had planned, due to their disturbed sleep but they were delighted to notice Shib had caught their breakfast and was busy roasting it over a roaring fire and it smelt delicious.

"That's smells wonderful Shib," Sam yawned as he wandered over to the ship and opened the hatch.

An hour later they were washed, dressed, and enjoying the rich meat. With the aid of some Agregorian spices Sam found in his cargo hold, even Nef enjoyed his meal.

"They're awake and moving around over there," Shib said as he peered through a scope he had found in Sam's ship. It looks like Jake is practicing the moves you taught him Nef. There are three men with him and a woman."

"We'd better start our hike around to their rear," Crib said.

"It's gonna be a little awkward," Sam replied. "It's a little later than I'd have liked. Ideally, we would already be in position

230

behind them and ready to make our move by now. It'll take us a couple of hours to reach the best position and by that time the place will be crawling with hikers and tourists. Shit."

"Now one of the men has gone for a swim," Shib reported.

Nef stood and began to remove his clothes. Manlee stood up and went to him.

"You can't do this alone Nef, there are three of them," he said.

"No, there is only the one at the moment," Nef replied as he stripped down to his underwear.

"What can we do?" Crib asked him.

"As soon as I have this one, the other two will come to investigate. Once they are down, you deal with the woman. How long will it take to walk around to their position?"

"I have a hover buggy on board," Sam replied. "We can go directly over the lake and be there in two minutes. What are you planning? Come on people I'm the law enforcement guy remember? I can't let you do this."

"It's okay Sam," Manlee smiled. "Nef is the perfect man for the job."

"But how? Come on don't hold out on me here."

"Sam," Nef said. "I'm Damiklonian remember?"

"So what?"

"So I like to swim, and I'm good at it." He looked at Sam and raised his eyebrows.

"Oh, I see," Sam said as he remembered Damiklonians can breathe underwater. "Wow, I never thought of that. Shit, umm okay look. You go do your thing with the guy in the water and then we hope the others go and investigate so you can deal with them too. We'll scope you out and get over there immediately those three are down and get the woman."

"Okay great," Nef said and headed towards the water.

"Hey Nef?" Sam called. "Are you gonna be committing a crime here today? Do I have to lose my memory or something and are those creeps over there gonna die?"

"Yes, no and no," Nef replied. "I really shouldn't do what I'm about to do but as you're law enforcement and I'm helping to catch a bunch of wanted pirates, you're in a good position to know whether I need to be punished or not. And no, they won't die. They'll be out just long enough to get them restrained and then I'll give them the antidote," he said as he patted the tube attached to his upper arm and smiled.

"Okay go," Sam nodded and Nef ran into the water and disappeared beneath the surface.

"I hope the fuck this doesn't go wrong," Sam whispered. "He really doesn't deserve to get into trouble."

"Don't worry Sam," Shib said. "He knows what he's doing and although very quick acting, his poison doesn't kill for several hours. There will be plenty of time to give them the antidote."

"Have you ever known him bite anyone before?"

"He told me he bit someone once, years ago," Manlee replied. "Before he ever came to work on the Mayan Queen. He was imprisoned for a while but the guy he bit was a rapist and had tried to rape Nef's friend's little daughter, so they let him off without any punishment as he was acting to protect an innocent from harm."

They watched the figure splashing about in the water until it suddenly disappeared beneath the surface.

"Here we go guys," Sam said as he rushed into the ship and got the hover buggy fired up.

As they watched, the body suddenly flew out of the water and landed with a squish on the jetty. Nef retreated under the water beneath the jetty and waited.

"Okay guys, grab your guns while they're hot," Sam called as he edged the buggy down the ramp.

They trained their eyes on the distant shore and could just make out a figure approach the jetty cautiously. He leaned down and nudged the prone figure before turning him over onto his back. He stood up and called back to his colleague who stood and began walking towards the jetty. Nef reached a hand up, grabbed the man by the ankle, and yanked him into the water. The third man ran to the jetty and peered into the water calling out his colleague's name. Suddenly a face loomed up out of the water at him and he just had time to register the open mouth and wickedly long fangs aiming towards his neck, before he blacked out. Nef let the body drop onto the jetty, turned back, and waved to the opposite shore, before hauling the third unconscious pirate out of the water.

"Come on guys," Sam yelled as he leapt into the hover buggy and gunned the controls.

They sped over the surface of the water, Crib steering while Sam aimed his tranquiliser gun at the pirate's ship. They saw the woman saunter down the ramp and walk over to Jake, her back to them, unaware of her three colleagues lying unconscious just yards away. A dull 'throp' came to Crib's ears and the woman dropped forward and landed at Jake's feet.

The hover buggy raced up the shore and the men leapt out and ran to the jetty. Within minutes, all four of the pirates were in restraints and Nef was administering the antidote. After rummaging in Ink's pocket, they let Jake out of his restraints and he stood, the shock still evident on his face. Nef dried himself off before greeting Jake.

"You were amazing buddy," Jake said. "I couldn't believe what I was seeing. Thank you, I owe ya."

"You didn't think we were just gonna leave you here did ya?" Crib grinned as they shook hands.

"Did they mistreat you?" Sam asked as he wandered between the bodies, taking DNA samples with his mobile sampler.

"Actually no," Jake replied. "They threatened to, of course, but so far they hadn't actually done anything."

"I'm gonna get these guys back over to my ship and get them properly restrained. I'll call the Law Enforcement Agency, tell them I have them and that you are safe and well, then I'll hop back over here and pick you guys up. Give me twenty minutes."

"Thanks Sam," Jake said as he shook hands with him. "I appreciate this."

"No problem at all buddy," Sam smiled. "Just doing my job."

Whilst Sam was gone, the group sat and talked over the events of the previous day. Jake was amazed and delighted when Manlee told him that Sam was the man who captured and killed the leader of the group who captured and tortured him all those years ago and he laughed when they told him how surprised Sam was to find Manlee was the guy he'd wondered about for all the intervening years.

"My god, what are the odds of that?" Jake said.

"I couldn't begin to calculate," Manlee smiled.

"It must bring you some much needed closure though buddy."

"Yeah, it does," Manlee smiled. "It sure does."

"Hey Nef," Jake asked. "Are you going to get into trouble for biting those assholes? I'd hate to be the cause of more problems."

"Don't worry about that Jake," Nef said as he dressed. "Everything will be okay, you'll see."

"The woman in the square," Jake asked. "Does anyone know?"

"She didn't make it," Shib said quietly.

"Shit."

Sam returned and everyone climbed into the hover buggy for the return crossing. When they were sitting down, Sam turned and looked at them without a smile.

"What's up Sam?" Nef asked.

"Everyone is delighted and relieved that we have those bastards and that you're unharmed Jake. Tinnias Vaylo himself assured me you will not be getting into any trouble Nef so don't worry about that."

"Thank god," Jake sighed as he rubbed a hand through his hair. "I couldn't be the cause of more trouble, especially not a friend."

"He also informed me that the body of Stella Bodecki is now in the Agency Headquarters. The scientists on Tellizon 4 luckily knew how to handle evidence without contaminating it. There is just one thing that casts a further cloud over these events."

"What?" Crib asked.

"Come on," Jake said, "just let us have it."

"Stella's body was interfered with sexually. After death."

Everyone fell silent and Jake went white and almost passed out. Manlee held him up and encouraged him to breathe deeply and then put an arm around his shoulders as he cried.

"Oh fuck," Ace hissed after a long silence. "I want to kill those fuckers myself."

"Who did it? Do we know?" Shib asked.

"Desmond Rappnail," Sam replied. "Commonly known as Ink."

"We have to make them tell us who the inside man is," Crib reminded everyone.

"Don't worry," Sam replied as he steered the hover buggy back across the lake, "we will."

They reached the shore and the group were dismayed to find the ship's hatch closed and locked.

"Let me in Sam," Crib hissed. Manlee put a hand on his shoulder but Crib shrugged it away. "Let me in, please."

"Come on," Manlee urged. "Come with me and have a hot drink." He steered him away and sat him down by the still smouldering fire.

Nef handed him a drink. "They'll get far better punishment in prison than we could ever give them buddy," he said.

"How the hell am I ever going to come to terms with having caused all this?" Jake asked. "Huh? Can you tell me that?"

"You didn't cause any of it Jake," Ace replied. "Those assholes in there did and don't you ever forget that okay?"

"But if I hadn't," he began but Shib cut him off.

"If you hadn't come aboard the Mayan Queen they'd have got to you some other way, or they'd have taken some other movie star next week or next month or next year. You can't take responsibility for other people's actions. All you can do is make sure everything you do is responsible, honourable and right."

"I don't even know if I've been able to do that," Jake said as he wiped his eyes.

"Then you can start now," Nef said, "and I'll help you whenever I can. If I ever see you acting like an asshole I'll punch you in the face if it'll make you feel better." There was a pause before everyone started to laugh.

The sound of engines made everyone turn and look up to see a Law Enforcement Agency ship landing nearby. The hatch opened and Tinnias Vaylo leapt out and ran over.

"Are you okay Jake?" he said as they shook hands. "Did they harm you in any way?"

"I'm fine thank you," Jake replied. "They treated me okay."

"Thank heavens for that. I'm so sorry this happened to you whilst a guest on our world. There will be a full enquiry I can assure you."

"Thank you. I'm just happy to be back with my friends and looking forward to a hot shower and some decent coffee."

"Now that, we can provide," Tinnias smiled. "If you'd all like to come with me, I'll see you back to your rooms. Sam here will be taking his guests to lockup and he'll re-join you later."

"Thanks Sam," Jake said as they shook hands. "For everything. A real nice quick job you did here."

"My pleasure buddy," Sam replied.

"Thank you Sam," Manlee smiled, "for ten years ago and for today. It's a real pleasure to meet you at last."

"I'm real happy to have met you Manlee," Sam grinned. "I can't tell you how often I've wondered about you."

"Good job buddy," Crib grinned as he slapped Sam on the back.

"Nice work Sam," Ace smiled.

"You are very good at your job Sam," Shib said. "It has been an interesting experience for me, thank you."

"And for me too Shib. My first experience of working with someone like you."

"I hope I've been a good ambassador for my kind."

"No doubt about that buddy."

Tinnias and his guards set the Agency shuttle down in the middle of the square and the crowds fell silent.

"We decided to bring you all in via the main square so everyone can see you're well and unharmed. There are hundreds of guards everywhere and sniper drones are patrolling the air. No one will get to you again whilst on Sigma Prime Jake, I promise you."

"Sure thing," Jake grinned. "Let's go."

237

The hatch opened and the crowd went crazy. The media cameras flashed and microphones appeared from everywhere. Jake smiled and waved to the crowd before stepping forward to the media.

"Are you all right Jake?" a voice called.

"I'm unharmed, thank you."

"What about the guys who took you? Where are they?"

"They are in custody."

"Can you tell us what happened?"

Jake shot a look at Tinnias, who frowned slightly. "Well obviously I can't go into details at this time, suffice to say that this whole sorry experience is now over and those who were responsible are now in the custody of the Law Enforcement Agency."

"We were worried about you Jake. Do you have a message for your fans?"

"I'd like to say thank you to all my fans. I know each and every one of you gives me your time, energy and affection. I know many of you wait for hours to see me and most of you leave disappointed. I know you all hope and dream to meet me and despite never realising those dreams, you never lose your affection for me or the hope. I want you all to know I appreciate the energy and love you give me, every single one of you. You are all important to me because without you and the love you give me, I couldn't do what I do. We are a partnership, me and every single one of you. Never, ever believe that I don't care. I would dearly love to meet with every single one of you but there aren't enough hours in the day. I love you all."

"Who are your friends here Jake?" another voice called.

Jake turned to his friends and grinned. "These guys are real special. This is Crib, Ace, Manlee 18, Nef and Shib. Say hello guys." They all nodded and smiled at the cameras.

"Will you be continuing your time aboard the freighter or will you be going home?"

"Hey I signed on for three months. I have work to do. I have a role to research and I intend to do just that. I'm going to do what I set out to do and with the help of my good friends here, the next movie is going to blow your socks off."

Tinnias steered Jake and the group gently towards the Law Enforcement building and by the time the doors closed behind them, many fans had autographs and signed photographs and Jake had received many kisses and hugs. Even Nef signed an autograph and everyone had posed for photographs.

"Right, coffee," Jake said as the group headed up to their rooms.

Over the course of the next day, the Law Enforcement Agency panel interviewed the group and Sam Sinclair sat in on them all, making notes silently for the most part. Here and there, he would whisper to the panel and ask for more information and when it came time for the group to depart back to the Mayan Queen, he joined them in their rooms.

"Hey guys," he said as he entered. "Can you come with me for a moment?"

"Sure buddy, what's up?" Jake asked.

"Just follow me, all of you." He led them down to a room on the ground floor, where Captain Nagle sat drinking coffee.

Jake looked at the Captain and then at Sam. "So we're here Sam, what's up?"

Sam looked at Captain Nagle. "Well Captain?"

Captain Nagle looked up at Sam and then at Jake and the others. "Jake. I umm. I'm Patricia Porter's uncle."

Jake went white and flopped down into a seat. "Her Uncle?"

"Yeah."

"And all this was because of something that happened eighteen years ago?"

"No Jake," Sam replied. "Nagle here isn't your inside man after all."

"He's not?" Nef exclaimed. Everyone looked shocked.

"No I'm not," Captain Nagle said.

"But then why, and how? I mean umm," Jake faltered.

"Who is Patricia Porter?" Shib asked.

"I dated her when I was seventeen," Jake replied. "We were stupid and careless and she got pregnant. I married her but we lost the baby and our relationship never recovered from the loss. We got divorced a year later. It was amicable and I took care of her financially. It was a mistake for both of us and losing the baby killed what little chance we had of making it work. We were far too young and I was far too engrossed with my new movie career."

"She never got over you Jake," Captain Nagle said. "She used to hope and pray you'd go back to her and she followed your career closely. She'd queue up outside movie theatres and travel to where you were filming in the hope of seeing you and maybe getting to talk to you but it never happened. She got more and more depressed and eventually, she became a drug addict and nothing we could do would get her out of it. She died of an overdose two years ago and I've blamed you every second since that day I found her slumped over in the cellar of an abandoned factory. I hated you for her suffering Jake and I was more than happy to hand you over to those pirates but I'm not your inside man."

"Then who is?" Manlee asked.

"Zeke," Sam replied. Everyone gasped in shock. "His name is Zeke Mackie, as you already know and the pirate's pilot is named Kreeve Mackie. They are brothers. At one time Zeke used to make a little money by being a movie extra and has been in a couple of well known movies, in crowd scenes or walking along a street, that sort of thing. He got a part as an extra in Lost Treasures, one of your movies Jake, and asked if he could have a

240

speaking part but they turned him down. He always blamed you for ruining his chances of a movie career and when he saw his brother, who was the black sheep of the family due to his chosen career, he told him you were to be joining the Mayan Queen for three months. Kreeve promised him a cut of the ransom money they hoped to get from you."

"Fuck," Jake hissed as the pieces finally fitted together.

"Jeez, I'd never have suspected him," Nef exclaimed.

"Neither would I," Ace said as he shook his head. Manlee and Crib looked at each other in shock, both lost for words.

"Is he in custody now Sam?" Shib asked and Sam nodded.

"Yes, he will be staying with us now and you can return to the ship without having to worry."

"My god," Jake whispered, "Zeke? Captain, I apologise to you. I thought it was you because you obviously hated me. I'm sorry about Patricia. If she'd have written to me or called or something, we could've been friends at least but she never did. I'd never have wanted an end like that for her. We were gonna have a kid together for fuck's sake."

"I'm sorry too Jake," Captain Nagle replied. "I'm just glad this is all over at last and we can all move on."

"Yes indeed," Nef nodded. "We can all move on and that is what I intend to do Captain."

Captain Nagle looked at him and frowned. "Huh?"

"I'm resigning my position Captain," Nef said, "and I give you the required six months' notice."

"But Nef," Captain Nagle replied. "We can work this out."

"It's not because of what's happened Captain. I hold no grudges against you or anyone else. It's just that I've had an offer that will take my life in a totally new direction. One that will mean I can be something of an ambassador for Damiklon and one that means I can continue to make sure this idiot keeps out of trouble," he said as he turned to Jake.

Jake grinned and took hold of Nef's hand. "So you're accepting my offer?"

"Yes, if it's still open."

"So you're not content with just corrupting my android, you're poaching my Chief Engineer as well," Captain Nagle said.

"Umm yeah, it looks like it," Jake replied.

"Corrupting me Sir?" Shib asked as everyone laughed.

"Okay let's get back shall we?" Captain Nagle suggested.

Sam Sinclair watched the shuttle take off and head up into the clouds. He smiled to himself, pleased that this job had come to a favourable conclusion and happy to have met another Damiklonian. He thought of the friend who had died in his arms as his hand went instinctively to the necklace hidden safely beneath his shirt. The shock of meeting Manlee 18, who he had always assumed to be long dead from his horrific injuries, would stay with him for a long time to come and confirmed what he knew to be true, that the chase is always worth it.

Inside the shuttle, the group smiled as they made plans for the remainder of Jake's three-month stay. In time, he learned not to drop the crates of cargo and soon he had twenty-five men working out daily in the gym. He apologised to Aamy, who eventually explained why she was so upset and he took her into his arms and held her.

"You are way too good for me to do that," he whispered.

"Thank you Jake."

"I'm sorry it upset you, and thank you for all the love and energy you give me. I couldn't do what I do without you and everyone like you." He bent his head and kissed her passionately. "That one is just for you Aamy, just for you and no one else."

"I'll treasure it always," she smiled.

Captain Nagle let Jake visit the bridge and Arsh even let him have a go at the helm to steer the ship. Throughout the whole three months, Jake practised with Nef every day and

Manlee shadowed his every move taking thousands of photographs. When it was time for the trip back down to Earth, Jake felt like a real cargo hand and knew that his time aboard the Mayan Queen would not only ensure his next movie blew the Entertainment Council out of their seats, but it had also changed him in ways he couldn't begin to explain. He said his goodbyes in the shuttle bay and remembered the day came aboard and there was no one to greet him. Today the bay was full of people wishing him well and Captain Nagle was amongst them. He stepped forward and pinned something to Jake's shirt.

"This is a little gift from Mayan Freightlines," he smiled. "You're one of the family now Jake." Jake smiled as he looked down at the little metal pin in the shape of a stylised bird.

"Thanks Captain. Thank you for putting up with me. I've learned a lot since I've been here and I'll miss everyone." He shook hands with Captain Nagle and went to say goodbye to his friends.

"Thank you fellas, it's been awesome. You all have my number okay? If you don't call me, there'll be trouble. I love you guys." He went to Nef and they embraced. "Three more months Nef. I'll be there to meet you okay? Don't be late."

"I'm looking forward to it," Nef grinned. "Keep up the practice huh?"

As Shib steered the Al Grazia shuttle out of the Mayan Queen and headed towards home, Jake looked down at planet Earth below him and nodded. Ace was right, he thought, it never stops being awesome.

THE END

COMING SOON

BYGORA VANDOS
Sinclair V-Log LB734/A

Sam Sinclair didn't usually play the role of detective. His job was just to chase and catch a specific target and deliver them into the hands of the Inter Galactic Law Enforcement Agency, so when his boss offered him an undercover job, he accepted happily.

Together with his new partner Ren, Sam begins the slow process of investigating the secluded and secretive Calmarin Research Station. Although set up to apparently investigate the cause of dying trees in the locale, rumours run rife among the local people about what really goes on up at Calmarin. What Sam and Ren discover after weeks of carefully working their way in, is one of the most terrible crimes against humanity that either of them have ever encountered and both vow to do their utmost to bring it to an end.

Sam finds many allies amongst the local people but with his cover blown and Ren taken prisoner, he no longer knows who can be trusted. As the job reaches its explosive climax and the personal cost to Sam takes its toll, the shocking truth finally comes out.